"Who's this?

Luke couldn't tell if the child in Kristen's arms was a boy or a girl, clad as it was in blue flannel pajamas, blond head buried in Kristen's blouse.

"It's Cody."

"Cody." Luke absorbed this with the uneasy caution of a man who suspects he might be walking into a trap. "You mean your sister's boy?"

Kristen nodded.

"What are you doing with him?"

"I kidnapped him," she said.

Luke blinked. "You *what?*"

"Kidnapped him. Just a few minutes ago. From the hospital."

Luke was having trouble figuring out what to make of this. Was the boy sick? "Uh, well, what did you bring him *here* for?"

"Because—" she said, either the strain of holding Cody, or the strain of something else making her voice breathless "—because you're his father."

Dear Reader,

Once again, we're back to offer you six fabulous romantic novels, the kind of book you'll just long to curl up with on a warm spring day. Leading off the month is award-winner Marie Ferrarella, whose *This Heart for Hire* is a reunion romance filled with the sharply drawn characters and witty banter you've come to expect from this talented writer.

Then check out Margaret Watson's *The Fugitive Bride,* the latest installment in her CAMERON, UTAH, miniseries. This FBI agent hero is about to learn all about love at the hands of his prime suspect. *Midnight Cinderella* is Eileen Wilks' second book for the line, and it's our WAY OUT WEST title. After all, there's just nothing like a cowboy! Our FAMILIES ARE FOREVER flash graces Kayla Daniels' *The Daddy Trap,* about a resolutely single hero faced with fatherhood—and love. *The Cop and Calamity Jane* is a suspenseful romp from the pen of talented Elane Osborn; you'll be laughing out loud as you read this one. Finally, welcome Linda Winstead Jones to the line. Already known for her historical romances, this author is about to make a name for herself in contemporary circles with *Bridger's Last Stand.*

Don't miss a single one—and then rejoin us next month, when we bring you six more examples of the best romantic writing around.

Yours,

Leslie J. Wainger
Executive Senior Editor

Please address questions and book requests to:
Silhouette Reader Service
U.S.: 3010 Walden Ave., P.O. Box 1325, Buffalo, NY 14269
Canadian: P.O. Box 609, Fort Erie, Ont. L2A 5X3

THE DADDY TRAP

KAYLA DANIELS

Published by Silhouette Books
America's Publisher of Contemporary Romance

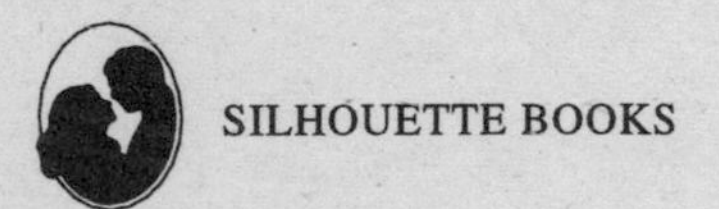

ISBN 0-373-07922-2

THE DADDY TRAP

This edition published by arrangement with Harlequin Books S.A.

Printed in U.S.A.

Books by Kayla Daniels

Silhouette Intimate Moments

Wanted: Mom and Me #760
Her First Mother #844
Secondhand Dad #892
The Daddy Trap #922

Silhouette Special Edition

Spitting Image #474
Father Knows Best #578
Hot Prospect #654
Rebel to the Rescue #707
From Father to Son #790
Heiress Apparent #814
Miracle Child #911
Marriage Minded #1068

KAYLA DANIELS

is a former computer programmer who enjoys travel, ballroom dancing and playing with her nieces and nephews. She grew up in Southern California and has lived in Alaska, Norway, Minnesota, Alabama and Louisiana. Currently she makes her home in Grass Valley, California.

For Jim,
my real-life romantic hero.

Chapter 1

Luke Hollister dug the heels of his hands into his bleary, red-rimmed eyes. Burning the midnight oil. That's what he would be doing literally, all right, if he couldn't figure out some way to reverse his bad luck before the power company cut off his electricity.

A knock at his back door roused him from the depressing sheets of facts and figures spread out across his dining room table. Lady Luck, showing up at last?

"Fat chance," Luke grumbled, shoving back his chair. "More likely a bill collector." He strode through the kitchen and switched on the back porch light.

He opened the door and got a rude shock. He would much rather have found a bill collector standing out there.

"Kristen." He kept his hand firmly attached to the door-knob, barring her entrance just in case she mistook his curt greeting for hospitality.

"Luke, you've got to let me in." Her half-whispered plea cut through the crisp late-night air.

Luke hadn't checked the weather report lately, but he was

pretty sure hell hadn't frozen over while he wasn't paying attention. "What do you want?" He didn't budge an inch from his position.

"I'll explain everything inside. Please! Turn off the light. And let us in!"

Luke peered closer and saw with a jolt that the bundle she was clutching to her chest like a sack of cement was a person. To be specific, a kid.

"Who's this?" He couldn't tell if that was a boy or girl clad in blue flannel pajamas, blond head buried in Kristen's blouse. September nights could be pretty chilly up here in the mountainous logging country of northern California. Those small bare feet were going to match the pajamas pretty soon. What was Kristen thinking of, hauling the poor kid around without proper clothing?

"It's Cody," she said. "My nephew."

"Cody." Luke absorbed this with the uneasy caution of a man who suspects he might be walking into an ambush. Who just heard a twig crack. "You mean..." He hesitated, reluctant to let her name cross his tongue. "You mean Sheri's boy?"

Kristen nodded. Luke noticed now her teeth were chattering. It wasn't *that* cold out there.

Hmm. "What are you doing with him?" He'd seen the youngster before, of course. But only from a distance. Except for that one unfortunate time he'd U-turned his shopping cart into the canned goods aisle at the supermarket and come face-to-face with Sheri and her son. Frankly, he'd been too distracted by Sheri's embarrassed green eyes and by the bitterness that churned in his gut to pay much attention to the boy.

Kristen shifted his weight in her arms. She was petite, only five-three or thereabouts, with a slender frame and delicate-boned limbs. Cody looked like a heavy, awkward burden for her to balance. And why was she carrying a kid who must be, what, seven years old now?

"I kidnapped him," she said.

Luke blinked. "You...what?"

"Kidnapped him. Just a few minutes ago. From the hospital."

"Whoa, now." Luke was having trouble figuring out what to make of this. Was the boy sick? "Uh, well, what did you bring him *here* for?"

"Because," she said. Either the strain of holding Cody or the strain of something else made her voice breathless. "Because you're his father."

Kristen Monroe drew the blanket over her precious nephew and tenderly kissed his forehead, next to the white bandage. It had been months since she'd been allowed close enough to touch him.

She grazed her fingertips over his pale cheek as if to transmit all the love she'd stored up for him during their long separation. Trying to still her trembling hand so as not to waken him, she feathered one finger down the length of his arm, the arm that had been broken earlier this year. His soft skin was warm, smooth, achingly vulnerable. Kristen could feel the blood pulsing through his veins. The suffering etched on his innocent, angelic features tore at her heart.

"You poor sweet thing," she murmured quietly. "I'm sorry, Cody. So very, very sorry..." Her throat closed up tight with guilt and grief. Thank heaven whatever drugs they'd given him at the hospital had allowed him to sleep through all this.

Thank heaven Luke hadn't slammed the door in her face the way it had looked like he'd wanted to at first. Yet Kristen had known somehow that she could count on him. In spite of the shabby way she'd once deceived him.

Now it was time to face the consequences of what she'd done. With one last look at Cody, Kristen shut the door of Luke's guest room behind her. Stalling for time, she made a vain attempt to comb her disheveled red hair with her fingers. Getting in Luke's door had been the easy part. Persuading him to go along with the rest of her plan was going to be the *real* challenge.

She traveled in slow motion back to the living room, anxious to postpone the hostile barrage of his questions. She'd stolen Cody on impulse, under the influence of a white-hot anger. Now that her adrenaline and outrage levels had subsided a little, fear was seeping in to fill the vacuum.

What have I done?

The question kept hammering at the inside of Kristen's skull. Even though she knew she'd done what was right.

The living room was deserted. Kristen made a quick visual survey, curious in spite of the desperate circumstances that had brought her here. She'd never been inside Luke's home before. He'd bought it several years after their friendship had come to a screeching halt because of Kristen's role in what her sister Sheri had done to him.

It wasn't the typical bachelor pad she'd imagined. No microwave dinner trays and crushed beer cans littering the floor, no girlie magazines strewn across the coffee table. True, the decor was undeniably masculine, a bit dark for Kristen's taste and lacking personal touches like photos or sentimental keepsakes that would have made it seem homier. But the place was fairly neat, with a big comfy sofa and lots of wood and real curtains at the windows.

Propelled by a sudden spurt of alarm, Kristen hurried over and closed the curtains.

''What's next? You going to rearrange the furniture? Alphabetize my spice rack?''

She spun around to find Luke lounging in the doorway between dining room and kitchen. His familiar, rugged features hadn't changed much during the years they'd done such a good job of avoiding each other. He was still as attractive as ever in that rough-around-the-edges way of his. Something brooding and vaguely rebellious in his dark good looks had always reminded her of James Dean.

The faded, well-worn jeans hugging his muscular thighs were nearly transparent in patches, held together by little more stitching than hope. Kristen swallowed.

Luke parted the beer bottle from his lips and lifted it in her direction. ''Want one?''

''No, thank you.'' She needed to keep her wits about her. Though something to take the edge off her jangled nerves would have been nice. She'd forgotten the unsettling effect Luke could have on her. ''I—I didn't want anyone to see me in here.'' She gestured lamely at the closed curtains.

''Ah.'' His dark brows shot up toward his coal black hair. ''That's right, I forgot. You're wanted for kidnapping.''

''Or I will be, as soon as the night nurse goes in to check on Cody.'' Kristen sent off an apology by mental telepathy. The poor woman was going to wind up in extremely deep hot water when Cody's disappearance was discovered.

''Enough small talk.'' Luke pushed himself away from the doorjamb. ''Tell me what this is all about, and make it good.'' He strolled past her and propped one lean haunch against the arm of that big comfy sofa.

He didn't invite Kristen to sit down.

She was too worked up to sit still, anyway. Dear God, what if they'd already discovered Cody was missing? What if someone had seen her bring him here? She had to convince Luke to help her, and she had to do it quick.

No time for testing the waters with her toe and easing in gradually. She would have to plunge right in. ''The reason I brought Cody here is that Sheri told me once, a long time ago...'' A hitch of grief stopped her for a second. It had been a year now since her sister had died. And Kristen still missed her every single day with an anguished, empty place in her heart that would never be filled. She forced herself to move across that gaping chasm and go on. ''Sheri once told me that Cody was *your* son, not—''

''Hold it right there.'' Luke swung up his palm like a traffic cop. Except he wore a far more menacing expression. ''Let's table that whole subject for now, shall we?''

''But—''

''I'm not interested in listening to any more of your sister's lies.'' His knuckles formed a white bracelet of bone around his beer. Kristen noticed he hadn't touched it since his first swallow. He aimed the neck of the bottle in her direction. "Or any more of *your* lies, either, for that matter."

Well, she had that coming, didn't she? "I'm telling the truth," she said quietly. She forced both hands to remain motionless on the back of his leather recliner chair, out in the open, as if that could persuade him she didn't have any tricks up her sleeve.

"Is that a fact?" Luke crossed one sturdy work boot over the other and settled back against the wall, striking the pose of someone about to hear a good story. "Like you were telling the truth eight years ago, when I'd call from out of town and ask for Sheri and you'd tell me she was working the late shift again? Or that she'd gone to the movies with one of her girlfriends? Or that she was visiting a sick friend in the hospital?" He thumped his head back against the wall and shook it in self-derision. "Man, I can't believe I was fool enough to buy your excuses every single time."

"Luke, I'm sorry." Kristen had wanted to tell him that for so long. But once the damage had been done, it had been too late for apologies. Too late to make amends for the pain she'd helped cause him.

It had always been a source of great sorrow, knowing that Luke would never forgive her. Now it might be a matter of life and death.

Kristen straightened her spine and made herself confront his simmering blue eyes head-on, ignoring the weakness in her knees. "I shouldn't have covered up for her," she admitted. "But Sheri was my sister."

"So that made it all right to lie for her?"

"No."

"To help her sneak around behind my back while I was out of town working my tail off to build my construction business, to build a future for *us,* blissfully ignorant of the fact that she was sleeping with Derek Vincent the whole time?"

Kristen forced herself not to flinch in the face of his blazing, completely justifiable resentment. She'd taken the coward's way out once before. She wouldn't do it again.

"Sheri *wasn't* sleeping with Derek," she told Luke. "Not before they got married. That's how she knew that Cody was *your—*"

"Enough." Luke came up off the arm of the sofa as if shot from a cannon. He set his beer down with a *thunk.* "I don't know how this ludicrous claim of yours fits into whatever game you're playing, but let's cut to the chase, shall we?" Beneath the sleeves of his black T-shirt his biceps flexed while he alternately knotted and loosened his fists.

Funny. Though Luke was clearly stronger than Derek, capable of inflicting far greater damage, Kristen wasn't the least bit afraid of him. Not physically, anyway.

He towered over her, close enough so she could inhale the not unpleasant scent of sweat and sawdust that clung to him as snugly as his T-shirt. "Tell me why Cody was in the hospital," he said. "Tell me why you took him."

Luke hadn't laid a finger on her. But the intensity of his gaze and the subtle, raw force of his masculine power touched something primitive inside Kristen, warming her like an intimate caress. It took every ounce of her self-control not to back away from him.

"Cody was in the hospital because Derek beat him." Bile rose in her throat when she answered Luke's question.

His pupils dilated sharply, dark openings into his soul. Kristen saw disbelief, then the first tentative flames of anger. "You're telling me his own father hit him hard enough to put him in the hospital?"

You're his father, she wanted to protest. But continued insistence right now would only antagonize Luke further.

"Derek hit Sheri, too," Kristen said. "For most of their marriage. Then, after she died, he started in on Cody."

Luke's square jaw shifted. Like the San Andreas Fault right before an earthquake. "You knew about this abuse?"

Kristen wasn't fooled by the deadly calm in his voice. "Sheri didn't tell me at first, but I could see something was wrong.'' She dug her nails into the back of the recliner. ''After about the hundredth time I confronted her, she finally admitted it.''

Luke brought his face close to hers. A tiny vein pulsed beneath the tanned, taut skin at his temple. ''If what you're claiming is true,'' he demanded through clenched teeth, ''then why the hell didn't you do something about it?''

Kristen refused to cringe from his accusing expression. ''I tried to. Believe me, I tried.'' To her dismay her voice broke on the last word. Tears flooded her eyes. She didn't want to cry in front of Luke.

Too late. Before Kristen could rein in her runaway emotions her shoulders were shaking and her throat was so clotted with sobs she couldn't squeeze out one coherent peep.

Luke reared back as if he'd uncovered a rattlesnake in the woodpile. Good grief, what was he supposed to do now? He didn't know the first thing about comforting weeping females. So he did what he always did and opted for action. He scurried to the kitchen to get Kristen a glass of water.

On the way back he cursed himself for the sympathy that had elbowed its way past his anger. What was it about seeing a woman cry that turned his common sense to mush?

Common sense warned him that Kristen was up to no good. That she'd come here trying to entangle him in some self-serving scheme Luke hadn't figured out yet.

Common sense also warned him he'd be a prize idiot if he let himself believe that the poor kid sleeping in his extra bedroom might actually be his own flesh and blood. No, Kristen was just trying to use him somehow, trying to manipulate him with the outrageous claim that Sheri had borne him a son.

A son! Luke's heart picked up its pace even as he assured himself it was impossible.

Still, he couldn't deny that something bad sure seemed to be going on here. And at least part of what Kristen had told him must be true. Either that, or she was the world's greatest actress. Those tears were real.

''Hey, hey, come on now. Here you go. Have some water.''

He guided her into the recliner chair and stuck the glass in her hand. When he touched her he could feel invisible vibrations trembling through her body like aspen leaves in a strong wind. For some reason it made Luke want to protect her. Old habit, probably. He'd known Kristen nearly all his life, and for a long time she'd been like a kid sister to him. Even though she'd betrayed his trust, apparently he hadn't been able to sever the threads of their connection as cleanly and completely as he would have liked.

He dragged over a dining room chair to sit next to her. She sipped her water, staring into her glass as if all the secrets of the universe were swimming around at the bottom. Luke guessed she was embarrassed.

Either that, or she was busy concocting the next chapter of her story.

She offered Luke a wobbly smile when she finally set down the glass. "Sorry to go all soggy on you." Her green eyes, pink-rimmed and puffy but still beautiful, glittered with the remnants of tears. Like sparkling emeralds. Like Sheri's eyes.

Luke's defenses slipped a notch or two. "Let's start from the top, okay?"

Kristen bit her lower lip and nodded. She pushed her hair back from her face, sending copper glints shimmering like a fistful of new pennies as it tumbled across her shoulders. She cleared her throat and stared straight ahead, not looking at Luke, as if this were the only way she could proceed without bursting into tears again.

In profile he couldn't help but notice the pleasing sculpture of her features. Well-defined cheekbones, the delicate stroke of her jawline, the cute way her nose turned up just a tiny bit at the tip...

Kristen might not possess the head-turning, cover-girl glamour of her older sister. But the gawky, insecure teenager Luke used to tease about her shyness had developed her own kind of beauty. He was surprised to find himself attracted to it.

"I begged Sheri for years to leave Derek, but she wouldn't, because she was afraid he would get custody of Cody." Kristen's soft voice quivered with the strain of holding her emotions in check. "You don't exactly need a bookmaker to predict the odds of who would have won a court battle in *this* town. On one side, the heir to the Vincent lumber empire and all his high-priced lawyers. On the other, a onetime waitress from the wrong side of the tracks, who'd be lucky to get a legal-aid attorney to take her case once Derek put the pressure on."

"I see," Luke said. Unfortunately, he did. All too clearly. Whisper Ridge, California, was a one-company town. And that one company had been owned by the Vincent family for generations.

"As you know, Derek took over as head of Vincent Lumber a couple years ago when his father died." A spark of anger brought a measure of animation back to Kristen's face. "After that, Derek started knocking Sheri around more often, as if he were taking the stress of his new responsibilities out on her."

Tiny crescent moons appeared at the base of her nails as she gripped the chair arms. "Finally Sheri agreed to let me help her, to take her and Cody to a battered-women's shelter over in Pineville." Kristen's eyes darted back and forth, as if she were watching a fast-forward replay of past events. "We set it up to meet in secret one morning at the library. I waited and waited for them to come, but they never showed up."

Luke braced himself for what he suspected was coming. The anguish in Kristen's voice tore at him like claws. "Later that day Derek called and told me Sheri was dead."

Kristen's face crumpled. Luke flashed back with excruciating detail to the moment he himself had learned of Sheri's death. He'd been treating himself to a well-deserved cup of coffee and slice of homemade peach pie at the local diner when he'd overheard two waitresses expressing shock about Sheri Vincent's accident. Luke had carefully set down his fork, abandoned his pie, and walked straight out of the diner in a beeline for the nearest liquor store.

He still winced when he remembered that hangover. Hearing this new ironic twist to the tragedy brought it all back. On the very same day Sheri had finally found the courage to seek help, she'd died in a crash after losing control of her car.

"What happened tonight?" Luke asked. The past he could do nothing about. He was still trying to make sense of the present. "Why'd you take Cody out of the hospital?"

"I didn't intend to, originally. I just wanted to see him, to make sure he was really going to be all right." Kristen hoisted her chin to a defiant angle. "But I couldn't let Derek have him back. Not after I sneaked into Cody's room after visiting hours were over and heard him cry out in his sleep—"

"Wait a second." Luke patted the air in a hold-your-horses gesture. "Why'd you have to *sneak* into his room?"

Kristen's cheeks bloomed with angry roses. "Because Derek has forbidden me to see Cody for months now. I didn't even know my own nephew was in the hospital until this afternoon when I was delivering flowers from my shop and bumped into my friend Jenna, who works in the hospital kitchen. She mentioned seeing Cody's name on the meal roster and acted like I must know he was there. So I went up to see him, but the doctor had left orders he wasn't to have any visitors." Kristen's mouth puckered as if she'd bit into a lemon. "No doubt the doctor was following *Derek's* orders."

Luke rubbed the base of his neck and frowned. "I don't get it. Why won't Derek let you see Cody?"

Kristen flew from the chair like an arrow shot from a bowstring. Every taut muscle in her body appeared to thrum with agitation. "Because I tried to stop him from abusing Cody, that's why." Fireworks of frustration exploded in her eyes. "Soon after Sheri died I noticed Cody had lots of bruises all the time. Knowing how Derek had treated Sheri, it wasn't hard to figure out what was going on." She curved her palm across her forehead as if checking for fever. "I finally got Cody to admit that Derek hit him, even though the poor kid was scared to death of telling the truth." She curled her fingers into a fist. "So I reported Derek to the police."

Luke rose slowly to his feet, mirroring the anger that was building inside him. "And?"

"Derek denied it, of course. And Cody was too terrified of him to tell the cops what he'd done." Her lips twisted in disgust. "Naturally, the cops were hardly about to take *my* word over the word of someone who could put half their relatives out of work with a snap of his fingers."

Luke's brows yanked together in a scowl. "So Derek retaliated by forbidding you to see Cody."

Kristen's eyes glittered, though not with tears this time. "He refused to let me come to the house anymore, and wouldn't let Cody go anywhere by himself except to school. Even then Derek drove him both ways. So I went to the grade school one day and talked to Cody through the chain-link fence at recess. Except somehow Derek got wind of it." The color drained from Kristen's face, leaving her pretty features pale and haunted. "So he made Cody call me and tell me his daddy would hurt him if I ever talked to him again."

The outrage that had been smoldering inside Luke burst into flame. "That son of a—"

"I couldn't risk that!" Kristen cried. "I knew Derek wouldn't hesitate to take it out on Cody if I tried to interfere, so I—I had no choice but to stay away and pray with all my heart that Derek would stop hurting him." She plowed her hands through her long auburn hair and knotted them into fists. "It just about killed me, but I *had* to, for Cody's sake."

The torment that had ripped her soul apart was clearly etched in Kristen's face. She let her hands fall helplessly to her sides. "When I found out Cody was in the hospital," she went on, "I wanted so much for the story Derek told them to be true—that Cody'd fallen out of a tree. But while I was in his room he cried out in his sleep, 'Please don't hit me, Daddy,' and right then I knew what I had to do."

She dropped a hand to Luke's arm, and the steel in her grip matched the steel in her voice. "I swear to you, Luke, I will never, *ever* give Cody back to that monster."

Luke didn't doubt her for a second. He'd once stumbled across a mother black bear and her cubs while out hiking in the woods one summer. He recognized the ferocious, deadly protective gleam in Kristen's eye as the same one that had warned him to back oh-so-carefully away from Mama Bear.

It wasn't a look Luke cared to argue with. Even if he hadn't sympathized with the agony Kristen must have suffered, terrified for her nephew's safety yet cruelly prevented from helping him.

The least he could do was hear her out. "What is it you want from me?" he asked gruffly. "Money? A ride somewhere?"

Luke was acutely aware of the warm pressure of her hand on his arm. He was surprised by how good it felt there. Probably because he'd led a monk's existence for so long he was reacting all out of proportion to a woman's touch.

Kristen was studying him with an odd intensity that raised wary hackles on the back of Luke's neck. Suddenly he was certain that what she wanted from him was something a whole lot more complicated than cold hard cash.

"As a last resort I might have no choice except to run away with Cody forever. But he deserves better than a life in hiding." A ghost of sadness passed through Kristen's eyes, as if she were envisioning a future of secrecy and loneliness and looking back over their shoulders. "But there's a way to win legal custody of Cody from Derek." She squeezed Luke's arm. "That's where you come in."

All at once her grip felt like the jaws of a trap. So they were back to this again. Luke glared at her. "If you think I'm going to go along with some cockamamie scheme to pretend I'm his real father and sue for custody—"

"No. That's not what I need your help for."

"Then—?" He knew he was going to be sorry for asking.

Kristen looked him straight in the eye. "I want you to help me prove that Derek Vincent killed my sister."

Chapter 2

Luke's muscles stiffened beneath Kristen's fingers. Slowly he detached his arm from her grasp, as if he considered her mentally unbalanced and feared his withdrawal might send her right over the edge.

She wanted to reach for him, to draw him back. But she reined in her foolish impulse.

The suspicion that had faded from his steel blue eyes was back in full force. He put a deliberate distance between them and folded his arms across his sturdy chest. "What are you talking about?" he asked. Every rigid line of his posture proclaimed his skepticism.

Kristen squared her shoulders. "I'm talking about murder."

"Murder." Luke pronounced the word carefully, like someone learning a foreign language. "But Sheri died in a car accident." He studied Kristen from beneath his furrowed brow. "Are you suggesting Derek was at the wheel or something?"

If only it were that simple. "I'm saying Sheri didn't die when her car went off that cliff. I'm saying she was already dead when it happened." Frustration wrapped its arms around

Kristen like a straitjacket of despair. "And I'm not *suggesting* anything. I *know.*"

"Is that a fact?" Luke cocked his head at a doubtful angle. The patronizing note in his voice grated like fingernails on a chalkboard. "And just how, pray tell, do you *know* this?"

"Because it doesn't make sense any other way!" Kristen burst out. Then she remembered the all-important need to keep her presence here a secret. Quickly she lowered the volume of her exasperation. "Why would Sheri have been driving her car along Lookout Road at the exact same time she was supposed to be meeting *me* clear across town?"

Luke shrugged one broad shoulder. "Maybe she changed her mind about letting you help her. Maybe she decided to stay with Derek after all."

"Then why did she call the school that morning and tell them Cody was going to be out sick that day?" Kristen struggled to keep emotion out of her arguments. Logic was the only tool that would carry any weight with Luke. "Calling the school was part of our plan, so they wouldn't tip off Derek too soon by contacting him to ask where Cody was."

Luke still wasn't buying it. "Maybe Cody actually got sick. That could be why Sheri decided not to go through with your plan that day."

Kristen resisted the urge to grab those well-built shoulders and shake some understanding into him. "If Cody had gotten sick at the last minute, Sheri would have called me. And she would *never,* under any circumstances, have left him home by himself the way the police found him after the accident." She shook her head. "The so-called facts just don't add up."

For half a second Kristen glimpsed a wavering question mark in Luke's eyes. She was disappointed but not surprised when it vanished. Luke had made it plain he wanted nothing to do with her. But if Kristen succeeded at convincing him her suspicions were well-founded, he would have no choice but to become involved. Luke wasn't the kind of man to let murder go unpunished.

No wonder he was so reluctant to believe her.

"Let me see if I've got this straight." When he rubbed his jaw, its sandpaper roughness made a faint rasping sound. "You think Derek had something to do with Sheri's death."

Kristen spread her hands. "It's the only explanation that makes sense." She outlined her case with the passionate energy of a prosecutor pleading her case before a jury. "Derek must have come home unexpectedly from work that morning and found Sheri getting ready to leave him. So he lost his temper and ended up beating her to death." Steady, Kristen. Focus on the facts, not your reaction to them. "Maybe Derek meant to kill her, maybe he didn't. But once Sheri was dead, he had to make it look like an accident. So he left Cody at the house, drove her body to a deserted stretch of Lookout Road and sent the car over a cliff to make it look like that's how she died."

At least Luke didn't dismiss her theory right away. Kristen held her breath while he frowned in thought, crossed over to the dining room table, drummed his fingers against the polished oak. When he produced a deep sigh, hope flared inside her. Maybe she had him.

"Have you told all this to the police?" he asked.

"Of course! I spelled it all out for them, I pestered them for weeks, I demanded they do something." The injustice of it still appalled Kristen. "The cops insisted there was no proof. That there was only my word that Sheri intended to leave Derek that day."

"They didn't find anything suspicious at the accident scene?"

"If they did, they weren't sharing the information with me." Kristen hissed a disgusted stream of air through her lips. "As long as Sheri's death appeared accidental, they were hardly about to launch a murder investigation against the high-and-mighty Derek Vincent, for the same reasons they ignored me later on when I told them he was abusing Cody."

Luke got the picture. But Kristen painted the rest of it for him, anyway. "Vincent Lumber owns half this town. Every cop on that force has a brother or a father or a wife who works for the company. Who do you think would pay the price if some cop started poking into Sheri's death? Derek wouldn't hesitate to fire the guy's relatives. Or evict them if they happened to live in company-owned housing. Or pressure the bank to foreclose on them if they'd fallen a bit behind in their mortgage payments.''

Kristen was so steamed up Luke could practically see smoke coming out her ears. ''Derek Vincent can singlehandedly destroy anyone he chooses without even breaking a sweat.'' Sarcasm dripped from her words like acid. ''Unfortunately, the police required more proof than the rantings of his hysterical, grief-stricken sister-in-law to go after him.''

Luke probed his cheek with his tongue. ''And you want *me* to help you find that proof?'' It was finally sinking in, the magnitude of the favor she was asking.

Kristen slapped her palm against the table, scattering a few of his unpaid bills. ''I already tried to do it alone. When the police refused to cooperate, I started asking questions myself, hoping to find other incriminating evidence or a witness that could break Derek's alibi for that morning. But one of the people I spoke to must have gone running to Derek.'' The delicate tendons in her neck convulsed when she swallowed. ''Derek proceeded to make it clear that if I didn't stop snooping around, Cody would get hurt.''

Luke jammed his fists into his pockets. ''He actually threatened the boy?'' The smoldering heat of his anger was building again.

Kristen made a disdainful sound in her throat. ''In that arrogant, veiled, cover-your-rear-end way of his. He told me he was sure I didn't want to see Cody *suffer* by having his father falsely accused of anything.'' Determination hardened her features. ''I wasn't going to let Derek stop me. I decided I would just have to be more discreet, was all. I wasn't going to let him get away with murdering my sister! But then...'' She pressed her fingertips to her temples. ''The problem is, you can't keep secrets in a town of four thousand. Derek found out I was still trying to find evidence against him. So he...he...'' She closed her eyes briefly, as if in pain. ''By then he'd already stopped me from seeing Cody. But the next time I spotted Cody from a distance,'' she said miserably, ''his arm was in a cast.''

Luke's temper was inching up into the danger zone. ''Are you telling me Derek broke the boy's arm?''

''I—I can't know for sure.'' Kristen let her arms fall to her sides in a gesture of defeat. ''But I was so scared I was responsible that I—I stopped looking into Sheri's death right away. Even if it meant letting her killer go free, I—I just couldn't risk what Derek might do to Cody.''

Luke didn't know which he wanted to do most—march straight over to the Vincent place and give the lord of the manor a dose of his own medicine, or pull Kristen into his arms and give her the comfort she plainly needed.

Considering the unexpected signals his body had been sending him ever since she'd arrived, that second option probably wasn't such a hot idea. Luke's feelings toward Kristen were such a complicated mix of resentment, suspicion and sympathy, he didn't dare add physical chemistry to that treacherous brew.

Giving in to this crazy desire to cradle her slender curves against him, to stroke her silky hair and mutter soothing words in her ear could only lead to trouble.

Besides, what reassurance could Luke offer her, anyway? For all he knew, the cops had written her off as a nutcase for good reason. Luke had only heard one side of the story, and previous experience had taught him that Kristen's version of the truth couldn't always be trusted.

Still, he could hardly deny that something—or some*one*—had done a real number on Cody. Kristen hadn't made up the part about the hospital—Luke had seen the plastic identification bracelet himself when he'd shown Kristen where she could put the poor kid to bed.

As for her claim that he was Cody's father...

Luke and Sheri had always taken precautions to make sure she didn't get pregnant. He couldn't speak for what she and

Derek had or hadn't done. Luke had paid just enough attention to local gossip to hear that Sheri's baby had been born prematurely, so he'd never had any reason to suspect that *he* might be…

On the other hand, if the kid *hadn't* been premature, even the most careful precautions *could* fail now and then, so—scientifically speaking, of course—Luke supposed he had to concede there *was* technically an infinitesimal possibility…

That Cody was his. Even though it seemed far more likely that Sheri had lied to Kristen, or that Kristen was lying to him.

But when Luke got right down to it, did it even matter, as far as deciding how to respond to Kristen's plea for help? No matter whose son he was, if Cody was being abused then Luke was sure as hell going to do everything in his power to stop it.

As for Sheri's death, it certainly wouldn't hurt to poke around a little bit himself, to see if there was actually any basis for Kristen's wild accusation that Derek had killed her sister.

Good grief, what was he considering getting himself into here? Aiding and abetting a kidnapper? Going up against a powerful, ruthless adversary who practically ran the whole town?

A slow, unpleasant grin crept across Luke's face. His grudge against Derek Vincent went way, way back, even before the jerk had stolen Sheri from him. Derek had been a few years ahead of Luke in school, a pompous, two-bit bully who'd tormented Luke on a regular basis until the day Luke finally grew big enough to whip the older kid in a fair fight. Derek had never forgiven the public humiliation he'd suffered at the receiving end of young Luke's windmilling fists. From then on he'd never missed a chance to inflict petty revenge by sneering at Luke's impoverished background or by sabotaging Luke's after-school jobs.

By his senior year in high school Luke had managed to save up enough money to buy a beat-up old Mustang convertible that he'd lovingly restored to gleaming perfection. Then one morning he'd come out of his house to discover someone had slashed all four tires and scratched a road map of squiggly, long-distance lines all through the cherry red paintwork.

He'd never been able to prove who'd done it, of course. But he'd known.

Just as Kristen claimed to know.

She was watching him closely now, waiting for him to commit himself one way or the other. Her tense stance made Luke think of a spooked deer, poised to take graceful flight if he made the wrong move.

If he didn't agree to help Kristen she would have no choice but to take Cody and run. And in the extremely remote chance that Cody *was* his son, Luke would lose him forever.

He couldn't let that happen.

"All right," he said. "I'll see what I can do."

And keep his fingers crossed that she wasn't playing him for a fool.

"Cody, honey? It's me. Aunt Kristen."

She perched on the edge of his bed, gently smoothing his tousled blond hair off his forehead. His skin felt unusually warm to her touch. Was he running a fever? Once again it overwhelmed her, the magnitude of what she'd done. For the time being, the responsibility for Cody's medical care was going to rest squarely on *her* shoulders.

An awesome burden, but not nearly as unthinkable as letting Derek get his hands on her nephew again. The human body *did* have an amazing ability to repair itself, after all. And it wasn't as if Kristen were depriving him of medication he needed to get well. Still, she could hardly gaze down upon his small, bruised, fragile limbs without the horrible fear that her reckless action might have made everything even worse.

Luckily Cody had slept through the night. With the first pearl gray light of dawn slipping through the curtains in Luke's guest room he'd begun to stir, rousing Kristen from her uneasy vigil on the floor beside his bed. Luke had loaned her his sleeping bag. She was probably just imagining it, but all night long the woodsy, masculine smell of him had seemed to envelop her like the down-filled cocoon itself. It was almost like lying in his arms.

Not that Kristen knew what that was like, or had the slightest chance of ever finding out.

Cody blinked groggily, then closed his eyes again. "Hurts," he whimpered.

Kristen would gladly have borne his pain a hundred times over if she could have taken it away from him. She'd already rummaged through Luke's supply of over-the-counter pain relievers and found nothing suitable for a seven-year-old. Luke would have to go out and buy something as soon as the drugstore opened.

Of course, the clerk would no doubt wonder why a bachelor like Luke Hollister was purchasing a product intended for children. In Whisper Ridge speculation like that spread with the speed and efficiency of satellite television. It wouldn't take long for the telltale gossip to reach the ears of those who were looking for her and Cody.

Kristen nearly wept. Already she could foresee a long list of complications she hadn't had time to prepare for, and it hadn't even been ten hours since she'd stolen Cody. How on earth was she ever going to keep him safe?

Then his lashes fluttered open and he looked up at her. His beautiful blue eyes brimmed with such confusion and pain and sadness it nearly broke Kristen's heart. And right then she knew she was capable of doing whatever it took to protect him.

He rubbed one eye. "Aunt Kristen?" His tiny voice wavered with bewilderment. It had been a long, long time since he'd seen her.

She took his limp hand in hers. "It's me, sweetie." That was all the explanation she could muster for a moment, so choked up was she with love and sorrow.

"Where...?" He seemed too exhausted to finish the question.

"We're at a friend's house," Kristen told him. "A good

friend.'' Okay, so Luke would probably object strenuously to that label. But she was eager to reassure Cody.

''I was…in the hospital.'' His eyes darted nervously around the room. As if he were looking for someone he didn't really want to see.

''Yes, I know. But *I'm* going to take care of you from now on.'' She squeezed his hand. ''Everything's going to be all right, Cody. No one's ever going to hurt you again. I promise.'' She made a crisscross motion over her heart and produced a smile, forcing herself to swallow any hint of animosity toward Derek. Cody was only a child. Despite what Derek had done to him, Cody still thought of him as his father. To put him in the middle of a war between her and Derek would tear the little guy apart.

''How's the patient?''

The deep male voice, still husky with sleep, startled Kristen. Cody's hand clenched convulsively around hers, surprising her with his strength. His eyes were wide-open now, alive with fear.

She raised their linked hands and pressed a kiss to his rigid, ice-cold knuckles. ''It's all right, honey. It's just Luke, the friend I told you about. This is his house.'' She nuzzled her cheek against Cody's hand, but he didn't relax his death grip on her.

Luke slouched casually in the doorway, blowing on a mug of what Kristen could smell was coffee. His feet and chest were bare, his unbelted jeans slung low across his flat hips. Those muscles that had looked so impressive beneath his T-shirt last night were even more magnificent in all their naked glory. An unexpected yearning made Kristen's mouth water. Must be the coffee.

''Cody's…'' She had to stop and clear her throat. ''Cody's still not feeling too perky, are you, kiddo?''

He gave a little jerk of his head, still clinging to her with his iron grip, silent and scared.

''Sorry to hear that.'' As Luke pushed himself off the door frame and into the room, Kristen saw his posture wasn't nearly as casual as he was striving for. "Anything I can do?" Though he spoke to Kristen, his gaze was fixed on Cody.

"He'll need some things from the drugstore. Clothes, too. I'll make a list." She wasn't too sure how Luke would react to his assignment as errand boy, but he *had* offered to help, hadn't he?

She needn't have worried. Luke nodded absently and sipped his coffee, clearly too absorbed by Cody's presence to chafe at her request. As he came closer to the bed, Cody shrank beneath the covers.

Kristen felt a pang of sorrow. His own father, and Cody was afraid of him! Not that it came as much of a surprise, considering how Cody had been treated by the man who'd raised him as his son. A tall, powerfully built male stranger towering over his bed was bound to conjure up all sorts of ominous images.

"Luke, this is Cody." The awful irony of having to introduce a man to his own child left the bitter taste of guilt in Kristen's mouth. If only she hadn't lied for Sheri all those years ago…if only she hadn't kept her sister's secret during all the years since…

If only. Surely the two most regretful words in the English language.

Well, it was too late to undo the past. Kristen's only goal now was to set things right for the future. "Cody, this is Luke." She winked at her nephew. "He may look kind of grouchy first thing in the morning, but he's actually a very nice guy."

A trace of amusement flickered in Luke's eyes as he exchanged glances with Kristen. A strange warmth stole through her belly. It had been a long time since Luke had glanced at her with anything but hostility.

"Pleased to meet you," he said gruffly to Cody. Then, obviously recognizing himself as the source of the boy's distress, Luke retreated a step from the bed. "I, uh, used to know your mom," he said in gentler though no less awkward tone.

Cody blinked at him warily. Those eyes, Kristen thought.

Those beautiful blue dreamboat eyes that'll someday break all the girls' hearts. She held her breath. Surely Luke must see that Cody has the same eyes as he does.

But no shock of recognition caused Luke to stagger backward, no instinctive spark of kinship lit up his craggy features.

"My mommy?" Cody echoed in a weak, tentative voice. He peered at Kristen for confirmation.

"Luke and your mommy were friends." Kristen patted his hand. "A long time ago." She felt some of the tension seep from Cody's thin limbs.

He risked another glance at Luke. "My mommy's dead," he said solemnly.

Luke's mug froze in midtrajectory, halfway to his mouth. A muscle twitched along his jaw. "I heard about that," he said, once he got his mug moving again. He cupped it gingerly between both hands, as if trying not to spill any coffee. "I'll bet you miss her a lot."

Cody nodded. His chin started to quiver. A panicky expression leaped across Luke's face—the look of a man who'd prefer to be anyplace else in the universe besides the one spot where he happened to be standing.

Kristen would have giggled if she hadn't felt so much like crying. When she tried to raise Cody up to give him a hug, he winced. "Ow!"

"Oh, Cody, I'm sorry!" For a moment she'd nearly forgotten his injuries. From the corner of one eye she saw Luke stiffen. He took a swift step toward the bed and tugged back the covers to get a better look. Cody cowered against Kristen, whimpering.

No wonder he was scared. Luke's nostrils flared in anger while he surveyed the little boy's bruises. His dark brows collided like storm clouds, and the hand holding back the covers bunched into a fist. His mouth was straight and hard as an iron crowbar when he asked, "Who did this to you, Cody?"

"Luke," Kristen warned.

"Did someone hit you?"

"Luke, please!"

Cody's face turned as white as the pillowcase beneath his head. "N-n-no!"

When Luke's hand abruptly descended to set his coffee on the nightstand, Cody recoiled against Kristen, burrowing his face into her blouse. Tremors racked his body like a life-threatening fever.

"Tell me the truth," Luke said sternly. "How did you get hurt?"

Cody whipped his head frantically from side to side, as if trying to bore through his aunt with his skull. A thin wail escaped into the room.

"Luke, for God's sake!" Kristen shielded her terrified nephew with her free arm. "Stop it. Leave him alone. Can't you see what you're doing to him?"

"We need to know what happened." Luke's jaw was set like a stubborn block of granite.

"This isn't the right time."

"Tree!" Cody's muffled cry emerged from the tangle of sheets and Kristen's clothing. "I fell out of the tree! That's how I got hurt!"

Luke opened his mouth as if to continue his interrogation, but Kristen silenced him with a ferocious scowl. Cody's continuing sobs were punctuated by a weak, smothered chant of "Tree, tree..."

"Go away," Kristen mouthed at Luke over the top of Cody's head.

He looked as if he were about to give her an argument, but the glare she fired off like a warning shot across the bow must have convinced him he wouldn't win. He let the bedcovers fall from his fist, retrieved his coffee and marched out of the room.

It took Kristen fifteen minutes to calm Cody down, and even then she only succeeded with a little help from nature. "What'd you say, sweetie?" She ceased stroking his hair and coaxed up his chin so she could hear him.

"I hafta go to the bathroom," he whispered into the front of his pajama top.

"Oh. Uh, okay." The guest bathroom was down the hall. "Do you want me to...help you?"

"Aunt *Kristen,*" he said with disgust. "I can go by *myself.*"

It was such a blessedly normal, tough-little-boy response that she came close to a genuine laugh. "I just meant, do you want me to help you *get* there. Does it hurt too much to walk? Do you want me to carry you?"

"I can walk," he said bravely, even though she could see the effort it cost him to struggle off the bed onto his sore muscles and aching limbs.

"This way." When Cody finally detached his limpetlike grip, Kristen found the hand he'd been clutching had turned numb. She shepherded him closely in case he stumbled or the pain became too much for him. He tottered across the room on his unsteady legs as if he were seventy-seven instead of seven. Rage and hatred pounded for Kristen's attention, but she did her best to ignore their insistent clamor. Time enough to deal with Derek later. Right now Cody needed her full concentration.

"I'll be right here outside," she promised as he clumsily swung the bathroom door shut. She considered pressing her ear against the wood to eavesdrop for any problems, then decided that would be going overboard. He could call out if he ran into trouble. She massaged her tingling hand, where the feeling was starting to return.

A wide-shouldered shadow blocked the light at the end of the hallway. Luke. As his work boots thudded toward her, Kristen saw he was fully dressed now, wearing a red T-shirt and a navy blue windbreaker with the sleeves pushed up to the elbows.

Whew. At least she wouldn't have to confront that distracting, broad expanse of bare chest again. Those Greek-god pectorals...that sexy sprinkling of dark hair...that sturdy ribcage tapering down into his jeans...

"You," he said, clamping his fingers around her wrist like a handcuff. "I want to talk to you."

"Ouch!" Pins and needles shot up her arm from her partially awakened flesh. "Let me go. I'm waiting for Cody."

Luke hesitated, but didn't let go. "He's in there?" He canted his head toward the bathroom door.

"Yes."

"Good. We can talk privately for a second." He headed back toward the living room, hauling Kristen behind him.

She dug in her heels. "Stop! I told Cody I'd be right outside."

"Take my word for it," Luke said over his shoulder without slowing down. "As a former seven-year-old boy, I can personally assure you Cody would be mortified if he knew you were hovering right outside the door, wringing your hands like you're afraid he might fall in."

"I was *rubbing* one hand because it went numb when—"

"Forget about that." Once he'd dragged her out into the living room, Luke let her go. He scrubbed his fingers through hair still damp from the shower, shoving it up in little black spikes. "Look, you're not doing that kid any favors by coddling him."

"*Coddling* him? Luke, the poor child's been through hell!"

"He says he fell out of a tree."

"Of *course* he does! Because that's what Derek *told* him to say, and he's terrified of Derek!"

Luke crossed his arms. He looked like a bouncer barring entrance to a trendy nightclub. "How do I know the boy isn't telling the truth?" Shrug. "Maybe Derek didn't hurt him at all. Maybe you just made up the whole story so I'd help you finagle custody away from his father."

Kristen's nails jabbed into her palms. "*You're* his father."

"Don't!" Luke speared a warning finger into the air. He took a deep breath, visibly struggling to control his temper. "Do *not* say that again. I mean it."

A tide of helpless despair rose inside Kristen. "You told me last night you would help us. I thought that meant you believed me."

"It meant I decided I ought to find out what's going on."

Luke's jaw jutted forward. "Clearly *someone's* up to no good."

"And you think maybe it's me." A blade of hurt slashed through Kristen. She couldn't blame Luke for not believing her at first, but to have him think her capable of using Cody as a pawn in some vindictive scheme—

"Fine," she said, jerking up her chin. "I'll take Cody and leave. I can protect him *without* your help." She spun around but got no more than two steps before Luke yanked her to a halt.

"You're not taking him anywhere," he informed her through clenched teeth. "Not until I get to the bottom of this."

His hand was a red-hot manacle around her wrist. He held her pinioned so close Kristen could smell the soap from his shower and see the blue embers smoldering in his eyes. There was a wild, dangerous gleam in them.

But she refused to back down in the face of danger. Not anymore. She held her ground without flinching.

Right up to the astonishing moment when Luke hauled off and kissed her.

Chapter 3

What the devil's wrong with you? yelled a voice inside Luke's head a split second before his lips collided with Kristen's. One moment he'd been so steamed up at her he was ready to chew nails, then all of a sudden he was kissing her as if his life depended on it!

In his cocky youthful days Luke had fancied himself quite a skilled kisser. Even before he and Sheri had started going steady in high school, young Luke had had ample opportunity to refine his technique. He'd prided himself on his ability to hold his own eagerness in check while he tenderly seduced a girl with his lips, enticing her with sweet whispers and lazy flicks of his tongue till she practically melted with desire and swooned right into his arms.

This kiss with Kristen didn't fall into that category at all.

This kiss was hard, reckless, impatient. Luke wasn't so much sharing it with her as *inflicting* it on her. He kept her wrist pinned against his side while his other hand got all tangled up in her thick hair, cupping the base of her skull to imprison her mouth against his.

Yet, except for one brief instant when Kristen had gone rigid with shock, Luke had felt no resistance from either her slender body or her warm, pliant mouth. If he had, he would have released her at once.

Luke might be sadly out of practice, but he still had no trouble recognizing when a woman was kissing him back. *That,* perhaps, came as the greatest shock of all. Sheri's little sister? Responding to him with a grown woman's passion, with an adult awareness of where this could lead?

Lust surged through him, a bolt of lightning that knocked him dizzy and charged every cell in his body with electricity. He melded his mouth even more demandingly to hers, seeking her tongue with a blind, senseless hunger that blotted out everything except his own ferocious need.

But Luke's instinct for self-preservation was too keenly honed to be ignored for long. His hormones had led him astray once before, hadn't they? Straight into the biggest mistake of his life.

Letting one woman become too important to him.

He broke off the kiss abruptly, with none of the finesse he'd once been so proud of. He cursed himself for a fool. Hadn't he already learned his lesson from *one* treacherous Monroe sister?

He let go of Kristen as if she'd scalded him. Except that her hair was still twisted around his fingers, the long strands ensnaring him like a clever trap. It took a clumsy minute for Luke to extricate his hand. The whole time he was uncomfortably aware that Kristen was studying his face from mere inches away, the curiosity in her eyes shifting first to uncertainty, then to hurt.

As soon as he freed himself, they both stepped backward.

Kristen tossed her head. "Well," she said, clearly trying to disguise her wounded feelings with a veneer of accusation, "I guess I don't have to ask what *that* was all about."

"Huh?" *Brilliant rejoinder, Hollister.* But her lips were still swollen from his kiss, her mouth glistening with moisture.

Luke was momentarily sidetracked by the herculean struggle it took not to seize her and kiss her again.

He got a grip on himself. "What are you talking about?" he asked. There was irritation in his voice, but it wasn't aimed at her.

"Not *what. Who.*" Kristen flipped a gleaming fistful of hair back over her shoulder with an air of false bravado that reminded Luke eerily of her sister. Sheri, too, had always put up a bold front to hide her vulnerability from the world.

"I'm talking about Sheri," Kristen said, jolting Luke with the echo of his own thoughts. "That was really for her, wasn't it?"

"You mean that, uh, that..." He made a few fumbling circles with his hand, as if a round of charades might save him from having to say the word out loud. "That kiss?" he finished, barely managing not to scuff his toe on the rug like an embarrassed adolescent. "No. I mean—"

What the heck *did* he mean, anyhow? That in a moment of weakness he'd given in to the crazy attraction he'd been fighting ever since Kristen had shown up on his doorstep last night? That he'd made a bad mistake by yanking her close to him? That the velvet heat of her skin, the irresistible curve of her mouth, the dazzling green sparks in her eyes had simply proven too much for him?

Much smarter just to keep her in the dark about the traitorous urges she aroused inside him. "Maybe you're right," he said with a one-shoulder shrug. "I shouldn't have done that. I'm sorry."

Was that disappointment that shimmered through her eyes? Or relief?

Whichever it was, she was concealing it now. "I really think it's best if Cody and I leave," she said, smoothing the front of her blouse as if Luke had pawed his hands all over it. "I'm sorry, too. Obviously this was a bad idea, coming to you for help."

Something akin to alarm set Luke's nerves jangling. Once Kristen got it into her head it was best to take Cody and run, there would be no way to stop her. Luke had to convince her to stay. For the kid's sake.

"Look, I promised to help you, and I'm a man of my word." He reached for her elbow, then thought better of it. She had the sexiest elbows he'd ever seen. At the last second his hand changed course and swung toward the kitchen instead. "Let me get you a cup of coffee while you make up a list of what Cody needs. I'll run out right now and buy the stuff."

Kristen's eyes narrowed with suspicion at his sudden cooperative attitude. Luke produced what he hoped was a disarming smile. "We'll forget about what just happened, all right? I promise it won't happen again."

Indecision wavered across her lovely features. Luke could practically hear the wheels spinning inside her head while she weighed her options. Her problem was, she didn't have too many.

He would be willing to bet his last dime, though, that Kristen would eventually choose whatever course of action she thought best for Cody—never mind that it might mean continuing her own awkward association with Luke.

She didn't disappoint him. "All right," she agreed at last. "Get me a pencil and paper, while I go check on Cody."

Luke delayed a moment to watch her walk down the hall, her glossy auburn mane dancing between her shoulder blades. His fingers twitched with the memory of what it felt like to curl themselves through that luxuriant, sweet-smelling softness. Even with her head held high and her spine ruler-straight, her hips swayed with a natural rhythm that set the blood pounding through Luke's veins again.

Before he could stop himself, he relived the hard, hot thrill of his mouth on hers.

I promise it won't happen again.

He'd sworn to Kristen he was a man of his word. But Luke had an uneasy hunch that this was one promise it was going to be darn near impossible to keep.

* * *

"Would you like to go in the living room and watch TV while we wait for Luke to come back?"

Cody shook his head in response to Kristen's question. Luke had left for the drugstore half an hour ago, armed with a short list of supplies. They'd decided it would be safer if he shopped for clothes later, in the neighboring town of Pineville, where the clerk wouldn't wonder why Luke Hollister was buying kids' clothing.

After venturing out to the bathroom, Cody had limped back to huddle beneath the covers in Luke's guest room. He lay there now, listless and uncommunicative, his dejected expression tearing at Kristen's heart. He wore the same tragic face as a little boy trying to be brave after learning his puppy dog has been run over.

Kristen had attempted to coax him out to the kitchen for breakfast, but he'd rejected even her repeated offers to bring him a piece of toast or a bowl of cereal to eat in bed.

"I'm not hungry, Aunt Kristen."

"Cody, you need to eat something, even if you don't feel like it."

"But I *can't.*" Then, inevitably, his lips would start to tremble and Kristen would squeeze his hand helplessly.

What was she going to do if Cody kept refusing to eat? What if his condition took a turn for the worse? What if she couldn't protect him from Derek after all?

One after another, doubts tormented her. Her one tiny measure of consolation was that at least now she had Luke on her side. Well, sort of.

Luke. Kristen's heart flipped over when she thought about how he'd kissed her that morning.

Except he hadn't really been kissing *her,* had he? Only technically. He'd as much as admitted that kiss had really been for Sheri.

How many teenage nights had Kristen spent mooning out her bedroom window, dreaming about what it would be like to kiss her sister's boyfriend? Now she knew. And it hadn't been anything at all how she'd fantasized so many years ago.

Of course, back then Luke hadn't held a grudge against her. He didn't suspect her of trying to involve him in some outrageous scheme. It was the *anger* in his kiss that had stunned Kristen, as much as the kiss itself.

Over the years she'd successfully conquered her schoolgirl crush on Luke, packing it away with her high-school yearbook, her rock-star posters and all the other relics of her adolescent era.

That's what she'd firmly believed, anyway. Until this morning when Luke had flung open her emotional storage closet with one rough, possessive kiss and started dragging out old feelings right and left.

Agitation propelled Kristen to her feet. She would *not* let herself fall under Luke's spell again. She should have pushed him away. How could she have indulged in even that brief moment of pleasure when poor Sheri was dead because of her?

If only she hadn't convinced her sister to leave her husband...

At least she still had a chance to save her sister's son. "Cody, I'm going to find a radio to bring in here so we can listen to it, okay?" It dawned on Kristen that the local radio station might be reporting the story of Cody's disappearance. Any information about what the police were saying could prove helpful.

"You won't go 'way, will you?" Cody's hand shot out from beneath the covers and latched onto her.

Kristen clasped it reassuringly. She *hated* that the only strong emotion to rouse her nephew from his lethargy was fear. "Sweetheart, I'm *never* going to leave you." She hoped her smile conveyed more confidence than she actually felt. "You're going to be safe from now on. I promise."

His big blue eyes flickered with halfhearted hope, as if he *wanted* to believe her, but didn't quite dare to. Kristen patted his hand. "I'll be back in a flash, okay?"

"'Kay."

Like the ongoing ebb and flow of the tides, another wave of fury swelled inside Kristen. No matter how much it cost her, she was going to make sure that someday Derek Vincent paid for what he'd done to Cody. To Sheri. To the two people Kristen loved most in the world.

She left Cody's room to look for a radio. After searching most of Luke's house, however, the only one she could locate was part of his expensive, high-tech stereo system. But then she would have to leave Cody alone while she sat out in the living room listening for news.

There was one room Kristen hadn't searched yet. She paused at the threshold of Luke's bedroom, reluctant to enter.

"For heaven's sake, it's just the room where he sleeps," she scolded herself under her breath. Well, actually, chances were Luke did more than just *sleep* in that rumpled king-size bed—although word would certainly have gotten around Whisper Ridge if Luke had had a stream of women parading through his bedroom. In the absence of such gossip, Kristen could only theorize that he must be seeking his female companionship out of town.

"Oh, grow up," she muttered. "His love life is none of your business." She made herself enter his room. "What are you afraid of finding in here? A pair of lace panties? Kinky sex toys?"

Still, it was a big relief when she spotted the radio alarm clock on the nightstand beside Luke's unmade bed. She could still see the depression in the pillow where his head had rested last night.

"Cut it out," she said, gritting her teeth. She only wanted one thing from Luke, and it definitely didn't involve sharing that pillow with him.

She unplugged the clock radio, even though Luke would now have to reset the time. Tough. She bolted from his room and was about to enter Cody's when a faint, unfamiliar sound caught her attention. Was it coming from outside the house? Or inside?

She tiptoed down the hallway toward the living room, radio clutched to her chest. The noise grew louder. The curtains were still drawn, but she dropped to her hands and knees anyway, just in case someone could see her shadow from outside. Abandoning the clock, she crept toward the kitchen, following the sound.

It was a metallic, irregular clicking. Some kind of kitchen appliance that had switched on automatically?

Suddenly Kristen froze, trapping a startled gasp in her throat. Once she'd moved within sight of the back door, she could see what was making that sound.

Someone was jiggling the doorknob.

Trying to get in.

For one desperate moment she nearly convinced herself it was only Luke. He'd forgotten his key, that was all. Except wouldn't he keep his house key on the same ring with his car keys?

Besides, the knob was rotating in a stealthy, controlled fashion, interspersed with long pauses. Luke would have rattled it impatiently, kicked the door, then gone around the house banging on windows to get her attention.

No, someone was definitely trying to pick the lock and break in. And Kristen didn't believe for one terror-filled second it was a burglar.

''That be it for you today?'' Ralph Myers, the middle-aged pharmacist, gave Luke a sociable smile while he rang up his purchases.

Luke hadn't felt so self-conscious since the first time he'd bought a box of condoms. ''Uh, yeah. That's it.'' It had taken him forever just to round up the few items on Kristen's list. He couldn't believe how many types of children's pain relievers there were to choose from. He wanted to make sure he got the best one, except he didn't have the foggiest idea how to tell the difference. Then he'd had to track down toothbrushes, toothpaste, bandages, antiseptic spray…

At least Kristen hadn't put any of those feminine products on her list. That's where Luke would have had to draw the line.

He accepted his change from Ralph and took his time stuffing the bills back into his wallet. He had one more thing he needed to do before he left the store.

Fortunately, Ralph was shorthanded today. He hurried back to stocking the shelves without waiting for Luke to leave the counter. As soon as Ralph was out of sight, Luke darted back down the pain medication aisle. Quickly he reached into his sack and switched the adult version he'd just purchased for a box of the children's kind. Same brand. Same price. Ralph would have been curious if Luke had brought a product meant for kids up to the cash register. And for a pharmacist, Ralph was sadly lacking in the discretion department.

Luke hustled out of the drugstore, flinching as the telltale bell over the door jingled behind him. He supposed he could have just slipped Cody's medicine into his pocket and walked out with it, but Kristen had already conned him into abetting a kidnapping. No way was he going to let her turn him into a shoplifter as well.

Still, he jumped into his pickup truck and peeled out of the parking lot as if he were driving a getaway car.

Going shopping had been the easy part, compared to going home. Luke dreaded facing Kristen again, after the way he'd lost his mind and kissed her that morning. What made it even worse was that, deep down inside, Luke still wanted to kiss her. Even though tangling with a cougar would be safer.

He eased up on the gas pedal a little.

Kristen rushed into Cody's room. ''Out of bed, sleepy-head!'' She tried to keep her voice cheerful so as not to scare her nephew any more than she had to, but the look on her face must have given her away. Or else the fact that her teeth were chattering.

Fear leaped into Cody's eyes even before she scooped him off the bed, sheet and all. ''No,'' he whimpered.

His featherweight body trembled in Kristen's arms as she fled down the hallway. They had to hide. Fast.

Someone had come looking for them.

Last night Kristen had left her florist's van parked at the

hospital and carried Cody the entire eight blocks to Luke's house. Had someone spotted their late-night arrival anyway?

Someone who might have mentioned it to the wrong person....

She stumbled into Luke's bedroom. It was farthest from the back door, and it had a big closet she'd noticed earlier. "Here we go, honey. We're going to stay in here for a while. Just like hide-and-seek, huh?"

But Cody clearly realized this was no game. He clung to Kristen's neck with the terrified strength of steel in his thin arms. Clumsily she maneuvered them both into the closet, shoving aside hangers so they could hide behind the clothes. Luke apparently hadn't done his laundry recently. Hopefully the jumbled pile of clothing on the closet floor would provide extra camouflage.

It went against Kristen's nature, though, to cower helplessly and wait for discovery. Whoever was looking for them possessed at least two brain cells, which were all it would require to think of checking the closet.

What about...?

She craned her neck to look up at the closet ceiling, and immediately spotted an access panel that must lead to the crawl space under the roof. If they could climb up through that somehow...

She shoved her way out of the closet and plopped Cody on Luke's bed. "Let go for just a second, okay?" She had to pry his arms from around her neck.

Then she grabbed the nightstand and hauled it over to the closet. There was a high shelf above the rod where the clothes hung. By scrambling onto the nightstand, she was able to reach the access panel and push it aside. A musty smell floated out of the darkness.

"Guess what! I found us an even better hiding place." Kristen swept Cody off the bed and climbed back onto the nightstand with him in her arms. "I know it looks spooky up there, but I want you to crawl through that hole, all right?"

His arms tightened around her neck. "Do it now," she commanded in the sternest voice she'd ever used on her nephew. There wasn't time to sweet-talk him into it. She hoisted Cody onto the closet shelf, then half shoved him through the opening. She winced, knowing what a painful impact this would have on his bruised little body.

"Aunt Kristen, aren't you coming?" His frightened voice drifted out of the crawl space.

"You bet I am." Kristen pushed the nightstand back beside the bed so it wouldn't look out of place. Somehow she would have to haul herself onto the shelf without it.

It had been a lot of years since she'd done pull-ups in gym class. For a few panicked seconds she didn't think she was going to make it. Even with adrenaline and fear propelling her, her muscles screamed in protest. On the third try she managed to hook one foot over the shelf and drag herself onto it, inch by agonizing inch.

Panting, she scrambled through the opening in the ceiling. Once she was inside the crawl space, she turned around and wriggled the upper half of her body back through it. By stretching one arm to its limit, she could just barely reach the closet door. Using her fingertips, she maneuvered it most of the way shut.

Then she scuttled backward as fast as her contorted position allowed, and pushed the access panel back into place.

Now the darkness was pitch-black.

She felt around for Cody and drew him close. "Okay, honey," she whispered. "We've got to be very, very quiet and sit still. Understand?"

Cody burrowed his face into her neck and nodded with a tiny animal sound. Of course he understood. He understood all too well.

Kristen held her breath. Over the frantic thumping of her heart she heard a noise again. Different this time. Even from up here, it sounded closer.

"Hey, Andy? Luke. Just wanted to let you know I'm going to be a little late showing up at the job site today." Driving home from the drugstore, Luke had remembered he ought to check in with his second-in-command, Andy Driscoll. Two weeks ago Hollister Construction had managed to land the contract to build a new recreation center over in Pineville. He was calling Andy there now from his truck.

"No, I was not out carousing all night." Luke grimaced sourly into his cell phone. "Don't I wish." True, he hadn't gotten much sleep—that much of Andy's guess was accurate. But what had kept Luke flailing between the sheets all night was the unsettling awareness that Kristen was sleeping right down the hall from him.

Along with the boy who *could* be, but probably wasn't, his son.

Luke was treated to a couple more of Andy's bawdy, good-natured wisecracks before he hung up. "Just make sure that foundation gets poured right," he retorted, "in case I don't get there in time."

After Luke broke the connection, he scowled. Kristen Monroe was a complication he didn't need or want in his life right now. If it weren't for the kid, Luke wouldn't have allowed the woman to set one dainty foot in his house, much less agreed to help her prove that Derek killed Sheri.

Kristen spelled trouble, and Luke had enough trouble on his plate right now, thank you.

Hollister Construction had been riding high until a year ago. Luke had finally achieved the financial success he'd struggled for all his life. He'd finally proved to himself and to...well, never mind. He'd proved he wasn't just some dirt-poor nobody from the wrong side of the tracks. Proved he wouldn't settle for being just another Vincent Lumber wage slave.

Luke had grown up watching how working for the company in a one-company town could grind a man down. He'd wanted a better life than his father had had, toiling long hours at back-breaking labor for a meager paycheck. Exchanging years of loyalty and hard work—sacrificing his health, even—all for some stingy pension.

His parents had moved to Arizona when his dad retired. But

Luke had stuck around, building up his business, buying a house, trying to make a name for himself in a town where only one name counted. On occasion, while contemplating life over a nice tall cold one, Luke would ask himself—particularly during the last twelve, trying months—how come he stayed.

Not to say that Whisper Ridge didn't have lots to offer. Magnificent scenery, for example. Good people. Clean mountain air. But when he got right down to the bottom of the beer bottle, Luke had to admit that what probably kept him here was sheer stubbornness.

He'd needed plenty of it lately. First had come the fire that had nearly wiped out his business in one night. Then the cancelled contracts. Followed by all those nasty glitches with his suppliers that always seemed to crop up at the worst possible moment. If his luck didn't turn around soon he might as well stand back and holler "Ti-i-m-m-ber-r!" while his construction business toppled into oblivion.

No, the last thing Luke needed right now was to get suckered into some scheme of Kristen's, to fall for her sexy green eyes and kissable lips, to swallow the dubious role she was trying to foist on him.

Holy cow. Could he actually be a father?

No! It wasn't true. It couldn't be. With a sharp wrench of the steering wheel, Luke turned onto his street. He wasn't about to buy Kristen's claim for a minute, not when the previous road he'd been led down by the Monroe sisters was littered with so many lies.

Luke had committed himself to helping the boy, that was all. No matter whose son he was.

It sounded to Kristen as if whoever was outside was probably making his way around the house now, checking for an unlocked window.

Dear God…it surely wouldn't take long to find one. Not in a town where plenty of people didn't even bother locking their *doors* at night. How could she have been so careless? She should have gone through Luke's house earlier, making sure everything was fastened as securely as possible.

She could also kick herself for not grabbing a weapon. She should have taken a knife from the kitchen, a hammer or screwdriver—*some* piece of hardware with deadly potential. It couldn't have been too difficult to find tools lying around Luke's house.

Kristen's leg was getting a cramp. She shifted carefully, trying to keep most of her and Cody's weight on the rafters so they didn't crash down through the ceiling. Dust tickled her nose. To her dismay, she felt a sneeze coming on. Quickly she pinched her nose until the urge passed. For now, anyway.

Maybe it was the police outside. Except the cops wouldn't be sneaking around trying windows. They would have announced themselves loudly, rapped on the front door, then simply smashed through it if they suspected Kristen and Cody were inside.

But even if it *were* the police, Cody was still in danger. Because the police would hand him right back over to Derek, and then Kristen would never get another chance to rescue him.

Especially after she was locked up in jail for kidnapping.

"He's not going to get you," she mouthed silently into Cody's hair. Weapon or not, she intended to put up a fight.

All at once Kristen lifted her head. The hair on the back of her neck stood up. Unless she was mistaken, she'd just heard a window scrape open.

Chapter 4

Luke pulled into his garage and got out of his truck carrying the sack from the drugstore. His backyard was screened by a mix of pine and fir trees, so he knew none of his neighbors were spying on him while he strode to the back door of his house. But he couldn't shake the creepy feeling that someone was watching him.

Kristen had him all paranoid. Why would anyone be watching *him*, anyway? He had no connection to the missing kid.

Still, he relocked the door once he got inside the kitchen. Never hurt to take precautions.

The house was silent as a tomb. Hmm. For some reason that struck Luke as ominous. Good grief, Kristen hadn't taken Cody and flown the coop while he'd been at the drugstore, had she? Maybe sending him on that errand had just been a ruse to get him out of the house.

He picked up his pace as he walked through the dining room. In the living room he almost tripped over something. Hey, what was his clock radio doing out here, upside down on the floor, its unplugged cord curling limply across the carpet like a dead snake?

Weird. Luke didn't like weird.

Then he heard a scuffling sound around the corner. "What the...?" He sprinted into the hallway just in time to see a hand disappear through the open window. "Hey!" He put on some of the famous speed that had made him a track star in high school, but by the time he reached the window, whoever had just crawled out had vanished.

Luke dropped the sack and went after him. "Ow!" He landed hard in the hydrangea bush outside the window, sending spikes of pain shooting up from his ankle. Muttering curses, he checked to the right, then the left, then the right again. No sign of the intruder. If Luke had ever been a Boy Scout, maybe he could have picked up the guy's trail. As it was, he didn't have a clue which way he'd gone.

Then he heard a car engine roar into life the next street over. It was as good a lead to follow as any. Luke charged across his backyard, fought his way through the prickly pine branches, then raced down the driveway of the property that backed up to his.

Just as he reached the front sidewalk, a car sped by—a sleek European luxury sedan that would have looked far more at home tooling up the autobahn than bumping along the potholed streets of Whisper Ridge.

Luke couldn't see the driver through the tinted windshield. He didn't need to.

"Son of a..." Lacking a solid target, he punched his fist through the air. If that bastard had done so much as touch one hair on either Cody's or Kristen's head...

Luke pivoted a hundred and eighty degrees and dashed back the way he'd come. He moved even faster than before, never mind that he'd been out of breath to start with. Dread put rockets on his feet.

He wrenched the back doorknob, then slammed his palm against the door in frustration. Locked, of course. He dug his keys out of his pocket. His hand was shaking, so that he wasted precious seconds trying to slot the stupid key into the lock.

Then he was back inside again, scanning each room as he hurried through the house. "Kristen? Cody?" He didn't bother keeping his voice down. Too late now to worry about someone discovering they were hiding here. Someone already knew.

The guest room was empty, the bedding strewn in disarray as if a tornado had swept Cody off the mattress. The dread in the pit of Luke's stomach congealed into fear. "Cody? Kristen?"

What was that? Luke thought he might have heard a distant reply. He yelled again, cupped a hand behind his ear, then followed Kristen's voice down the hall and into his own bedroom. "Where are you?" he demanded.

"Here."

Luke shoved open his closet door and starting whipping hangers right and left. "Where?"

"Up *here.*"

Surprised, he looked up. Kristen was peering down at him through the opening into the crawl space. Relief and traces of fear mingled on her face with streaks of dust.

"Are you all right? Where's Cody?" Luke moved quickly to reach for her.

"He's here. We're fine." She adjusted her position to make room for Cody. "Can you lift him down?"

"Sure."

"It's okay now, sweetie. It's safe. Don't worry. Luke will help you."

Judging by the scared look on Cody's face, he would have preferred to stay perched up there in the dark rather than submit to Luke's handling. But he obeyed his aunt and allowed her to lower him through the opening.

He slid awkwardly into Luke's waiting arms. A strange thing happened to Luke as the boy's full weight settled against him. A bubble of pressure expanded inside his chest, squeezing his heart. A feeling akin to...longing.

Luke had never held a kid before, never known what it felt

like to carry such an important burden. Why, Cody was completely dependent on him right now! What if Luke accidentally dropped him, or stumbled and fell? His safety was entirely in Luke's hands.

He'd never comprehended before how vulnerable kids were, how fragile. Cody hardly weighed more than a bundle of chicken wire. Except this bundle pulsed with life and warmth and emotion. His compact little body contained all the special qualities that made each human being unique.

Luke tightened his grip in a protective reflex. By God, he wasn't going to let that animal Derek Vincent get his hands on this sweet kid again!

Cody began to squirm. Obviously he didn't share the awe, the sense of revelation that Luke was experiencing. Luke gently sat him down on the bed. He wanted to pat the kid's head or something, rustle his hair, tell him everything was going to be all right. But he wasn't sure how to.

Now it was Kristen's turn. By the time Luke came back from the bed, she was already shimmying backward through the rectangular opening. Her tantalizing tush incited all sorts of ideas Luke had no business considering. Still, he had to grab her *someplace,* didn't he?

He helped her down. She twisted around at the last second and tumbled straight into his arms.

"Oh, Luke. Oh, thank goodness!"

Her soft breasts were crushed against his chest. She had her arms wrapped so tight around his neck Luke could barely breathe. He didn't complain, though.

Her voice was muffled in his shirt. "I heard a noise, then I found someone trying to break into the house through the back door, so we ran in here to hide, but then I heard a window open somewhere—"

"The hallway." Luke's response came out a bit strangled.

Kristen immediately loosened her hold and drew back to stare at him, her enormous eyes a vivid green in contrast to her pale complexion. She had a cobweb trailing through her hair and a smudge on the tip of her nose. She looked sexy as all get-out.

"You saw him?" she asked breathlessly.

"Only part of him. Disappearing through the window." Somehow Luke's hands were still bracketing her hips, even though she no longer needed him to steady her. "He must have got the window open and climbed in just as I got home. Then got scared off when he heard me inside in the house."

Kristen bit her lip. "Could you tell who it—?"

"I chased after him, but he had too big a head start." Luke stretched his mouth into a grim line. "I saw his car drive off, though. It was Derek."

Cody let out a faint moan.

Kristen dug her nails into Luke's arms. "Oh, no." Her worst suspicion confirmed. "I *knew* it was him." She peered quickly past Luke's broad shoulder. Cody sat frozen on the edge of Luke's bed, bare feet dangling above the floor, arms wrapped around his midsection as if he had a terrible stomachache. His eyes had that hunted, fearful look again, the look that always slapped Kristen like an accusation. It's *your* fault my mommy's dead. It's *your* fault that now my daddy hits me.

Of course, Cody wasn't really thinking those things. It was Kristen's own guilty conscience taunting her.

All at once she realized that she and Luke were standing awfully close together. *Much* closer than necessary. It might have been only natural for Kristen to hug him with gratitude and relief when she'd first hit the floor. But there was no cause for prolonging this rather intimate embrace. No reason why Luke's hands should still be curved possessively on her hips, branding her with their heat. No need for Kristen to keep clutching the biceps that bulged beneath his jacket sleeves.

And there was no excuse at all for the sudden flare-up of desire that whipped through her, urging her into the strong, seductive shelter of his embrace.

She uncurled her fingers and let go of him. Luke hesitated for barely a second, then removed his hands from her hips and stuffed his fists into his pockets. He was still slightly out of breath from chasing Derek, his rugged features flushed. A throbbing vein in his neck revealed his heart was still pumping in overdrive.

Before she could stop it, a vision crashed through Kristen's mind—the vision of Luke arching above her, making love to her right here in this bedroom, flushed and out of breath like he was right—

No!

She squinched her eyes shut as tightly as possible, but she couldn't shut off that inner vision. Why did all the unrequited yearnings of her schoolgirl infatuation have to pick *this* inconvenient moment to come back and torment her?

Those feelings hadn't led anywhere before, and they weren't going to lead anywhere now. She was only torturing herself with these unwanted hallucinations.

Kristen took a deep breath and opened her eyes. Luke was studying her with a wary look, one dark eyebrow cocked at an angle.

She felt as exposed as a bug under a microscope. Well, *this* bug wasn't going to stand around and be visually dissected. "Come on, Cody. We can go back to your room now."

Cody hooked his heels under the bed frame as if he intended to stay right here where it was safe.

"The coast is clear now. I promise." Kristen had been making an awful lot of promises to her nephew lately. Time would tell how good she was at keeping them.

Cody tentatively slipped his hand into hers. Kristen's first instinct was to pick him up and carry him, but then she remembered what Luke had said about coddling him. Maybe it *would* be better for Cody if she stopped treating him like a helpless infant.

It just killed her to see him in pain, though.

Hand in hand they walked slowly down the hall. Kristen knelt below the open window to retrieve the drugstore sack Luke had dropped. Luke reached over her and slammed the window shut, locking it with an emphatic flick of his wrist.

His arm brushed Kristen's shoulders when she stood up. Once again she had to fight the desire to lean into him, to press her cheek against his chest so she could hear the steady, reassuring beat of his heart telling her everything was going to be all right.

But, for Cody's sake, she had to stand on her own two feet without depending on anyone else. Cody was *her* responsibility, and hers alone, until Luke accepted him as his son.

Something that might never happen.

How could Luke see that child's adorable face, look into those hurt, innocent eyes, and not *want* Cody to be his?

Kristen sighed. "You know what?" she said to her nephew with forced cheerfulness. "I haven't had any breakfast yet, and my tummy's growling. How 'bout yours?"

Cody flattened his hand over his stomach as if to assess its condition. He gave a halfhearted shrug.

Well, at least he hadn't refused to eat again. "Let's go into the kitchen and get a glass of water for you to drink with your medicine. And I'll bet Luke has some breakfast cereal in his cupboard, don't you, Luke?"

"Uh..."

"Some bread, then. We can make toast."

"Er..." Luke rubbed the base of his neck. "See, I'd actually planned to go to the grocery store today...."

They reached the kitchen. "Well, what *do* you have to..." Kristen opened the refrigerator. "Oh."

Luke offered her a lame smile.

"For heaven's sake, what do you live on? Mayonnaise and moldy cheese?" That just about summed up the contents of his refrigerator.

"I might have a jelly doughnut left over from yesterday," he said with sudden inspiration.

"How handy! An entire day's allowance of fat *and* sugar, all in one completely nutritionless meal." Kristen let the refrigerator door swing shut with disgust.

"I *like* doughnuts," Cody said in a small, hopeful voice.

Both adults turned toward him in surprise. Kristen swallowed hard. This was the first spark of interest Cody had shown about *anything* since she'd taken him from the hospital.

Luke grinned. "So, you like doughnuts, too, huh?"

Cody nodded. "They're my *favorite.*"

"Yeah?" Luke crouched down on his haunches so he and Cody were eye to eye. "What kind do you like best?"

"Mmm..." Cody tipped his head to one side, considering. "Chocolate covered. With sprinkles."

"Hey, me, too!" Luke pointed to his own chest. "Guess that's why there's only a jelly one left." He winked.

"I like those, too," Cody said politely.

"Well, good." Luke pushed himself to his feet and crossed his fingers that that doughnut was still out in the truck where he thought he'd left it yesterday. Otherwise, he was about to make a trip to the bakery.

He would gladly buy a whole baker's dozen of doughnuts, all chocolate covered with sprinkles, if that's what the little guy wanted.

Kristen got a nervous look on her face when Luke headed for the back door. "Don't worry." He touched her shoulder and muttered in her ear, "He's gone."

"For the time being."

Luke felt a shiver pass through her. He gave Kristen's arm an encouraging squeeze, then remembered he wasn't supposed to touch her anymore. "I'll be right back."

For Pete's sake, why couldn't he keep his hands off her? He met attractive women all the time. Heck, Andy Driscoll was always fixing him up on blind dates with some out-of-town cousin or old schoolmate of his wife's. Luke had never had any trouble acting the perfect gentleman, even when his date made it plain she would willingly settle for a little less perfection and a little more...hanky-panky.

Truth was, Luke had got used to letting women pursue *him,* not the other way around. It was a lot safer that way. Gave him the upper hand, so to speak. Then, when the relationship inevitably cooled off, *he* wasn't the one left standing there with a broken heart.

So what made Kristen different? Why was it Luke couldn't seem to be in her presence for more than three seconds without feeling compelled to touch her? Without imagining all sorts of tempting possibilities?

For cryin' out loud, she was Sheri's little *sister*. Was that why Luke couldn't stop thinking about getting her into bed? Was this some sicko revenge fantasy to pay back both Sheri and Kristen for the way they'd once betrayed him?

Yeah, that must be it. What other explanation could there be for the dangerous attraction that kept drawing him to Kristen the same way a kid is drawn to matches?

Playing with fire. That's what he would be doing, all right, if he couldn't control his lustful urges.

Luke opened the door of his truck and rummaged through the clutter on the front seat. Aha! One stale doughnut, coming right up. At least it would tide the boy over until they could get him some real food.

Cody was finishing a glass of water when Luke got back to the kitchen. "You'll feel better soon," Kristen assured him, "now that you've taken some medicine." She curved her hand over the boy's forehead.

Luke had a sudden childhood memory of his own mother, checking him for fever with that same tender gesture. He'd never imagined it from her perspective before, or comprehended the concern she must have been hiding behind her comforting smile.

Mom and Pop were always hinting how they would love to have grandkids someday....

Forget it. Luke hated to disappoint them, but he wasn't about to make that kind of commitment with a woman. As for the possibility that he might *already* have fathered a child, well, that was just wishful thinking. Common sense warned Luke against getting his hopes up.

Besides, if he couldn't figure some way out of this mess with Derek, Kristen was going to vanish with Sheri's son forever.

''One jelly doughnut, as ordered.'' Luke produced the crumpled white bag with a flourish.

Cody's eyes lit up. ''Thanks!'' He opened the bag cautiously, as if experience had taught him not to get *his* hopes up, either. He nibbled the doughnut gingerly at first, but was soon chomping it with gusto. Clearly the fact that it was a day old didn't bother his taste buds.

Kristen's face shone with pleasure. Her smile illuminated her pretty features, turned her eyes luminous with love. Luke found himself watching *her* instead of Cody.

He shook himself with impatience. ''Can we talk alone for a minute?'' He angled his head toward the next room.

The pleasure on Kristen's face wavered. ''I guess that's a good idea.'' Her hand lingered on Cody's shoulder. ''Luke and I will be in the living room while you finish eating, all right?''

Cody swallowed as if a big lump of dough had just stuck in his throat. He bobbed his head in reluctant agreement.

''Good.'' Kristen's smile evaporated as soon as she turned and glanced at Luke. He ushered her through the dining room, into the living room where there was less chance Cody would overhear their conversation.

Some things a kid shouldn't have to listen to.

Luke bent down and picked his clock radio off the floor. ''Any idea what this is doing out here?''

Kristen knotted her hands together. ''I meant to take it into Cody's room, so I could listen for news reports about his disappearance, but then I heard Derek trying to break in, and—''

''There *aren't* any news reports.'' Luke set the radio on the coffee table. ''Not yet, anyway.''

''How do you know that?'' Her eyebrows feathered upward in surprise.

''I had the radio on in the truck while I went to the drugstore. The local station didn't mention a word about it during their news break.''

''That's odd. Unless...'' Kristen pressed her fingertips to her mouth in thoughtful silence. Before Luke could ask what those thoughts might be, she dropped her hand and said with agitation, "We've got to find some other place to hide, right away! Now that Derek knows we're here—"

"Did he actually see you?"

"No." Kristen frowned. "But he must have been darn sure we were here, or he wouldn't have taken the risk of breaking in." Her gaze searched his face with a probing intensity he found intrusive. What was she trying to do, read his mind? "Luke, don't you see what this means?"

He folded his arms across his chest. "It means we've got to move you both to another hiding place."

"Yes. But besides that." She studied him expectantly, like a teacher waiting for a slow student to come up with the right answer.

Luke wasn't about to oblige her. "I don't follow." But some traitorous mechanism in the back of his brain was starting to work on the logic puzzle she seemed so anxious for him to solve.

"Don't you understand?" She gripped his crossed forearms and gave him a little shake. "Somehow Derek must have found out that you're Cody's father."

No.

He couldn't have, because it's not true.

A dull blade of pain prodded Luke in the chest. A small jab so far, but an ominous warning there might be much worse to come.

He refused to acknowledge it. "I thought I made it clear I didn't want to discuss that subject." He shook Kristen's fingers off his arms.

She didn't back off. "Why else would Derek have come *here,* of all places, unless he knows about your connection to Cody?" She sidestepped in front of Luke when he tried to move away. "Derek would have suspected immediately that I was the one who stole Cody." Her words tumbled out in a rush, as if she feared Luke might escape before she could finish. "But why would Derek have figured I would come to *you* for help, when you and I haven't spoken two words to each other in eight years?''

Luke analyzed the logic of this, weighed it, then rejected it. His suspicion of her was still too deeply ingrained an instinct.

Especially when she's telling you something you don't want to hear, huh, pal?

Shut up, he snarled back at that traitorous inner voice.

''Maybe someone saw you come here last night,'' he said with a shrug, offering Kristen a completely reasonable alternate theory. ''Someone who told Derek.''

''*Why* won't you listen to the truth?'' Kristen fisted her hands in despair, then abruptly switched tactics. ''Look, if you don't want to be a father to Cody, that's fine. That's not what I'm asking. I'll gladly raise him myself, once we get him away from Derek.''

''No, it's *not* fine.'' Luke scowled at her. ''You think I'd shirk my responsibilities? Let someone else raise my kid?''

''No, but—''

''I've got damn good reasons to assume you're lying to me.'' Luke brought his face belligerently close to hers. ''Or else that Sheri lied to you about the identity of Cody's father.''

Regret shimmered briefly in her eyes. ''Luke, I don't blame you for—''

He flailed an arm through the air to cut her off. ''You think I'm stupid enough to get attached to that kid?''

''Shh! He'll hear you!''

He lowered the volume of his voice, but not its intensity. ''You think I'm going to make the mistake of caring about what happens to him, when this whole mess could turn out to be just another pack of lies?''

''I think you already do,'' Kristen said quietly. ''Care about what happens to him.''

Luke blinked as if she'd slapped him. After a moment of stunned silence, he blew an exasperated stream of air through his lips. ''Well, of course I do. He's an innocent kid! Anyone can see he's scared to death of that rotten bully he's got for a...father.''

Kristen edged closer. Like a lioness stalking her prey. ''Even if there *is* another way to explain how Derek knew we were here, why wouldn't he simply send the police to look for Cody?'' She looked as if she were about to clutch Luke's sleeve again, then thought better of it. ''This is a *kidnapping,* for heaven's sake! Derek's obviously trying to keep it secret and handle it without involving the authorities, or else the news would be all over town.''

Luke drummed his fingers against the back of a chair. ''And in this hypothetical scenario of yours, what exactly does Derek have to gain by keeping his kid's disappearance secret?''

''Derek's *afraid* to call the police.'' Kristen paused to let this sink in, as if worried Luke might lose the trail of her reasoning. ''Why else would he dirty his lily-white hands by breaking and entering, not to mention risking a physical confrontation with you?''

Aha! Here was a flaw in her logic. ''What reason does Derek have to be afraid of the cops?'' Luke rocked back and forth on his heels, pleased to have trapped her in a contradiction. ''Last night you claimed he had the whole Whisper Ridge Police Department in his pocket.''

His triumph didn't faze her at all. ''Derek's not afraid of the *police.* He's afraid of what might come out, once they get involved and start asking questions.''

''What are you talking about?''

Kristen hesitated before replying, as if giving him a chance to work out the answer for himself. ''Don't you think the police would want to know why Derek was so sure I'd brought Cody here? Don't you think they would ask me the same question, after they found us?''

Luke had the unpleasant sensation he was tippy-toeing across quicksand. About to be sucked into an inescapable conclusion he was anxious to avoid. ''You had nowhere else to turn,'' he explained slowly. ''You thought you could play on my sympathies to persuade me to help you escape.''

Kristen shook her head. ''That isn't why I came to you for help. I brought Cody here because you're his—well, you know why.'' She swallowed. Luke's reaction had clearly made her think twice about completing that sentence.

Determination flared again in her eyes. ''I also brought Cody here because I knew you were a decent human being who would never let a terrible crime go unpunished if he could help it. Who wouldn't let someone keep on hurting an innocent little boy...'' Kristen's face crumpled on the last word.

Luke started to reach for her, then jerked himself back.

Kristen dabbed at her eyes and collected herself. ''I knew you wouldn't want Sheri's killer to go scot-free,'' she continued in a husky voice, ''even after the way she hurt you. And I knew that once you understood about Derek, you would do everything in your power to protect Cody.'' She lifted her chin. ''Even if he *wasn't* your son.''

Luke regarded her with a stony stare. ''What's the point of all this?''

''That Derek hasn't called the police because he's afraid of what I might tell them.''

Luke glimpsed where her reasoning was headed. Straight into that quicksand. But that didn't mean he had to follow. ''You said the cops already dismissed your accusations that he murdered Sheri.''

''That's not what Derek's worried about.''

''Then—?''

Kristen took a deep breath. ''Derek's afraid I'll tell them Cody's yours. He's afraid word will get out that his wife bore another man's child. He's afraid of the public humiliation, the whispers when he walks down the street, the snickers behind his back.''

The weight of her argument pressed down on Luke like an anvil, making it hard to breathe.

Kristen rushed on. ''You know what Derek's like. How he can't stand to be laughed at. How he thinks he's superior to everyone else.'' She spread her hands wide and exclaimed mockingly, ''The high and mighty Derek Vincent—whose wife got pregnant by someone else!''

She flicked a stricken glance toward the kitchen and immediately lowered her voice. "Luke, you *know* Derek would risk anything to protect his precious reputation." Bitterness crimped the corners of her mouth. "Whatever the cost, he's not about to let the whole town learn what he no doubt considers his dirty little secret."

Cody? A dirty little secret? Luke fumed. Why, that bastard ought to be *proud* to—

Damn it, he was getting off track here. He set his jaw stubbornly. "This is all speculation."

"No." The sincerity in Kristen's voice took on an edge. "Whether or not *you* believe Cody is your son, Derek does. That's the only explanation for why he came looking for him here. And it also explains why he hasn't involved the police yet."

"Maybe Sheri lied to *him,* too."

Kristen's brow furrowed with bewilderment. "Why on earth would she have done *that?*"

Luke snorted with exasperation. "Believe me, I'm the last person on earth who can make sense of Sheri's actions."

"Never mind. I'm through trying to convince you Cody's your son. All I care about is keeping him safe." Kristen tossed her hair over her shoulder in an impatient gesture. "One thing *is* certain. Derek's time is running out. He may have persuaded the hospital to hold off notifying the authorities so he could handle the situation by himself, but the hospital won't wait much longer. They have medical, legal and ethical obligations to report this kidnapping, and if they haven't called the police already, they will soon. Cody and I *have* to find another hiding place. Now."

She spun on her heel and walked away rapidly, her stride full of purpose and determination. At the dining room she paused to look back. Giving him one last chance. "Are you still willing to help us, Luke?" Her eyes blazed with defiance. With challenge. "Or do I have to take Cody and get out of town?"

Unspoken was the word *forever.* A word Luke had long ago banished from his vocabulary.

He felt the quicksand dragging him down....

But he had a chance to escape. He could wash his hands of this whole situation right now—give Kristen some cash, wish her and Cody well, send them on their way. No more agonizing over whether the boy might be his. No more struggling to control his troublesome attraction to Kristen.

She'd asked him a yes-or-no question. By uttering one single syllable, Luke could put the tangled web of the past behind him. Be done with Sheri Monroe Vincent and her legacy of lies once and for all. Easy.

The problem was, Luke had never been one to take the easy way out.

Chapter 5

"Thanks a million, Blake. And like I said, I'd sure appreciate your not mentioning this to anyone." Luke listened while the person on the other end of the phone spoke. "Yeah, that's it. A matter of life and death." He produced a feeble chuckle.

Kristen felt as tightly wound as a steel guitar string, and no wonder. During the last hour she'd had to cope with their narrow escape from Derek, then her argument with Luke, and now the suspense of waiting to hear if his phone call was successful. If someone plucked her, she would probably let out an earsplitting twang.

She forced her muscles to relax. Her jaws ached from clenching her teeth. "Did your friend agree to let us stay at his cabin?" she asked the instant Luke hung up.

"Yeah." Luke had built a vacation cabin several years ago for a wealthy out-of-towner named Blake Sizemore. The two men had become friends, although Blake's demanding business schedule rarely allowed him to spend much time at the cabin. It stood vacant most of the year, and it was vacant now.

It was isolated, yet only five or six miles from Whisper Ridge. The perfect hideout.

That's what they were hoping, anyway.

"Come on, I'll drive you out there," Luke said. "Then I'll head over to Pineville and buy some stuff for Cody to wear."

"Uh..." Kristen glanced down at her own garments, suddenly self-conscious about her wrinkled appearance. She hadn't packed for a kidnapping when she'd left home yesterday. "Maybe you could pick up a few things for *me,* too," she suggested.

Luke gave her a swift head-to-toe once-over and frowned. "You mean like frilly lace undies? Uh-uh. No way."

Irritation pricked her. "Look, the only clothes I have are the ones I've got on. Unless you're planning to solve Sheri's murder by this afternoon, I'm going to need something else to wear."

Luke assumed the stance of a roadblock. "I'm not Sherlock Holmes. And I'm not prancing into some ladies' clothing store to pick out a wardrobe for you."

"Oh, for heaven's sake." Kristen propped her hands on her hips. "While you're in the department store buying stuff for Cody, you can just grab me some slacks and blouses off the rack. I'll write down my sizes."

Luke stuck his face close to hers. "I didn't sign on for shopping."

Kristen glared right back. "I've already slept in these clothes one night, and I'm not going to do it again!"

By now they were nose to nose. "And just how exactly am I supposed to explain it to the cashier?" Luke demanded.

"Explain *what?*" Kristen's blood pressure was inching into the danger zone. So was Luke's, judging by the vein that throbbed near his temple. "Women buy clothes for their husbands all the time," she pointed out. "Why should it be any different the other way around?"

"It just *is,* that's all." His eyes smoldered like twin blue flames.

Kristen made a scornful sound. "What's the matter? Are

you afraid they'll take away your Macho Guy membership card if you handle a woman's clothing while the price tag's still on?''

''Very funny.''

''Be reasonable. You can't sneak into my house to get things, because the police or Derek might be watching the place. And even over in Pineville, it's too dangerous for me to be seen in public. *You* have to do it.''

Plainly Luke didn't appreciate being informed of what he *had* to do. No surprise there.

What did surprise Kristen was that he finally agreed. Grudgingly. ''All right. But no underwear!''

She rolled her eyes. ''Luke, I need clean underwear.''

''Can't you just wash it out in the sink? Women are always draping wet underwear all over the bathroom, aren't they?''

Kristen ignored the jealous pang his observation aroused. Obviously Luke had made himself at home in plenty of female residences.

''Just buy it,'' she said. Something in her tone must have warned him not to argue further.

He didn't. ''Let's go,'' he mumbled.

It didn't take long to get ready—one advantage of traveling light. The few items from the drugstore were all Kristen had to round up.

''We're going for a ride in Luke's truck,'' she announced to Cody back in the kitchen.

''Where are we going?'' The anxious wobble in his voice was unmistakable.

Kristen swiped a dab of jelly from the corner of his mouth and kissed the top of his head. ''Someplace nice. A cabin in the woods. Doesn't that sound like fun?''

''I guess so.'' Although *fun* didn't exactly enter into his expression.

''All set?'' Luke came into the kitchen, jingling his keys in his hand.

''Are you going with us?'' Cody asked, tipping his head back to look up at Luke.

"Sure, sport!" Luke feigned surprise. Or maybe he wasn't pretending. It sounded like Cody actually *wanted* him to come. Luke winked. "Think I'd trust a *girl* to drive my truck?"

Kristen made a face. "Oink, oink," she retorted.

Cody giggled. It was about the nicest sound she'd ever heard. Warmth melted some of the exasperation she felt toward Luke. He might be a male chauvinist pig, but he was a nice one.

"Let's go," he said, ushering them through the kitchen.

Kristen stopped to peek out the back-door curtains. "It's so exposed outside," she said, frowning. "How are we going to get into your truck without anyone seeing us?"

"We can't wait until dark, that's for sure." Luke nudged her aside to get the doorknob. "Even if you-know-who doesn't get up the nerve to come back, the cops might have the place surrounded by then."

For the first time, Luke sounded as if he actually *believed* her story. At least some of it.

"The backyard is surrounded by trees," he said. "If we move quickly, I doubt anyone will see us."

Kristen looked through the curtains again. The detached garage seemed awfully far away. "Isn't there some way Cody and I could, I don't know, *hide* in something?"

Luke's mouth twitched. "What do you suggest? That I roll you both up in a carpet and carry you out to my truck?"

"Well, no, but—"

"Stuff you in a bag of my dirty laundry?" He snapped his fingers. "I know! How about hiding you under the room service cart? That always works on TV."

Kristen scowled. "Will you please be serious?"

He clapped a hand to his heart in wounded innocence. "I *am* being serious. *You're* the one who's acting like we're in a spy movie."

"Couldn't you maybe...put us in a wheelbarrow or something, and, hmm, cover us with some kind of construction materials?"

Luke laughed, sounding genuinely amused. ''Like what? Bricks?'' He winced. ''Doesn't sound too comfortable.''

''I don't hear *you* coming up with any better suggestions,'' she said, distracted for a moment by how handsome he was when he smiled. Gleaming white teeth, sexy crinkles radiating from the corners of his twinkling blue eyes...

''By the time we work out some elaborate plan, the cops could be pounding on the front door. Let's just get out of here, all right?'' He sighed when Kristen still hesitated. ''I'll back the truck down the driveway and stop where it passes close to the house. That way you won't have to be out in the open as long. Okay?''

Kristen had two choices. She could stand here and argue with Luke some more, giving the police and/or Derek a better chance of trapping them.

Or she could go along with Luke's so-called plan.

''Fine,'' she said curtly.

''Don't forget to lock up behind you,'' he said. ''The way my luck's been running, the place'll be burglarized while I'm gone.''

Then he was out the door and crossing the backyard, moving with the easy, muscular grace of an athlete.

For a few vivid seconds, Kristen was back at one of their high-school track meets, jumping up and down in the stands with Sheri, both of them screaming, ''Go, Luke, go!'' as he breasted the tape to win the race.

Afterward, they would run to find Luke. Sheri would squeal and throw her arms around his neck. Luke would wink at Kristen over her sister's shoulder. Then he would lean down to kiss Sheri...slow, hot and masterful, like a conquering hero claiming his prize. Sheri, breathless and beaming with pride, would link her arm possessively through Luke's, skimming her fingers across his heaving chest and sweat slick muscles.

Kristen would hover in the background, fighting to keep her smile from sagging, while another little piece of her heart shriveled inside her.

Luke's truck roared into life, yanking Kristen back from the painful past. She took hold of Cody's hand. "On your mark," she whispered. Tires scrunched on the gravel driveway as Luke backed out of the garage.

"Get set..." She eased open the back door as the pickup neared the house.

"Go!"

They ran for it.

Luke took a roundabout back-roads route, thus avoiding potential encounters with anyone who might be on the lookout for them.

"Okay, you can sit up now." He turned off the pavement onto the winding dirt road that led up to Blackberry Lake and the surrounding vacation homes. It was September, so most vacationers would have left for the season. If he spotted an approaching vehicle, he would still have plenty of time to warn Kristen and Cody to duck.

They both sat up cautiously. It was crowded with three people in the truck, even if one of them was a kid. Every bump in the road jostled Cody against Luke's side. Sunlight filtered through the dense woods, dappling the boy's pajamas with an ever-changing pattern of shadows. His small bare feet made Luke feel protective for some reason. Got to remember to buy him a decent pair of shoes... Casually, he draped his arm along the seat back.

Kristen glanced at Luke over the top of Cody's head. "How much farther is it?"

"Couple of miles." It was slow going on this rutted road, which got even narrower as it wound uphill through the towering pine forest. Good. The last thing they needed was a lot of traffic whizzing near the cabin.

"Is this road closed during the winter?" Kristen asked.

"Nope." Luke swerved around an especially deep pothole. "Not to worry. Besides, you won't be here that long."

Uncertainty marred Kristen's brow. "Aren't you going to be staying here with us?"

Luke shot her a startled look. "Hell—er, *heck*, no! Where'd you get that crazy idea?"

Drat. Now he'd gone and hurt her feelings, without meaning to. He could tell by the way her back stiffened up.

"Well," she said, "I just thought maybe you'd stay here to protect us...."

"From what? Raccoons?"

She was starting to get annoyed with him, which was just what Luke had intended. Hostility he could handle. But whenever Kristen gazed at him with those gentle, injured eyes like a wounded doe, Luke's guts got all tied up in knots.

She clicked her tongue. "You know perfectly well from what."

Ah, much better! That feisty emerald spark was back. She aimed a meaningful glance at Cody, warning Luke not to discuss too specifically the danger they were in.

Luke curled his fingers tighter around the steering wheel. "How am I supposed to do any investigating into Sheri's—uh, into that matter we talked about—from way out here?"

Kristen stared straight ahead through the windshield. "I didn't mean you had to stay with us every single minute."

She sure was cute when she pouted. Always had been. And would probably haul off and slug Luke if he ever told her so.

"Anyway," he went on, "think how suspicious it would look if I dropped out of sight, too. I need to stick to my normal routine as much as possible, which means going home to my own house at night."

Her exquisite profile shifted slightly, as if in grudging concession.

Share a cozy, secluded cabin with this woman? Good grief! Luke shuddered to think what a disastrous effect *that* setup would have on his peace of mind. Not to mention the havoc it would wreak with his hormones. He was already having trouble keeping his hands off her luscious body. How would he ever control his rampaging libido if he had to sleep under the same roof with her?

Hearing her turn on the shower in the morning...picturing

her standing there under the steamy spray with her eyes closed, sliding the bar of soap all over her long, sleek, wet limbs....

Luke's foot inadvertently stomped the gas pedal, jerking them all backward. "Sorry," he mumbled.

Kristen turned sideways in her seat. "You're right," she admitted. "You can't stay out here with us. I just wasn't thinking. I mean, I thought...never mind." She fiddled with a lock of her coppery hair, caressing it with an unconscious sensuality.

"Here we are," Luke announced with relief. The driveway entrance was screened by thick manzanita growth. You had to be deliberately watching for it, or you'd drive right by.

Branches scraped the sides of the truck while he eased forward in first gear. "Blake hasn't been up here this year," he explained. "That's why the brush needs trimming back."

Kristen peered ahead, but the thick forest still screened any view of the cabin. "When did you build this place for him?"

Luke thought back. "Mmm, four or five years ago, I guess. He's never had much chance to use it. Too busy with work." A trace of bitterness crept into his voice. "Lucky him."

Kristen tilted her head. "What do you mean?"

Luke concentrated on the bumpy, overgrown driveway. "Nothing."

He should have known she wouldn't drop it. "Hasn't the construction business been good lately?"

"Not my *particular* construction business." A vague pressure clamped down on the base of his neck. Probably the onset of a headache.

"But I thought you were doing so well! I read about you in the local paper all the time, I've been following your—uh, I mean..." She cleared her throat. "Word gets around town, of course. About your success."

Luke's mouth twisted as if he'd bitten into a pickle. "You must have heard about the fire, then."

"Yes, that was awful." She shook her head in sympathy. "Six months ago, wasn't it?"

"A year."

''Really?'' She blinked. ''I didn't realize it had been that long...but you must have had insurance, right?''

''Sure, but it takes a while to rebuild.'' He would never forget the crushing weight of defeat he'd felt that night. As suffocating and hopeless as those thick, black clouds of smoke. Tools, machinery, lumber, all his business records. Gone.

''I lost a lot of customers right afterward. Guess they couldn't wait for me to get back on my feet.'' Luke would rather eat splinters than admit it out loud, but he'd been hurt by how quickly his customers had dumped him. ''On top of everything else, I started having a run of bad luck with my suppliers. They'd promise to deliver stuff by a certain date, then some problem would come up so they'd have to delay or cancel the order. Which made me fall even further behind with the few jobs I still managed to land.''

Kristen sounded taken aback. ''Luke, I had no idea.''

''Yeah, well, I haven't exactly been anxious to broadcast my financial woes. Bad for business.''

She frowned. ''When did all this start?''

''This stretch of bad luck, you mean?''

She nodded.

''The first disaster was the fire.'' He gave a harsh laugh. ''I can tell you the exact date, in fact. One year ago tomorrow.''

Kristen performed some mysterious calculation on her fingers. Her eyes widened. ''Less than two weeks after Sheri died.''

They both glanced automatically at Cody. Luke shrugged. ''I guess so, now that you mention it.''

''Hmm.'' Kristen patted Cody's knee. ''And all these other problems with your business came after that?''

''There are always problems when you're in business. But all the major stuff, yeah. Happened during the last year.''

Kristen drummed her fingers on the armrest.

''What are you getting at?'' Luke asked curiously.

''Nothing,'' she said. But she looked troubled.

Moments later, they pulled up in front of the cabin.

Kristen had been inside a number of the summer cottages that rich out-of-towners had built in the woods near Blackberry Lake. Not for years, though. And never to spend the night.

She and Sheri had come up here with their mother when they were little. Rita Monroe had worked as a cleaning woman. She couldn't have afforded day care even if such a thing had existed in Whisper Ridge back then, so during the summer, when her daughters were out of school, she'd had no choice but to bring them to work with her.

Money had always been tight in the Monroe household, even before Kristen and Sheri's father had been killed in a logging accident the year Kristen started kindergarten. Afterward, money was even tighter, even though their mother worked herself to the bone mopping people's floors and dusting their furniture and scrubbing their bathtubs.

Summertime, things were a little easier. Starting in June, lake people would hire Mama to open up their cabins for them, sweeping away the cobwebs, airing out the linen before they arrived for their annual sojourn in the mountains.

All summer long she got extra work up here, and sometimes people even gave her tips, too. That meant once in a while her two girls got dessert with supper. Never Mama, though. She always claimed she didn't want any because she was on a diet, even though she was skinnier than any model you ever saw in a magazine.

On rare occasions, Mama might even splurge and buy *both* girls a new dress or a bathing suit or a pair of shorts, so that not every single outfit Kristen wore had been handed down from her older sister.

It hurt Kristen to think of her mother now. To remember how sick she'd been near the end, and how hard she'd kept on working to support her daughters, even with her bad heart. Even though the doctor had warned her she was working herself to death.

The doctor had been right. Rita Monroe wouldn't quit working, but her heart finally did. On a gorgeous spring day when

Kristen was a sophomore and Sheri a month away from graduating.

"Mama, you wouldn't *believe* this place," Kristen whispered while she surveyed the ritzy hideout Luke had brought her and Cody to.

Ten-foot-high ceilings with skylights. A huge stone fireplace. Three spacious bedrooms, each with its own private bath. Hardwood floors, antique light fixtures, Oriental rugs that looked as if they belonged in a museum. The furniture was big and masculine—couches and chairs upholstered in a nubby oatmeal fabric, with overstuffed cushions you could sink right into. No television, though. That was the one concession to roughing it.

Though the cabin didn't sit right on the water, Kristen could glimpse the lake through the magnificent picture window in the living room. *Cabin?* More like a palace. Luke had done an incredible job building this place.

Before leaving on his shopping expedition to Pineville, he'd gone around the outside of the cabin and turned on the well and electricity. Kristen and Cody now had all the comforts of home. Except food.

In the kitchen, Kristen searched through the rustic maple cupboards until she found a shelf of assorted canned goods. She picked out a can of soup and examined it, but couldn't decipher the date encoded on the bottom. She pulled open drawers until she found a can opener. Suspiciously, she sniffed the contents of the can.

Well, it smelled fine. She rustled up a saucepan, and in no time at all the soup was bubbling on the stove. "Cody," she called. "Lunchtime!"

She called again a moment later, but got no response. Uneasiness stirred in her stomach. She was sure no one could have followed them here, and yet—

She switched off the stove burner and hurried toward the bedrooms. "Cody?" After their arrival, Luke had scouted up some old outdoor magazines to entertain him. Not very exciting reading for a seven-year-old, but Cody had seemed content to look at the pictures.

Kristen had checked on him twenty minutes ago, but it would only take a minute for someone to break into the bedroom window and snatch him. Cody was in no physical shape to put up a struggle.

Uneasiness shifted into dread. Kristen burst into his bedroom, half convinced she would find it empty, curtains billowing in the breeze from an open window.

Cody lay sprawled on the floor with his eyes closed.

Kristen's heart leaped into her throat. Did he have some internal injury she hadn't known about? She flung herself down beside him, anxious to shake him into consciousness but afraid she might injure him further by moving him. She listened to his steady breathing, watched him for a minute, and finally concluded he was only sleeping.

Relief flooded her, turning her knees to jelly. She pressed her fist to her mouth to muffle a sob. Would she ever be able to stop worrying about him? To quit jumping to horrible conclusions every time he was out of her sight?

No. Not until Derek was no longer a threat. Hatred trickled into Kristen's bloodstream like acid. If it took the rest of her life, she would make that monster pay for what he'd done. She would protect this darling little boy. No matter what.

But you didn't do such a great job protecting Sheri, did you? taunted the familiar voice of her conscience. If you hadn't interfered, talked her into leaving Derek, she would still be alive today. Cody would still have his mother.

Tears blurred Kristen's vision. She would never stop blaming herself for Sheri's death. Never.

She kissed a fingertip and transferred it to her sleeping nephew's cheek. Someday Cody would learn the truth about how his mother had died. And then *he* would blame Kristen, too. Maybe even hate her. For the same reason she hated herself.

She pushed herself upright on unsteady legs. Sleep was the

best thing for Cody right now, to give his body time to heal. Lunch could wait until later.

Back in the kitchen, the soup was still hot, but Kristen had no appetite for it now. What was taking Luke so long to get back?

She paced in front of the picture window, too edgy to admire the distant view of the lake through the trees, or the backdrop of mountain peaks. The clock on the mantel seemed to be running in slow motion. Maybe the batteries were worn out. Except that didn't explain why her own watch was keeping such slow time as well.

Had the police come after Luke and hauled him in for questioning? Had Derek tracked him down, threatened him, maybe even attacked him? When things didn't go the way Derek wanted, there was no telling what he might do. Kristen could clearly imagine the storm of fury and frustration that must be raging inside him right now.

Ears alert for the slightest sound, Kristen heard the approaching engine while it was still some distance off. She flattened her hand over her accelerating heart. It had to be Luke, of course. But if it wasn't…

When the front end of his truck nosed through the gap in the woods, relief poured through her again. She stumbled across the porch on rubbery legs, nearly tripping down the front steps in her eagerness to meet him.

He flung open his door before the pickup had even rolled to a full stop. "Kristen, what's wrong?" He seized her arms when she rushed around to the driver's side.

"Nothing! I…" She tried to catch her breath. With her hands braced against Luke's chest, she could feel his heart thumping beneath his T-shirt. She couldn't believe how glad she was to see him.

"Is Cody all right?" Luke gripped her arms tighter.

"Yes! I just—I was worried about you."

"Me?" A puzzled frown creased his forehead. "What for?"

Kristen was still breathing faster than normal. ''Because it took you so long to get back, that's why.''

''For Pete's sake!'' Indignation swept his rugged features. ''*You're* the one who gave me a shopping list a mile long.''

''It wasn't *that* long.''

''Yeah? Well, sometime *you* should try picking out clothes for somebody else. I had to make sure I got the right sizes, the right colors—''

''Did you go to the grocery store, too? Because there's not much to eat in the cupboards—''

''Of course I did. It was on your famous list, wasn't it? But how was I supposed to know what kind of breakfast cereal Cody likes, or—shh!'' Luke silenced her with a stern glare, even though *he* was the one doing all the talking.

The dashboard radio was still on. Luke's glare hardened into a grim frown. ''The local station started broadcasting this about an hour ago.'' He leaned in to turn up the volume.

''—And for our listeners just tuning in...

''Cody Vincent, seven-year-old son of Derek Vincent, owner of Vincent Lumber, disappeared late last night from Whisper Ridge Hospital, where he had been undergoing treatment for injuries suffered in a fall from a tree yesterday.''

A chill tiptoed up Kristen's spine.

''Police suspect kidnapping and are asking local residents to be on the lookout for Cody, who's just over four feet tall, with light blond hair and blue eyes, last seen wearing blue pajamas. If you have any information as to his whereabouts, please contact the Whisper Ridge Police Department at—''

Luke reached into the truck and switched off the radio.

Kristen drew in a long, shaky breath. ''So. The news is out now.''

''Yeah.'' Luke rubbed her arms as if to comfort her. ''Either Derek or the hospital finally called in the cops.''

Kristen's skin felt like ice. Now *everyone* would be looking for them. It struck her once again, the enormous magnitude of what she'd done.

She swayed forward. Luke was right there to steady her.

"Easy," he said. "Everything's going to be all right." He dropped a quick, spontaneous kiss on her forehead, looking as surprised by what he'd done as Kristen was.

She felt the lingering imprint of his lips. The quality of the air around them seemed to shift, like the electricity that charges the atmosphere right before a thunderstorm.

Kristen could tell by the startled awareness on Luke's face that he felt it, too. Her hands slid up his chest as if of their own accord. His fingers tightened on her arms. Slowly, he pulled her closer. His blue eyes were hypnotic...magnetic...a force of nature Kristen was helpless to resist.

"Don't," she whispered. But even as she said it, she was moving forward, into the heat and the strength and the sheer, elemental male force that radiated from him. Letting the electricity draw her in, envelop her, capture her with the power of her own desire.

Luke's breath caressed her lips. "I don't want to," he muttered. "But so help me, I have to."

So do I. It was Kristen's last coherent thought as his face dissolved into a dark blur, as their mouths came together, as the world began to spin so that the only solid anchor she could cling to was Luke.

Chapter 6

Their first kiss had been hot, hard, angry.

This kiss was outright seduction. Except Kristen wasn't sure who was seducing whom. All she knew was that, despite the chaos and fear that had recently turned her life upside down, she would be quite content to stand here forever in this wooded clearing, kissing Luke.

The sun was warm on her back and so were his hands, kneading, exploring, tracing the length of her spine with strong, capable fingers. Kristen's hands weren't still, either. It seemed as if she'd waited her whole life for this chance, and she wasn't about to waste it. She needed to *feel* Luke Hollister. Every hard, sexy square inch of him.

When he teased open her lips and sought her tongue with his, Kristen welcomed it gladly. Heat poured through her like molten honey, turning her limbs to liquid. She clutched his sturdy shoulders, then slid her hands down his powerfully built arms, physically acquainting herself with the magnificent body she'd been forced to admire from a distance—until now.

She skimmed her fingers over his rock-hard biceps, their

muscular contours sculpted by years of hard work. The wiry dusting of hair on his bare forearms rasped deliciously against her fingertips. She savored the hard angles of his elbows, the bones in his wrists, the tendons flexing beneath his tanned skin. She treated herself to a thorough Luke Hollister anatomy lesson, while his hands aroused her body and his mouth did magical, impossible things to hers.

''Mmm...so sweet,'' he growled, flicking his tongue over the sensitized skin of her earlobe. ''You taste so good....''

Desire spiraled up inside her. Her head tipped back like a sunflower whose stem has grown too weak to support it. Luke buried his face in the curve of her throat, kissing, sucking, teasing her with his lips and tongue, driving her wild.

She heard a faint animal sound, like the contented purring of a kitten, and realized she was making that noise herself. Except she was a far cry from content. She was...starving. Desperate. Aching with need.

And only one man could give her what she craved.

''Luke,'' she murmured in a voice that sounded drugged. ''Oh, Luke...'' I've wanted you for so long, she thought. But she wasn't so far gone as to reveal *that* secret out loud.

He sought her mouth again and kissed her with deliberate, lazy assurance, as if moving in slow motion. As if they had all the time in the world.

''Mmm, you taste good, too,'' she told him between kisses. Heavens, was that sultry voice actually hers? ''Like...'' She ran the tip of her tongue over her lips. ''Like...chocolate.''

''Oops!'' Luke nuzzled his nose against hers. ''Caught me.''

''A chocolate...doughnut, to be specific.''

''Don't worry,'' he said with a grin. ''I bought a whole box of 'em at the grocery store.'' Then his grin slipped off his face. ''Do that again,'' he commanded.

''What?''

Their mouths came together, parted.

''That thing with your tongue,'' he urged.

''My tongue?''

"And your lips."

"Oh." Kristen complied, gliding her tongue across her lips.

"Slower," Luke said.

"Like this?"

"Uh..." He gulped. "Yeah. Like that."

She raised herself on tiptoe and teased her tongue across *his* mouth this time. "How about like that?" she whispered.

Sweat glistened on his forehead. "Oh, man." His eyes burned with fever. "Feel what you do to me." He captured her hand and brought it down below waist level.

Shock crashed through her. Not shock at the bold, throbbing feel of him, but astonishment at the force of her own sexual response. With the speed of a lightning bolt, desire infused every cell in her body with primal, urgent, white-hot need.

Kristen was stunned by how much she wanted Luke. And by how close she was to making a very big mistake.

She yanked her hand from his body, dragging herself back from the steep precipice of disaster.

"No! I'm—sorry." She felt herself blushing furiously. The color of her cheeks probably matched her hair. "I can't do this."

Luke was breathing hard. "Who says you have to?" he asked with annoyance. His face was red, too, but not from embarrassment or remorse. He shrugged, trying but failing to make it look indifferent. "I've never forced myself on a woman, and I'm not about to start now."

"Of course not. I mean—" Kristen's pulse hammered at her temples, making it hard to think.

"Let me give you a piece of friendly advice, though." *Friendly* was the *last* word she would use to describe Luke's expression. "Be careful who you try that stuff on." A muscle flickered along his jaw like the forked tongue of a rattlesnake. "Not all guys are as...well-behaved as I am."

"Try *what* stuff?" Kristen stared at him. "You make it sound like I was...playing some kind of game or something."

"Weren't you?" He turned his back to start unloading bags from the pickup truck.

"No!" She couldn't blame him for being mad at her, but she wasn't going to let him get away with that implication. "Are you accusing me of—of leading you on?"

"That's one way to put it." He shoved two sacks into her arms. "I can think of some other, less flattering ones."

"Why is it *my* fault?" She teetered off balance for a moment, juggling the load in her arms. "*You* were, uh... participating, too."

Luke grabbed a couple more sacks before sticking his face into hers and replying, "*I'm* not the one who chickened out."

"Chickened out? You think I'm *afraid* of you?" Kristen stumbled after him, struggling to keep pace with his long stride.

"Would you rather I came up with a less innocent interpretation?"

"Like what?"

Luke took the front steps two at a time. "Like maybe this cuddly, come-on act of yours is just part of your scheme. A way to manipulate me, to twist me around that pretty little finger of yours to get me to do what you want."

His accusation lashed her like a whip, but Kristen wasn't about to show he'd drawn blood. "How dare you!" she demanded with as much indignation as she could summon.

"Easy." Luke shouldered his way through the front door. "All I have to do is keep reminding myself whose sister you are."

"And you'll never be able to forget that, will you?" Kristen couldn't quite hide the bitterness in the question she hurled at him. Sheri's little sister. That's all she'd ever been to Luke. That's all she would ever be.

"Forget how you and she banded together to make me feel like the world's biggest chump?" He dumped the sacks on the kitchen table. "Not likely."

Luke might pretend it was all a matter of pride. That what had really irked him was the public humiliation of being jilted for Derek Vincent.

Yet Kristen had witnessed firsthand how deeply Sheri's betrayal had devastated him. She'd been stuck with the unhappy task of breaking the news that Sheri had eloped with Derek Vincent while Luke had been working out of town that weekend. She'd glimpsed the stunned, bewildered pain that had wrenched his features during those few, frozen seconds before anger had taken over.

Luke braced his hands on the edge of the table. His knuckles were white. "If you're playing games with me again," he warned as Kristen set her bags down in front of him, "it won't just be Derek and the cops you have to worry about."

She wasn't playing games. But she wasn't about to explain the real reason she'd pulled back, either.

Guilt was a burden Kristen had chosen to bear by herself. Sharing it with someone else would make it too easy. The fact was, Kristen didn't deserve to find happiness or pleasure in her life. Not after the way she'd destroyed Sheri's.

If she hadn't convinced her sister to leave Derek, Sheri would still be alive. That was a terrible truth Kristen would have to live with forever. She couldn't change the past. She couldn't bring Sheri back. But at least she could pay the price for what she'd done.

Luke made her want things she had no right to. How could she kiss him, find joy in his arms, gratify her own selfish desires when it was her fault poor Sheri was dead?

What made it even worse was that Luke was the man Sheri had once loved. The man she should have married.

The idea that Kristen might someday find happiness with Luke was highly unlikely, to say the least. Luke didn't even trust her! But how could she betray her sister's memory even by daydreaming about it?

Daydreaming? Ha! That steamy seduction in the driveway just now hadn't been any daydream. It certainly hadn't been a fantasy that Luke had wanted her—Kristen had felt the hard proof of it herself.

And it hadn't been her imagination where all those arousing kisses and bold caresses had been leading.

Straight into bed.

Kristen couldn't let that happen. Ever.

"I'm sorry I gave you the wrong idea," she told Luke. She busied herself putting groceries away, so she wouldn't have to meet his eyes. "I just don't think it would be smart for us to...get involved."

"Huh. Well, you're sure right about that." His ready agreement stung. "Guess we need to make more of an effort to remember it." He slapped his palm on the table as if that settled the matter. "I'll go bring the rest of the stuff in from the truck."

Kristen was relieved when he left. But she couldn't shake a twinge of regret, too. Regret for what could never be.

The matter was all settled. Now, if she could only convince her foolish heart that was true.

"Be with you in just a sec." Phil Clausen was covered with grease. He squinted up into the engine of the car hoisted on the lift, made a few adjustments with a wrench, then turned to give Luke his full attention. "What can I do for you, ol' buddy?"

Phil was a few years older than Luke, the brother of one of Luke's school chums. He'd started fixing cars for a living when he got out of high school, eventually saving up enough to open his own garage. A few years back, he'd increased his already lucrative business by landing the contract for servicing the police department's vehicles.

The cops also consulted him whenever they needed an automotive expert.

Luke rolled his question around his mouth, then finally spit it out. "You checked out Sheri Vincent's car, didn't you, right after the accident?"

Phil's eyebrows made a subtle jump toward the baseball cap that covered his thinning hair. Aha, his expression seemed to say. "Yep." He wiped his hands on a filthy rag that probably left more grease than it removed. "Wondered if you were ever gonna come 'round and ask me about it."

Luke chafed at the underlying assumption in Phil's remark.

Just because he and Sheri had once been the Romeo and Juliet of Whisper Ridge High School, that didn't obligate him to go around grilling people for details about her tragic accident. Sure, he'd been shook up by it. But Sheri had ceased to be any of Luke's business the day she'd stood up next to that skunk Derek Vincent and said, "I do."

Luke's neck grew hot. Here's where the conversation got tricky. "You, uh, find anything unusual about her car when you examined it?"

Phil leveled his gaze at Luke while he fished a stick of gum from the front pocket of his dark green coverall. "Unusual?" He unwrapped the gum, still eyeing Luke.

"Unusual. You know, funny. Strange. Peculiar."

Phil stuck the gum in his mouth and chewed blankly. Good grief, was Luke going to have to recite him the whole thesaurus?

"You sound like Kristen," Phil said finally.

Luke tried not to react. "Kristen? What do you mean?"

"She came around here right after the accident. All upset, of course. Asked me if I'd found anything suspicious with her sister's car."

"What did you tell her?"

Phil scratched the back of his neck. "I told her no."

"And...that was accurate, right?"

Phil wavered as if trying to decide whether to look offended or amused. He came down on the side of amusement. "Yeah, that was accurate, all right. I mean, the car was smashed up bad, just like you'd expect after it had rolled down the side of a cliff. Sorry." His grimace mirrored Luke's. "Maybe I could answer your question better if you'd spell out just what it is you're trying to get at."

"That's the problem. I'm not sure, exactly." Luke couldn't figure out a way to play the next card without revealing part of his hand. "Did you...find anything to suggest why the car ran off the road in the first place?"

"Nah." Phil's gum snapped loudly. "Cops said there weren't any skid marks where she went off the road, like she'd braked real hard for some reason. But she could have swerved suddenly to avoid hitting an animal, maybe.'' Phil shook his head sadly. ''Happens a lot, unfortunately. People don't realize how easy it is to lose control of a car. You take your eyes off the road for a second, just to tune the radio to a different station or something, then you look up and realize you've drifted into the other lane. So you panic, overcorrect the steering wheel, and *bam!*'' He smacked his fist into his grease-stained palm.

But that wasn't what had happened to Sheri, according to Kristen.

No use beating around the bush. Luke would have to come straight out with it. ''What I'm wondering,'' he said, ''is whether the car might have been tampered with.''

Those last two words hovered in the air like the smell of motor oil.

Phil nudged back the brim of his baseball cap with one grimy knuckle. He squinted at Luke the way he'd been squinting at that engine a few minutes ago. ''You mean, were the brake lines cut or something?''

His incredulous tone made Luke feel like an idiot. But he forged ahead. ''Was there, uh, anything to indicate...that Sheri herself didn't drive the car over that cliff?''

Phil gawked at him. ''Boy, you are barking up the wrong tree. There's no way someone else could have been in that car with her and walked away from the accident.''

Luke forced himself not to envision her car, veering over the edge of the cliff, bouncing end over end down the steep, rocky slope till it came to rest in one final, annihilating crash.

With Sheri inside.

For a second he felt like he might lose the lunch Kristen had fixed for him.

He clamped his back teeth together. ''Could someone have rigged the car to move by itself? Like if Sheri was...asleep. What if someone else drove her out there to Lookout Road? Could they have...I don't know...wedged something by the accelerator to make the car move forward without a driver at the wheel?''

Phil tugged his cap brim down over his eyebrows and studied Luke from beneath it. He chewed his gum about a dozen times before replying. ''Now you *really* sound like Kristen.''

''What'd you tell her?'' Darn it, he didn't want to be linked with Kristen in anyone's mind. Phil was a decent enough guy, but keeping a secret in this town was like trying to patch a leaky radiator with masking tape. It just wouldn't work.

''I told her the same thing I'm about to tell you.'' Luke could almost hear the gears whirring in Phil's brain while he tried to figure out why two people, a year apart, had shown up trying to second-guess the cause of Sheri Vincent's accident. ''Her car had an automatic transmission. In this wild scenario of yours—and I stress, this is purely hypothetical...'' He waited till Luke verified this with a nod. ''All someone would have had to do—theoretically speaking, of course—is aim the car toward the cliff, shift the transmission into Drive, and hop out. The car would have slowly moved forward even *without* anyone stepping on the gas pedal.''

Well, all this proved exactly nothing, Luke thought. Derek *might* have sent the car over the cliff the way Kristen claimed. Or Sheri's death could have been exactly what it looked like. An accident.

The only thing Luke had accomplished by talking to Phil was to make the guy curious. And it would just make him even more curious if Luke asked him to keep quiet about his visit here today.

Word had got back to Derek once before, when Kristen had started asking questions about Sheri's death. It was only a matter of time before Derek found out Luke was doing the same thing. Except this time that bastard wouldn't have Cody as a hostage. He wouldn't be able to stop Luke the way he'd stopped Kristen.

Luke rather relished the prospect of confrontation with his old enemy. How immensely satisfying it would be to serve

Derek a helping of the same violent treatment he'd been dishing out for years!

Except with *his* luck, Luke would wind up in jail. And without his help, Kristen would have no choice but to take Cody and run.

Luke was bound and determined not to let that happen, for reasons he didn't care to examine too closely right now. Maybe he would never dig up enough incriminating dirt to bury Derek once and for all. But by God, he was going to keep shoveling.

"Thanks for the information, Phil."

"Sure." The mechanic looked as if he were eager to ask a few questions himself. But Luke wasn't about to give him a chance. He started back to his truck, but had only gone a few steps when Phil hauled him up short. "Hey, speaking of the Vincents, awful news, huh? About the kid."

Luke hoped his acting skills were better than his detective ones had proved to be so far. "Yeah, sure is. Awful news. Have they, uh, gotten any kind of ransom note yet?"

"Not that I've heard."

Luke shook his head. "Terrible. Sure hope they find him." He lifted his hand in farewell. "See you around, Phil."

He hoped he was just imagining that speculative gleam in Phil's eyes, the suspicious slant of his mouth. But as Luke strolled the rest of the way to his truck, forcing himself not to hurry, he couldn't shake the unpleasant sensation he had a target pinned to his back.

With the bull's-eye right between his shoulder blades.

He would make them pay. All of them.

She deserved it for interfering. For sticking her nose in where it didn't belong. It was her fault, the things he'd had to do. She'd forced him to resort to extreme measures.

He'd thought he'd solved the problem months ago, that he wouldn't have to worry about her anymore. He'd seen the stark terror in her eyes when he'd threatened the little brat.

God, but that terror had been sweet! She'd been so weak,

so helpless, while he'd felt the power surging through him. What a turn-on! It excited him, just to remember how afraid she'd been of him. Afraid of what he could do to her.

Of what he would do to her now, once he got his hands on her.

He was going to make her pay for all the trouble she'd caused him.

The kid would pay, too. For being a sniveling, cowardly little twerp who couldn't keep his mouth shut. For looking like his mother. For existing in the first place.

As for Hollister…

Man, oh man, was he ever looking forward to making him pay! His punishment so far had been minor compared to what lay ahead. Hollister had been a thorn in his side way too long. Time to teach him a lesson. Make him suffer the consequences.

He would make them all suffer. Oh, yes.

Just as soon as he found the kid.

"This is good."

Kristen burst out laughing. "Don't look so surprised." It felt good to laugh. Laughter was a kind of promise that things would get better someday, no matter how dismal they seemed right now.

Luke took another bite of the casserole she'd cooked. Kristen hadn't known whether or not to expect him back at the cabin for dinner, considering the…strained atmosphere between them when he'd left that afternoon.

After Kristen had cut short their passionate encounter. After Luke had accused her of playing games. After they'd both vowed to keep each other at arm's distance from now on.

Truce? Well, maybe. They were certainly on the same side when it came to protecting Cody. So why did it feel to Kristen as if she and Luke were constantly fighting at cross-purposes?

Maybe because she was constantly fighting so hard against herself. Against her own foolish dreams and desires.

"I didn't know you could cook," Luke said between mouthfuls.

"My mommy could cook," Cody piped up.

Luke stopped chewing as if the casserole had turned to wood shavings. With effort, he swallowed. "She did have a way with fried chicken, as I recall." He looked as if he weren't hungry anymore.

Kristen beamed at her nephew, pleased to see that at least *his* appetite was improving. "She used to bake cookies with you, didn't she?"

"Yeah! Chocolate chip and oatmeal raisin and peanut butter..." Cody's enthusiasm disintegrated. "I wish..." His voice trailed off as he poked at his food. But it was hardly necessary for him to complete his sentence. The two adults knew what he wished.

Kristen shot Luke a glance full of sorrow. Compassion gentled his craggy, attractive profile as he studied Cody. "I'll bet those cookies were mighty tasty," he said quietly.

Cody blinked rapidly, eyes fixed on his plate. He nodded.

"My mom used to bake cookies, too." Luke coughed into his fist. "'Course, she never let me help. She complained I ate so much raw cookie dough, most of it disappeared before she even got it in the oven."

One corner of Cody's mouth lifted. "My mommy used to look somewhere else and pretend not to see me, so I could sneak some."

Luke chuckled. "She did, huh?"

Cody looked up. "Is your mommy dead, too?" he asked solemnly.

Luke felt the amusement drain from his face. "No." He met Kristen's eyes for a second. "My mom lives in Arizona. With my pop."

"Oh." Cody went back to playing with his food again.

Observing him, Luke acknowledged he had all the proof he needed that Cody hadn't got hurt by falling out of a tree. Whatever doubt Luke might still have harbored that Derek was responsible for Cody's injuries had been wiped out by one simple fact.

Cody hadn't mentioned his father once, at least not when Luke was around. He hadn't wondered out loud where Derek was, or expressed any desire to see him, or asked when he could go home.

Cody's total silence on the subject of his father spoke a lot louder than words. By now Luke was convinced that Kristen had told him the truth about Derek abusing the boy.

But that didn't mean he had to believe anything else she said.

"Sweetheart, aren't you going to finish your supper?" Kristen reached over to tip up Cody's chin.

He shook his head and mumbled, "Can I go to bed now?"

"Are you feeling worse? Does your head hurt?" Concern laced her voice.

"No." He kicked the toe of his new sneaker against the table leg. "I just wanna go to bed, that's all."

"Okay." She shoved back her chair. "I'll come help you put on your pajamas."

That got a reaction out of him. "I can put them on by myself, Aunt Kristen." He climbed down and scurried out of the dining room as if worried she might follow.

Kristen's face twisted with a mix of emotions. "I'll come tuck you in, in a little while," she called.

"'Kay." His voice drifted back from the direction of the bedrooms.

She began to clear the table, making what seemed a deliberate effort to avoid looking at Luke. When he finally caught her eye, a sheepish smile nudged up one side of her mouth. "Okay, okay. So maybe I do try to coddle him."

Luke refrained from I-told-you-so's. "He acts like he's feeling better." He stood to give Kristen a hand with the dishes.

"Yes, thank goodness." She led the way into the kitchen. "By the way, he really enjoys that handheld video game you bought for him today."

With perfect timing, a series of electronic bloops and bleeps emerged from Cody's bedroom.

The two of them laughed in unison. "See what I mean?" Kristen's eyes sparkled. The laughter magically smoothed some of the harsh worry lines from her face, making her look more like the teenager Luke remembered.

"I'm glad he liked it." He scraped the remains of their dinner into the trash. "I must admit, I had to ask the salesclerk for advice. Buying toys for kids isn't something I've had much practice with."

"You'll get the hang of it." The implication behind her cheery statement seemed to strike them both at the same time. What she meant, of course, was that Luke was going to have more practice buying toys for *Cody*.

The way a father would.

Resentment simmered inside him, his automatic response to Kristen's assumption that someday he would accept Cody as his son. Except this time Luke's resentment died down before he could even warn her off the forbidden topic.

She must have read his face, though, judging by the way she tried to backpedal. "I mean, you did such a great job with the shopping today! All the clothes you bought fit perfectly...." She drowned out the rest of her own words by noisily jostling the dishes and silverware together as she plunged them into the sinkful of hot, soapy water.

"There *is* a dishwasher, you know." Luke pointed to the appliance he himself had installed.

"Is there? It didn't even occur to me...." She brushed a loose strand of hair from her eyes with the back of one sudsy hand. Her lips pursed with rueful consideration while she studied the dishwasher. "I've never had one. Wouldn't even know how to operate it."

"I'll show you next time." Luke sidled up to the sink and unstrapped his watch. "For now it's probably easier if I just help you—"

"No!" Alarm leaped into her eyes. She edged away from

him. "I mean, the dishes can wait till later. I told Cody I'd tuck him in."

"Oh. Well, I'll start working on them while you're gone." Luke picked up the dishcloth.

"All right." Kristen hastily dried her hands on a towel, as if the cozy confines of the kitchen had suddenly become too much for her. Luke suspected she wouldn't be back until the dishes were done. He had to admit, standing elbow to elbow, hip to hip, sharing this traditional domestic chore probably wasn't such a hot idea. He pictured Kristen's hands, slippery and sleek and glistening with soap…her skin glowing rosy pink from the hot water…damp tendrils framing her face…

Can it, he instructed his imagination.

Kristen paused by the dining room table, then tilted her head thoughtfully. "Why don't you come with me?" she suggested.

"Uh…" Luke wasn't exactly clear what was involved with tucking a kid into bed, but he was pretty sure it didn't require two people.

Then he heard himself say, "Sure. I'll come," and realized he was already drying his hands.

He followed Kristen toward Cody's room with the uneasy reluctance of a man who suspects he might be walking into a trap.

Chapter 7

Kristen smoothed Cody's hair off his forehead. Tomorrow morning she would have to change that bandage again. "Can I get you anything? A glass of water?"

"No, thank you."

She arranged the bedcovers beneath his chin. "Sweet dreams," she said, wishing she could believe they would be.

Luke hovered a safe distance behind her. Kristen swallowed a smile. He acted about as comfortable as a lumberjack at a baby shower. Still, he had agreed to come say good-night to Cody. Maybe they were making progress here.

How ironic, she thought wistfully. Here she was, trying to encourage Luke to accept Cody as his son, when success would mean that she herself would lose Cody. With Derek in jail, Kristen would be the logical person to raise her nephew...as long as Luke refused to claim him.

It wasn't as if she still *needed* to convince Luke he was Cody's father. He'd already agreed to help them. A small, selfish part of Kristen whispered that she could keep the child she loved all to herself.

But she couldn't do that. It would be wrong to keep father and son apart, even if it meant she would wind up alone. It was *her* fault Cody's mother had been taken away. The very least she could do was give him back his father.

Kristen rose from the edge of the bed and moved to the doorway. She was reaching for the light switch when Cody blurted, "Leave it on!"

Her hand hovered. "But you won't be able to sleep with the bright light in your eyes."

"Yes, I will! Honest."

Kristen could hardly blame him for being afraid of the dark. In Cody's world, monsters lurked even in the daylight.

"I've got an idea." Luke snapped his fingers. "Be right back." He winked at Kristen when he passed her on his way out of the room. The casual, intimate gesture did something funny to her heart.

Under ordinary circumstances, Kristen would gladly have indulged her nephew and left the light on all night. But these were hardly ordinary circumstances. They couldn't take the chance of someone noticing and coming to investigate why the normally vacant cabin had a light blazing in the middle of the night.

"Here you go." Luke returned with a heavy-duty flashlight. "Now, most people would call this a flashlight. But what it is, see, is actually a light saber."

Cody pushed himself up on his elbow to get a closer look.

"See how it works?" Luke showed him the switch, then demonstrated his swashbuckling technique. A circle of light danced crazily over the ceiling, the floor, the wall behind Cody's head. "Here. You try it."

Cody took the flashlight and made a few experimental swipes through the air.

"Hey, you're a natural!" Luke exclaimed. "You're gonna make space commander before you know it." He slipped the flashlight beneath the covers. "Now, you keep this light saber right next to you, so you'll have it handy whenever you need it."

"Okay." Cody snuggled next to the flashlight, hugging it like a teddy bear.

After a moment's hesitation, Luke gave him an awkward pat on the shoulder. "Good night, buddy."

"G'night." Cody was already yawning as Luke came over to Kristen and switched off the light.

"See you in the morning," Kristen called softly.

She left the door ajar when she and Luke stepped out of the room, so Cody would have some light spilling in from the rest of the house.

"That was a nice thing you did," she murmured.

"No big deal." Luke waved his hand in dismissal.

"You've certainly got a way with children."

He shot Kristen a wary glance, as if he suspected a trick. But underneath it, she could tell he was pleased.

On impulse, she dropped her hand to his arm. His muscles tensed beneath her fingertips, as if she'd transmitted a high-voltage charge.

She let go immediately. But even that brief moment of contact had stirred up those impossible yearnings she was trying so hard to bury.

A vision shimmered before her eyes, a vision of the three of them living together as a real family. She and Luke would tuck Cody into bed every night, then stroll back to the living room with their arms around each other. They would sip hot chocolate or brandy while they shared the day's events in close, loving companionship.

At the end of the evening they would turn off the lights and go to bed themselves, slipping out of their clothes, coming together eagerly in the darkness....

Kristen wrapped her arms around her stomach and nearly moaned. Her longing for that vision was so intense it was almost a physical ache.

"You all right?" Luke was watching her closely, concern etched on his brow.

"Yes, I—it's just...everything that's happened. Sometimes I feel...overwhelmed."

He guided her onto the sofa without actually touching her, then took up a safe position in a chair on the opposite side of the coffee table.

So much for her vision of close, loving companionship.

''I talked to Phil Clausen today,'' Luke said.

''The mechanic?'' Kristen sat up straight. Proving Derek had killed Sheri was far more important than her ridiculous, hopeless fantasies. ''What did he tell you?''

''Same thing he told you, apparently.'' Luke gave her a brief rundown of the conversation. ''So there's no mechanical evidence either to prove or disprove your theory about how Sheri died.''

Kristen dug her fingernails into one of their host's expensive throw pillows. ''I don't need proof. I *know*.''

Luke poked his tongue into his cheek. ''Yeah, well, the cops need proof. And so do I.''

''You still don't believe me?'' She tried not to take it personally. But it *was* personal.

''Let's just say I'm withholding judgment.''

''How can you—''

Luke bounded to his feet. ''Kristen, for Pete's sake, you can hardly expect me to swallow everything you say hook, line and sinker.''

''You still don't trust me.'' She plucked furiously at the pillow.

Luke paced back and forth. ''Look, you can't just wipe out eight years of distrust overnight.'' He plowed a hand through his hair. ''Especially when you're asking me to believe things that are so farfetched.''

They'd been discussing Sheri's murder. But the quick, furtive glance Luke sent toward Cody's bedroom gave him away.

Kristen jumped up and marched past him, heading for the door.

''Where are you going?'' Luke demanded.

''Outside. Where Cody can't overhear us.'' She held open the screen door. ''Care to join me?''

''Do I have a choice?'' he grumbled.

On the front porch, moths and other night insects tapdanced against the window, drawn by the light from inside. The faint illumination cast shadows over Luke's strong features, emphasizing every bold plane and stubborn angle.

Kristen folded her arms. It was chilly out here, but her simmering anger kept her warm.

"I don't blame you for doubting that Sheri was murdered. Like you said, there isn't any physical proof. *Yet.*"

She took a deep breath, inhaling the scent of pine and the mossy smell of the lake in the distance. "But how can you believe I would be so cruel and deceitful as to swear Cody's your son, if it wasn't true?"

Luke's mouth moved as if he were sampling the flavor of various responses and not finding any of them too pleasant. "You don't exactly have the world's greatest track record in the truth department," he said finally. "I'd be a fool to accept everything you say at face value."

"Luke, I was nineteen years old!" she cried.

"Old enough to know better."

"Young enough to make a mistake." She might as well have tried to argue with a block of granite. "You must really hate me," she said slowly, trying not to let him hear how much pain that caused her.

Luke exhaled a gust of air. He turned aside to rest his hands on the porch railing, looking up at the stars instead of at her. "No," he said, sounding halfway surprised. "No, I don't hate you. Not anymore."

"But you still think I'm a liar."

Silence, except for a chorus of frogs croaking somewhere close by.

Well, she had her answer, didn't she?

"Please, don't take your resentment of me out on Cody," she pleaded. "He needs you. And I think maybe...you need him."

Luke's spine jerked ramrod straight. "I can't be his father."

"Can't?" Kristen prodded his chest to make him turn and look at her. "Or won't?"

Even in the dim light she could see the smoldering gleam in his eyes. ''Don't keep pushing me on this.''

''I've seen how good you are with him. And how he responds to you.''

''Stop it.''

''He needs a real father, not some overbearing tyrant who uses him for a punching bag.''

''I said stop it!'' Luke seized her arm.

''It hurts to think about, doesn't it?'' Kristen's heart pounded faster. ''Now you know what I've had to live with all this time.'' Hot tears seared her eyelids.

Luke's fingers dug deeper into her flesh. His mouth was compressed to an angry slash. But Kristen wasn't afraid. Not of him.

She pressed on, heedless of the consequences. ''You keep accusing me of not telling the truth, but I don't think you really want to hear it.'' Emotional pressure built inside her chest, threatening to explode. It was all so unfair, what had happened to Sheri. What Cody had suffered.

Kristen had been helpless to stop it. No one would listen to her. Not the police. Not the social workers.

And now, not Luke.

''You want the truth?'' Bitterness etched her tone like acid. ''I'll give you the truth, Luke.'' She made one all-or-nothing effort to wrench out of his grasp, then wrote it off as hopeless. ''The truth is, you don't *want* to believe Cody's your son. You don't *want* to believe everything I've told you.''

The gleam in his eye turned into the glint of sharpened steel knife blades.

Kristen pushed her face up to his. ''Because then you'd have to face the fact that your child has been raised by a man you despise. That your old enemy has been abusing your son.''

Luke emitted a growl deep in his throat, like the warning signal of a wolf about to attack.

Fury and fear and frustration made Kristen reckless. ''You're *afraid* of having to live with that knowledge for the rest of your life,'' she taunted. ''*Aren't* you?'' She was breathing so hard she felt dizzy. "Isn't that the *real* truth, Luke?"

For a few endless seconds neither of them moved, as if time had screeched to a stop. Kristen felt the heat and power and anger pumping off Luke's body in waves.

Then in one swift motion he thrust her away from him. She clutched the railing for balance as he stormed across the driveway, flung open the door of his truck, and roared off with pinwheels of gravel spinning in his wake.

"Now you've gone and done it," Kristen whispered into the night. She wiped a tear from her cheek. "You've driven him away for good."

Luke paid a visit to the county medical examiner the next morning. Dr. Brookings peered at him over the top of his horn-rimmed glasses. "No," he said in a stern voice, "no, I did not find any evidence to suggest that Sheri Vincent was already dead before her car went over the cliff."

Seated in front of the man's desk, Luke tried not to fidget under his disapproving scrutiny. He felt like a kid who'd been called on in class and forced to 'fess up that he hadn't done his homework.

Dr. Brookings drew off his glasses. "What on earth would even make you ask such a question?"

Luke shifted his feet. Well, you see, Teacher, the dog ate my assignment....

"Certain information has recently come to my attention," he said. "Information that has made me wonder, uh, whether there might be an alternative theory about how Sheri died." Maybe he ought to go into politics. Those sure were a lot of words to say absolutely nothing.

Furrows creased the doctor's balding pate. "Are you questioning my official findings?"

"No! I mean, I looked up the official police accident report this morning, but to tell the truth, I couldn't make hide nor hair of all the medical mumbo jumbo—er, I mean terminology.'' Way to go, Hollister. Why not try to put his back up even further?

Dr. Brookings chewed on the earpiece of his glasses. ''Does this have something to do with Sheri's sister?'' he asked.

''Kristen?'' Luke aimed for an expression that combined innocence with bewilderment.

''She came to see me, not long after the accident. Asked me the same thing you're asking, except she was far less reticent than you are.''

''Oh?'' Keep those eyebrows up there, Hollister.

''Yes. She claimed that...someone...had knocked her sister unconscious, possibly even killed her, and then sent the car over the cliff to make her death look like an accident.''

''That's what she said?'' Luke noticed how careful the doctor was to avoid mentioning Derek. Even someone with the power and authority of the medical examiner, it seemed, was reluctant to spatter the tiniest speck of mud on the illustrious Vincent name. ''What did you tell her?''

''That her sister's injuries were consistent with the accident.''

''Meaning...?''

''That I had no reason to suspect Sheri Vincent had suffered any physical trauma prior to the crash.''

''I see.'' Luke scooted forward in his chair. ''But you also didn't find anything to prove she *wasn't* injured or dead before the crash, correct?''

The doctor hesitated. ''Correct.''

''So your findings as to whether or not Sheri might have been dead before the crash are inconclusive.''

The doctor reddened. ''I had no reason to assume otherwi—''

Luke held up his hands. ''I understand. So, what you're saying is that it's possible. That Sheri *could* have died before the crash.''

''I'm not saying anything of the sort.'' Like everyone else in town, Brookings had a whole slew of relatives employed by the Vincent Lumber Company.

"Doc, all I'm asking is whether it's *possible.* In theory. Technically speaking. Hypothetically." Luke hunched forward over the doctor's desk as if to thwart any eavesdroppers. "All I need from you is a one-syllable answer. *Could* Sheri have been dead before her car went off that cliff?"

For a minute he thought the doctor wasn't going to reply. His nearsighted eyes darted back and forth as if straining to see all the potentially unpleasant consequences of his answer. "Yes," he said finally, barely moving his mouth muscles.

Luke stood up. "Thank you." Not that the doctor's grudging admission had proved a darn thing. All it did was keep Kristen's theory alive.

His hand was on the doorknob when the doctor's voice stopped him. "Does this have something to do with the kidnapping?"

"Kidnapping?" Luke's stomach plummeted toward the floor.

The doctor had put his glasses back on. "It seems quite a coincidence, your sudden interest in Sheri Vincent's death. In light of the fact her son's recently been kidnapped."

Luke was a pretty good poker player. Sometimes when the chips were down, you just had to bluff. "You really want to know?" He walked back toward the desk. "Actually, you might be able to help. Maybe I ought to just tell you everything."

"Never mind." Brookings folded immediately. Clearly he didn't want to become tangled up in something that might antagonize Derek Vincent. Better to remain ignorant, whatever it was.

Luke turned to leave. The doctor had buried his nose in a stack of papers as if he'd already forgotten Luke was there.

Just as well.

Luke had never been much for examining his own feelings. That is to say, he generally knew *what* he felt, but didn't always bother with the *why* part.

Driving out to the cabin that morning, he couldn't even

begin to sort out the emotional tug-of-war taking place inside him. It felt as if invisible ropes were yanking him in all directions.

He wanted to accept Kristen at face value, to believe that the only items on her agenda were protecting her nephew and bringing Derek to justice. But the scars of past betrayal were a constant sore reminder that she couldn't always be trusted.

To complicate matters, Luke found he desired her with a powerful craving that verged on obsession. What else could he call it, when he couldn't stop thinking about her? When every time he got within kissing distance of her, his pulse began to sprint and his blood caught fire?

Luke had vowed never to let any woman have that kind of power over him again. Especially a woman whose last name was Monroe. But even though Kristen seemed to think he was only attracted to her because she was Sheri's sister, Luke was disturbed by feelings he'd never experienced before.

As for his feelings toward Cody…

Was Kristen right? Was he denying the possibility he was Cody's father because to accept it would mean accepting the rest of the unthinkable truth?

A red haze filtered over Luke's vision, so that for a moment he had trouble seeing the road ahead of him. He slowed down, forcing his breathing into a calmer pace as well. Every time he tried to wrap his mind around the concept that Cody might be his son, the idea was so huge, encompassing so much that was terrible and wonderful at the same time, that in the end his mind simply shied away from it.

Kristen had accused him last night of being afraid. Maybe he *was* afraid to believe it, for fear his heart would rip right in two.

Approaching the intersection with Highway 17, Luke glanced in his rearview mirror as he braked to a halt, a purely reflexive habit to make sure some spaced-out driver wasn't about to plow into him.

He saw something even more ominous than the front grille of a semi bearing down on him. Tailing him at a prudent distance was the same car he'd seen speeding away yesterday after the attempted break-in at his house.

Derek's car.

Luke cursed under his breath. He'd checked to make sure he wasn't being followed when he'd left the medical examiner's office, but apparently he hadn't checked carefully enough. Either that, or Derek had lucked out and spotted him by accident.

It didn't matter now. The arrows on the sign at the intersection pointed left toward Blackberry Lake, right toward Pineville. Even though Luke's trusty pickup didn't have a chance of outrunning Derek's high-performance sedan, he could probably ditch the jerk with some fancy stunt driving. But that would just prove he had something to hide.

Like a poster boy for motor-vehicle safety, Luke flicked on his right turn indicator, came to a complete stop, checked the road in both directions. Then he turned and headed toward Pineville at the leisurely pace of Grandpa out for a Sunday drive.

Kristen had been listening for it all morning, so when she finally heard it in the distance, she figured it was just her imagination again. But no, the engine sound persisted, gradually growing louder, until she could separate the thread of it from the skein of other background noises—birds chirping, wind rustling through the trees, a jetliner cruising thirty thousand feet overhead.

"Cody, let's go back inside for a minute." Kristen had cajoled him into helping her collect some of the native plants growing near the cabin—goldenrod, yarrow, Indian paintbrush. Creating a decorative arrangement was a good excuse to get Cody out into the fresh air and sunshine, and also gave Kristen a project to take her mind off the perilous situation they were in.

"Can I carry the flowers?" Cody asked.

"Sure. Watch out for those yellow star thistles, they're prickly." She handed him the plastic pitcher they'd been using to collect foliage. ''Come on, let's go.'' She thought she recognized the growl of Luke's pickup, but no sense taking chances. She hustled Cody across the driveway and up the porch steps, shutting and locking the door behind them.

She peeked through the curtains, heart beating fast, until the familiar truck pulled up outside. Now her heart had a *different* reason to speed.

''It's just Luke,'' she said over her shoulder.

''Can I show him the flowers we picked?'' Cody carefully clutched the pitcher in both hands, as if it held a bouquet of the world's most exotic roses instead of a ragtag assortment of what most people would consider weeds.

Kristen smiled. ''You sure can. I bet he'll be impressed.'' And if she knew Luke, he would make a big show of pretending he was. Luke had a lot of good qualities Kristen had long admired, but the instinctive rapport he'd displayed toward Cody had come as a surprise. Who would have thought that tough, gruff Luke Hollister would have a soft spot for kids?

Too bad the same couldn't be said for the way he felt about *her.*

Kristen pushed through the screen door and went out to greet him. After the way he'd roared out of here last night, it seemed wise to extend an olive branch. They came face-to-face in the middle of the driveway, leaving a generous buffer zone of gravel between them. Like two fighters squaring off before the main event.

''Luke, I'm sorry about last night. About what I said.''

He opened his mouth, then snapped it shut, as if he'd been prepared for a confrontation but now had to rethink what he'd planned to say. He wore jeans again, but he'd replaced yesterday's T-shirt with a plaid, short-sleeved cotton shirt that buttoned down the front. The top couple of buttons were undone. Kristen found herself gazing at the tantalizing shadow of chest hair in the V of his open collar.

With a muted sigh, she jerked her gaze back up to his.

''No need to apologize.'' He shoved his fingers through his

hair so the short black strands fell every which way. ''Who knows? Maybe you were right.''

Kristen wasn't sure what he meant, but she didn't want to dredge up any of the touchy subjects they'd fought about, either. Better to give this cease-fire a chance to take hold instead of accidentally starting another battle.

''Want to come inside for lunch?'' she asked. ''I was just about to make sandwiches.''

''Sure. I'm starved.'' He fell in step beside her, still maintaining that buffer zone between them. ''I would have been here sooner, but I stopped off to talk to the medical examiner, and afterward I spotted Derek following me, so I had to take some evasive action.''

Kristen stumbled. Luke's hand shot out to steady her. ''Derek followed you?'' she gasped.

''All the way to Pineville.'' A satisfied smirk hitched up one corner of his mouth. ''He got to spy on me while I chatted with Andy for an hour.''

''Andy—?''

''Andy Driscoll, my foreman at the site of the recreation center we're building.''

''Oh...right.'' They started toward the cabin again.

''Derek finally got tired of slouching behind his steering wheel halfway down the block,'' Luke continued. ''After he left, I gave him about fifteen minutes' head start, then took the scenic route to get here, just in case he was cleverer than I thought.''

''He didn't talk to you?'' Kristen's mind was racing. If Derek had told the cops he suspected Luke was involved in Cody's disappearance, then *they* would have been following him, not Derek. That must mean Derek still hadn't revealed Luke's connection to Cody. Obviously, with his pride at stake, Derek's fear of public humiliation was greater than his desire to get Cody back.

For now, anyway.

''Nope, Derek didn't talk to me. Guess he was afraid of

blowing his cover.'' A cloud of gloom moved in to displace the satisfaction on Luke's face.

''What's wrong?'' Kristen asked.

Luke rolled one shoulder as if trying to shake off whatever was bothering him. ''Nothing for you to worry about. Problems at the construction site, that's all.''

''What kind of problems?''

Luke gave the bottom porch step a frustrated kick. ''The concrete company was supposed to come pour the foundation yesterday. Instead, they called Andy and told him they weren't going to be able to do the job after all. Some screw-up with their scheduling.''

''Can't they do it today? Or tomorrow?''

''Supposedly they're too busy. If I wait until they have time to do it, we'll have fallen way behind. This project has a tight deadline. If I can't finish the rec center on schedule, I can kiss goodbye any chance of winning other city contracts in Pineville.''

Kristen worried her lip. ''What are you going to do?''

''Get someone else to pour the foundation.'' Luke massaged the nape of his neck. ''Unfortunately, there seems to be a sudden boom in the concrete business. All the local guys are booked up—Andy checked. So we'll have to hire someone from the next county. That's if *they're* not booked up. Plus, they'll charge more for coming the extra distance.'' Luke chuckled, but it wasn't a happy sound. ''Well, one thing I can count on, anyway. My streak of bad luck is still holding out.''

Kristen kneaded her temples. ''Did you ever think...that maybe all these problems you've been having aren't just because of bad luck?''

He shook his head. ''What do you mean?''

''Well...'' She hesitated, then plunged ahead. Luke already thought she was some kind of paranoid conspiracy nut. ''Look, I don't have any proof—yes, I know, what else is new?'' She gave him a sour smile, then sobered. ''But I've been thinking about what you told me. How all these problems with your business started about a year ago.''

"So?"

"Shortly after Sheri died."

"As it happens, yes."

"That's my point. Maybe these problems didn't just *happen.*"

Luke shook his head again. "I don't follow."

The more Kristen thought about it, the more it made sense. "Derek came home unexpectedly that day and discovered Sheri preparing to leave him. All along I've believed that that was what made him lose control and kill her." She swallowed, but it didn't ease the ache in her throat. "What if Derek also found out something else that day?"

Luke frowned. "Like what?"

Kristen looked him straight in the eye. "What if Sheri was in such a panic to convince Derek to let her and Cody go, that she told him Cody wasn't his?"

Thunderclouds gathered on Luke's brow.

"Don't get mad at me," she said quickly. "Just think about it. What if Derek found out a year ago that Cody was yours? And deliberately set out to destroy you?"

She saw a glimmer of unwilling acceptance in his eyes. "You're saying –"

"I think Derek set the fire that burned down your business." Kristen gripped Luke's arm. "I think he's been sabotaging you behind the scenes. Pressuring your suppliers to back out of their deals with you. Warning people not to hire you in the first place."

Luke's jaw nearly hit his chest. "You honestly think that son of a b—"

"These disasters haven't just been bad luck." Kristen shook his arm. "It's been Derek, the whole time. Trying to ruin you."

Chapter 8

Cody's shy voice interrupted them. ''Look what me and Aunt Kristen picked in the woods!'' The screen door banged shut behind him as he came out on the porch, proudly bearing what looked to Luke's dazed eyes like a pitcher stuffed full of weeds.

His mind was reeling like a punch-drunk boxer's from the astonishing statement Kristen had just hit him with. Derek? Was it actually possible that Derek Vincent had been behind all of his business reversals in the last year?

As the idea filtered into Luke's stunned brain, he was forced to admit it made a vicious kind of sense.

He would have to decide what to do about it later. Right now he needed to focus on Cody, whose smile was already dimming in the face of Luke's blank expression.

''Hey, whatcha got there, pal?'' Luke covered Kristen's hand, meaning to gently detach it from his arm, but somehow he found himself still holding it while they climbed the steps.

''Aunt Kristen's gonna show me how to make a flower 'rangement.'' Cody held out his scraggly bouquet for Luke's inspection. "She has a store that sells flowers, so she's really good at it."

Luke winked at her. "I'll bet she is."

"Once, for my birthday, she made a 'rangement that had balloons and candy and Winnie the Pooh and *everything!*"

Luke had never heard so many consecutive words bubble out of Cody's mouth before, let alone with such exuberance. "Your aunt Kristen's pretty talented."

"Yeah, I know!"

Luke nudged Kristen in the ribs. "Looks like you've got yourself a fan club here."

She blushed. "More like a mutual admiration society." She wrapped her arm around Cody and hugged him against her, prickles, thorns and all. "Ready for lunch?" She dropped a kiss on the crown of his head.

"Are you gonna eat with us?" Cody peered up at Luke with a hopeful expression.

"Is that an invitation?"

"Uh...yes."

"Well, then, I'd be delighted!" And he was, too.

Cody beamed. "Yay!" Even Luke couldn't fail to notice the hero worship shining in his eyes. Now, what the heck had he done to make the kid look at him that way?

Kristen fluttered her lashes as if about to bust out in tears. "Go wash your hands, honey, while I make our sandwiches."

"Okay."

Luke held open the screen door so Cody could use both hands to carry the pitcher inside.

"Put it on the kitchen counter and we'll arrange it later," Kristen called. She lowered her voice and said with a matchmaker's gleam in her eye, "Speaking of fan clubs, Cody seems awfully taken with *you.*"

"Cut it out. It won't work." But Luke's protest lacked the heat of his previous warnings to stay off the dubious subject of his fatherhood.

He backtracked mentally to analyze Kristen's theory about his business woes. Derek was too clever to have left behind traceable evidence that he or someone he paid had burned down Hollister Construction. The fire investigator's report had been inconclusive as to the source of the blaze.

But it shouldn't be too hard to discover whether or not Derek had been behind all the misplaced orders, cancelled contracts and scheduling screw-ups that had plagued Luke's business for a year. By asking the right questions, he figured he would be able to tell whether or not Derek had put pressure on his suppliers and subcontractors, even if they denied it. Especially since he planned to look them straight in the eye while he asked.

And if it turned out Derek *had* been sabotaging him all this time…

He must have a reason, right? The bad blood between them ran back a long, long way. But why this sudden determined campaign to ruin Luke? It could hardly stem from a business transaction gone sour—Luke would no more deal with Vincent Lumber than he would make a pact with the devil, even though buying wood from an out-of-town supplier meant inconvenience and added cost.

But what personal grudge could Derek possibly hold against him? *Luke* was the one with the grudge, after the arrogant snake had stolen Sheri from him. Afterward, Luke had made a point of steering clear of his rival, hadn't come within fifty feet of the guy in years. Not too difficult, considering they didn't exactly travel in the same social circles.

So why, out of the blue, did Derek have it in for him?

Unless…

Luke's skin went clammy. His pulse stumbled. There *was* a logical explanation for Derek's sudden surge of animosity, all right. That's if Kristen's guess was accurate. If Sheri had blurted out to Derek on the day she died that Cody was—

"Luke, are you okay?" Kristen peered at him with an anxious look on her face. "You're white as a ghost."

He needed to sit down, before his legs buckled and *really* gave her something to worry about. "Just hungry," he said, though at the moment his stomach would have violently rejected food. ''Did you mention something about sandwiches?''

''Of course.'' She didn't sound exactly reassured, but at least she didn't pursue it. ''Ham and cheese? Or peanut butter and jelly?''

His insides roiled. ''Surprise me,'' he said, clamping his back teeth together.

As they moved inside, Luke noticed he was still holding Kristen's hand. Now, how had *that* happened? He ought to let go. Touching her was a trap.

Instead, he linked his fingers more securely through hers.

After lunch Cody took a nap. Kristen could tell he was feeling better today, but it was clear all the recent upheaval in his life had drained him of his energy reserves. Before going to his bedroom, however, he'd made Luke promise to stay until he woke up.

Kristen hummed a happy tune while she put away their sandwich fixings. It was so wonderful to watch Cody develop a bond with his real father. And she could tell by the wonderment that sometimes entered Luke's eyes that he was starting to accept the possibility that Cody was his son.

Kristen's humming faltered. If they couldn't prove Derek guilty of murder, she would have no choice but to take Cody and run, to separate him from his real father forever. She would *never* let Derek have him back.

Of course, there could be a chance that if she had to take such drastic action, Luke might come with them. Kristen's heart leaped even as her mind shot down the idea. No. Luke wasn't the type of man to live in hiding, always peering back over his shoulder for fear Derek might catch up with them.

Luke Hollister had never run from a fight in his life. He would insist on staying in Whisper Ridge and battling Derek face-to-face, hauling in an army of lawyers and private detectives if necessary. But the law was on Derek's side now. If Cody was found, Kristen would be forced to hand him back, at least temporarily.

She couldn't risk it. It only took seconds to hurt someone, or worse. No, if Luke couldn't come up with some solid evidence for the police pretty soon, Kristen and Cody would have to flee. Just the two of them.

Luke came back in the kitchen, dusting his hands together. "I adjusted the temperature on the water heater. The water should get nice and hot now."

"Thanks." The kitchen felt smaller when Luke was in it. His massive shoulders and muscular physique seemed to displace more air than a normal human being's. Maybe that explained why Kristen always found herself breathing a bit harder whenever he was around.

He fingered the jumble of wild plants she and Cody were going to arrange later. "Ouch!"

"Uh-oh. Did one of nature's little defense mechanisms prick you?"

"Darn right it did." He popped the tip of his finger into his mouth and sucked it.

When their eyes intersected across the room, desire unfurled in the pit of Kristen's stomach. Both she and Luke had been on their best behavior today. No arguing, no touching—well, except for a little friendly hand-holding.

Keeping their distance didn't help, though. Kristen would still want Luke even if he were clear across the solar system. Even though she had no right to.

From across the kitchen his unwavering gaze seemed to caress her, to explore her from head to toe, to pry into intimate places he had no business looking. Kristen's skin grew warm. The desire in her belly percolated outward, making her blood fizz and her nerves tingle. Every cell in her body yearned for him.

Good heavens, if Luke could make her feel this way just with his eyes, how on earth would he make her feel if she ever gave him free rein with his hands, his mouth, his seductive masculine power?

Something akin to panic made Kristen pivot around and whip open the refrigerator. She pretended to rummage through its contents, giving herself an excuse for a nice bracing slap of chilled air in her face.

"I swung by your shop this morning while I was in town," Luke said.

Now *that* had a chilling effect. Kristen shut the refrigerator. She wasn't even sure she'd locked up the store when she'd left that last time to make deliveries at the hospital. Her unplanned vanishing act also meant that a number of customers had paid for flowers that wouldn't be delivered now. It nagged Kristen's conscience, but couldn't be helped. "Hopefully Derek hasn't thrown rocks through all the shop windows," she said, striving for nonchalance.

"No." Luke inspected his pricked finger. "But the place was swarming with cops."

Kristen inhaled sharply. "Oh, no." She'd realized, of course, that she would be the prime suspect in Cody's "kidnapping." But the presence of the police in her shop confirmed it, made it real.

"Well, *swarming* might be an exaggeration." Luke propped his hands behind him and leaned back against the counter. "There were a couple of patrol cars parked out front. The door was open, and I could see uniforms moving around inside."

"So now they're looking for *me*."

"Seems like, yeah."

Kristen's mouth twisted. "Maybe I should have sent an anonymous ransom note to throw them off track."

"I doubt that would have helped."

"I know." She raked a hand through her hair, then noticed her fingers were trembling. "It's just—I feel like a hunted animal or something. With the hunters closing in."

Luke hesitated, as if debating with himself. Then he reached into his back pocket and extracted a folded sheet of paper. "These are all over town, too." He came over and handed the paper to Kristen.

She unfolded it with shaky fingers. A black-and-white photo of Cody beamed up at her with a gap-toothed grin, below the word *Missing!* in bold black letters. A fist squeezed Kristen's heart. The photo had been taken not long before Sheri died, at Cody's sixth birthday party. The shot had been cropped to display mostly Cody's face, but in the background Kristen could make out part of the special Winnie-the-Pooh floral arrangement she'd created for him that day.

He looked so excited, so happy, with that goofy party hat cocked at an angle atop his blond head, a dab of frosting near the corner of his mouth. Little did he know what tragedy fate would soon hand him.

His image blurred. "Here. You take it." Kristen shoved the flier in Luke's direction. "I don't want it around where Cody might find it."

"Sure." He folded the paper and carefully slipped it back into his pocket, as if it were something precious he intended to keep.

"I see Derek couldn't even come up with a recent photo of Cody." Scorn edged her voice. "That one was taken over a year ago."

"I thought he looked younger."

"He's changed a lot during the past year." Kristen didn't understand why that Missing! flier had upset her so much. Whenever a child vanished, it was standard procedure to plaster his picture everywhere. Yet it had come as a downright shock, holding physical proof in her hands that people all over town were looking for Cody. Another development that made their situation seem even more horribly real. Like the police combing her shop for clues.

"Kristen, don't worry."

To her surprise, Luke put his arms around her. It was a big brother sort of hug, nothing sexual about it, the same kind of hug he used to give her when he was her big sister's boyfriend. Kristen reacted the same way she had back then. She closed her eyes, clumsily circled her arms around him, filled her lungs with that wonderful male fragrance of sweat and denim. And prayed with all her might Luke couldn't sense how much she wanted him.

His heart thumped a steady, reassuring cadence against her

ear. Kristen hadn't felt safe for a long time, but she felt safe here in Luke's arms. He patted her back as if to say, "There, there," as if to demonstrate this was purely a hug meant to comfort, nothing more.

It *was* comforting, snuggling against Luke. Somehow, if only for a few brief moments, he made Kristen feel that everything was going to turn out all right.

Unfortunately, however, that wasn't *all* Luke made her feel.

Reluctantly, she uncurled her fingers from his shirt and disengaged herself from their embrace. "You mentioned earlier you spoke to the medical examiner," she said, adjusting the new blouse Luke had bought her yesterday. "What did he tell you?" They hadn't been able to discuss it during lunch, not with Cody there.

"He gave me the same kind of wishy-washy answer I get whoever I talk to." Luke pulled a face. "Nothing to show Sheri was dead or injured before the crash. Nothing to prove she wasn't. Anything's possible, blah, blah, blah."

"That's what he told me when I talked to him a year ago."

"Yeah, he mentioned that." Luke moved into the dining room, pulled out a chair and straddled it backward. "Look, we've got to start comparing notes. Everyone I talk to, you've been there before me. We're wasting time by covering the same ground twice."

Kristen sat at the table next to him. "Besides the police mechanic and the medical examiner, I also spoke to Cody's teacher, Pam Morrison. I mean, she was Cody's teacher *last* year, when he was in first grade."

"You learn anything from her?"

"She confirmed that Sheri *did* call the morning she died to say Cody was sick and would be staying home that day. That was part of our escape plan, so no one would contact Derek to find out why Cody wasn't in school."

"Meanwhile, you and Sheri and Cody would be on your way to the battered-women's shelter in Pineville."

"Right." Kristen's stomach took a familiar, sickening

lurch. If only their plan had worked. ‘‘What Pam told me proves that Sheri intended to go through with it.’’

Luke drummed his fingers on the back of his chair. ‘‘Unless Cody coincidentally did wake up sick that day…’’

Kristen’s hair whirled as she shook her head. ‘‘Sheri would never have left him home by himself if he’d been sick. She wouldn’t have left him alone under *any* circumstances.’’ She leaned forward and flattened her palms on the table. ‘‘Sheri was a good mother, Luke. No matter what faults she may have had, you have to believe that. She was a wonderful mother to your—to Cody.’’

Luke gripped the back of his chair hard enough to turn his knuckles white. ‘‘Let’s move on, shall we?’’

‘‘All right.’’ Best not to become sidetracked by emotion right now. ‘‘Sheri would never have left Cody home alone,’’ Kristen reiterated, ‘‘yet that’s how the police found him after the accident. His teacher agreed it was odd that Sheri would have been driving someplace by herself with Cody home sick.’’ Kristen smacked the table for emphasis. ‘‘And Cody *wasn’t* sick. I saw him myself, right after I got word of the accident. He was terribly upset, of course. But not physically ill.’’

Luke flexed his fingers. ‘‘So we have an oddity. But no proof.’’

‘‘Nothing that would stand up in court, if that’s what you mean.’’ Kristen fought to keep the resentment from her voice. She *knew* what had happened to Sheri. Why wouldn’t Luke believe her?

He reached over and covered her hand with his. ‘‘I’m not trying to poke holes in your theory,’’ he said gruffly. ‘‘I’m just playing devil’s advocate because we need to look at our evidence from the cops’ point of view.’’

Our. Luke had said *our* evidence. Maybe he did believe her, after all.

With renewed hope, Kristen continued down the list of people she’d interviewed about Sheri’s death. ‘‘Derek’s secretary,’’ she said, pinching her lips in disgust. ‘‘I think she’s the one who went running to Derek and told him I was asking questions about Sheri's so-called accident."

"That's when Derek threatened to harm Cody if you didn't drop your investigation?"

"Yes." Anger welled up inside her. She saw it darken Luke's face, too.

He stroked his thumb on the back of her hand. "Vanessa What's-Her-Name is his secretary, right?"

"Taylor," Kristen supplied. "Vanessa Taylor. Remember Ricky Taylor, from high school? Vanessa's his mother."

"She manage to tell you anything useful before she scurried off to Derek?"

"Are you kidding?" Kristen made a scoffing sound. "She's Derek's loyal lieutenant. Probably hoping he'll marry her someday as a reward for years of devoted service. She wasn't about to give me a straight answer. I asked her what time Derek had left the office that morning and what time he'd returned." Kristen batted her eyelashes with exaggerated innocence. "Vanessa claimed he'd never left, he'd been there the whole time, and she'd swear it on a stack of Bibles."

Luke narrowed his gaze. "You think she was covering up for him?"

"Of course! Vanessa would say anything to protect her boss and keep her precious job." Kristen sprang from her chair, too agitated to sit still. "Derek had to have left his office that morning in order to have killed Sheri. He would have passed right by Vanessa's desk coming and going. There's no way she didn't know he was gone for a while. She's lying."

Luke frowned as if deep in thought. "Maybe someone else saw him leave Vincent Lumber that day. It might help if we could get a look at his schedule, find out who he met with that morning. Maybe he walked one of his visitors out to the car and drove off himself at the same time."

Kristen propped a hand on her hip in a skeptical pose. "You don't seriously believe Vanessa will let you page through Derek's appointment book, do you?"

"I, er, wasn't planning to ask permission."

Kristen grabbed his shoulder. "Luke, be careful. So far *you're* not in any trouble with the law."

"I don't plan to get caught."

If the stakes weren't so high, Kristen would have begged him not to risk it. "Just...watch out for patrolling rottweilers, okay?"

"I'll stuff my pockets with doggie biscuits before I go in." He patted her hand. "Don't look so worried. I'll be fine." He guided her back into her chair. "Tell me who else you've spoken to about Sheri."

Kristen tented her fingers against her temples, trying to remember. "Her doctor. I mean, her regular doctor. He wouldn't talk to me at first, gave me all that stuff about patient confidentiality." Her lips twitched. "After I went ballistic and pointed out his patient was dead, he finally opened up."

"What did you ask him?" Luke stacked his arms on the back of his chair and rested his chin on them.

"I asked if he would agree to tell the police that Sheri had a history of injuries from Derek's beatings."

"Did he say yes?"

"Hardly." Exasperation made her scowl. "For one thing, Sheri consistently denied Derek had hurt her. She always had some story lined up about walking into a door or falling down the stairs."

"Surely her doctor suspected she wasn't telling the truth." Luke raised his head. "Didn't he have a legal obligation to report possible abuse?"

Kristen helplessly flipped over her palms. "Sheri begged him not to. She was terrified of losing Cody if she and Derek ever wound up in court together. She convinced her doctor he would only make matters worse by reporting her injuries to the police."

Luke stroked his jaw. "Tough position she put him in."

"Maybe. But his professional ethics apparently weren't troubled enough to make him tell the police what he knew even *after* Sheri was dead." Kristen's temper climbed. "He hemmed and hawed with me quite a bit, but he made it clear it would take a legal subpoena to force him to admit what he suspected about the ongoing abuse Sheri suffered.''

''And we would have to produce other incriminating evidence against Derek first, before the district attorney would issue such a subpoena.''

''Kind of a catch-twenty-two, isn't it?'' Kristen shrugged unhappily. ''Like everyone else in town, Sheri's doctor won't cross swords with Derek unless he's forced to.'' Bitterness welled up in her throat. ''Of course, I'm a fine one to criticize, aren't I? Considering I couldn't stop Derek from killing my sister, either.''

The words spilled out before Kristen could stop them, before she'd even realized they were floating around her subconscious.

Luke sat bolt upright, as if someone had zapped him with an electric charge. ''What's that supposed to mean?''

''Nothing,'' she replied with a weary shake of her head.

Luke scraped his chair around and sat on it the proper way, scooting forward so their knees were touching. ''Kristen, are you telling me you actually blame yourself for Sheri's death?'' His voice was harsh with dismay.

''I'm not telling you anything,'' she said with a sigh, focusing on a point past his shoulder. ''Never mind. It's not important.''

''It *is* important.'' He gave her shoulders a gentle, insistent shake. ''Sheri's death wasn't your fault. You do know that, don't you?''

Kristen clenched her teeth to keep her chin from trembling. She shook her head wordlessly.

''Honey, listen to me.'' Luke shifted her, forcing her to meet his eyes. They burned into her like lasers. ''Derek killed Sheri, not you. How can you possibly blame yourself?''

The way he said *honey* seared Kristen like an accusation. *Derek killed Sheri.* At least now Luke believed her. But in the end, he would *blame* her, too.

Pain and remorse flooded through her, gathering strength, threatening to sweep her away. Kristen did her best to keep it dammed inside, but the tide of her guilty misery was too strong.

"*I'm* the one who convinced Sheri to leave Derek." She pounded a fist to her breastbone. "If I hadn't done that, he wouldn't have killed her."

Luke's fingers dented her flesh. "What were you supposed to do? Keep letting him beat her?"

"At least she would still be alive!"

"You don't know that." Luke spoke firmly. "He might have found some other reason to kill her by now. You did the right thing, convincing Sheri to leave."

"How can you say that, when she wound up dead?" Kristen's body vibrated as if high-tension wires ran through it. "I pushed her into leaving. Sheri kept telling me something terrible would happen if she tried to, but I wouldn't listen. I begged her and nagged her and wouldn't stop until—" A sob choked off the flow of her words.

Luke framed her face with his hands. "Kristen—"

"Until I drove her to her death!" She knocked his hands aside and lurched to her feet. Shame and sorrow made her want to run away and hide, to lock herself up in a dark closet forever. Except she still couldn't hide from herself. And she had Cody to protect.

She shied away when Luke tried to catch her arm. His touch couldn't comfort her now. It would only add to her torment.

"This is wrong," he said, bunching his fists as if to keep from reaching for her. "I'm not going to give up until I make you see the truth. You did the best you could for Sheri. Leaving Derek was the right thing to do—the *only* thing to do. You're not responsible for his actions when he found out about it. *He* is."

"I should have been more careful. We should have waited until he was out of town on business."

Luke stuck an admonishing finger in her face. "Every additional day Sheri spent in that house put her in danger, not to mention what it did to Cody. The kid wasn't deaf, dumb and blind! Think how it must have affected him, knowing his father was hitting his mother on a regular basis.''

''I *did* think of that,'' Kristen said fiercely. ''That's one of the reasons I was so desperate to get them out of there. But now Cody doesn't even *have* a mother, thanks to me.''

''It was a risk that had to be taken.''

''That's easy to say, isn't it?'' she cried. ''When Sheri was the one who paid the price.''

''Would *you* have stayed in an abusive marriage?'' Luke's glare honed in on her like a prosecuting attorney's. ''Would you stay with some bastard who beat you for fear he might kill you if you tried to escape?''

Kristen hesitated. Ironic, but the only man she could imagine being married to was Luke.

''Sure,'' he went on when she didn't answer, ''maybe you'd stay alive, but what kind of life would you have? Can you honestly tell me you'd be better off not taking the risk?''

Numbness settled over Kristen, so that she almost felt calm. ''The difference is, Sheri didn't make that decision on her own. I forced her into it.''

''She was a grown woman. You didn't force her.''

''But if I hadn't—''

''In the end, it was Sheri's choice.'' Luke's expression turned bleak. They were discussing the woman he'd loved. ''And no matter what the tragic consequences turned out to be, it was still the right choice.''

Kristen wished she could believe him. But letting herself off the hook would be too easy. She could never, ever forget the fact that she was the one who'd fought for, planned and set in motion the events that had led to her sister's death.

''Please, Luke. Just...go now.'' She couldn't bear the probing intensity of his gaze one minute longer. He made her feel trapped in the merciless spotlight of Judgment Day.

But the stubborn shift of his jaw warned Kristen this soul-searching examination of her guilt wasn't over. Not by a long shot. ''Okay. I'll leave, if that's what you want,'' he said grudgingly.

What I want is you! her heart cried silently. She ached for Luke to take her in his arms, to absolve her of blame, to promise she and Cody would be safe with him forever.

But she couldn't let herself yield to that longing, even if Luke had been willing to participate in her fantasy. Sheri's memory prevented it.

Tears stung Kristen's eyelids.

"I'll be back this evening," Luke said from the doorway. "I told Cody I'd be here when he woke up from his nap. I mean to keep my word."

"I'll explain that you had to leave for a while." Please, please go, before I collapse into a weeping puddle on the floor.

Kristen peered through the window while Luke strode to his truck. Even though she wanted him to leave, a hollow feeling crept around her heart. It was starting to happen every time she watched him drive off.

Instead of leaving, though, he reached into the pickup, then jogged back across the driveway with something in his hand. Kristen met him at the door.

"Here, you keep this." He dropped his cellular phone into her hand and curled her fingers around it. "It bugs me to think of you stranded out here, without any way to call for help in an emergency."

"Thanks." She eyed the phone uncertainly.

"You know how to operate it?"

"Um, not exactly."

"Here, I'll show you." Luke's demonstration involved standing quite close, with frequent contact between his fingers and hers. Kristen forced herself to concentrate. If she ever had to use this phone, it would be for something serious.

"Now, if I need to call you, I'll use a signal." Grim amusement tugged up his mouth. "The last thing we need is someone trying to call me and hearing *your* voice answer."

"I could just wait for the other person to speak first, then hang up if it isn't you."

"Yeah, but that might seem suspicious. Tell you what. I'll

dial and hang up after the first ring, then call back right away so you'll know it's me.''

''Okay.'' Kristen studied the phone as if it were a hand grenade. ''But I'm still going to wait till I hear your voice before I say anything.''

''Wise precaution.'' Luke brushed a quick stroke on her cheek with the back of his finger. ''See you later, Agent Monroe.''

His touch lingered on Kristen's face for hours afterward, as if he'd left his permanent mark on her.

Chapter 9

Derek Vincent swatted aside the yellow crime-scene tape as if it were no more significant than a cobweb. The cops had already been here, and he doubted they'd be back. Not that he cared. They would just assume some punk kids had broken in.

The police hadn't found any clue about where Miss Troublemaker had taken the brat, either downstairs in her prissy flower shop or here in the apartment above it where she lived. He didn't expect to find any clues either. That wasn't why he'd come.

He jiggled the doorknob, only to discover it was locked. No problem. Years ago, while the bitch had been over visiting smart-mouth Sheri and the kid, he'd swiped her key ring long enough to make a copy of her apartment key, then returned it before she'd even known it was gone.

A necessary precaution in those days. No telling when his darling devoted wife might take it into her pretty little head to run blubbering to her sister after one of their domestic spats. He'd had no intention of standing outside banging on his sister-in-law's door to get in, broadcasting their private business to the whole town. No, all he would have to do would be to slip this nice little key into the lock, and *voilà!* His runaway wife would be back home where she belonged in no time.

He used the key now and entered the apartment. Late-afternoon sunshine slanted through the open curtains. He locked the door behind him, then shut the curtains. His visit here was purely symbolic. Dear old Kristen was temporarily out of his reach, but her home wasn't. It excited him, knowing how violated she would feel to see him tromping across her carpet, fondling her prized possessions, poking into nooks and crannies to ferret out her most personal secrets.

He'd never actually set foot in here before, and now he crossed his arms and regarded the cutesy, cramped apartment with satisfaction. The cops had done a pretty good job of trashing the place. Every drawer and cupboard stood open, contents shoved around, spilling out in careless disarray. ''Tsk, tsk,'' he scolded. ''Such sloppy housekeeping.''

His pleasure faded as he scanned her living room. All her stuff was here, but *she* wasn't, damn it! Through some miraculous, imbecilic luck she continued to evade both him and the cops. Not that they wouldn't track her down eventually. It wouldn't be much longer before he had his chance to even the score with her.

No, not *even* it. Derek Vincent, play to a tie? Never. He always made sure he came out ahead, and this time he intended to mop up the floor with his opponent.

She had framed pictures stuck all over the place, lining the walls, gathering dust on every flat surface. Pictures of his late lamented wife. Snapshots of the two sisters as teenagers. A photo of the dead woman who would have been his mother-in-law if she'd lived long enough.

That might have been amusing. He could remember her down on her hands and knees, scrubbing floors at the Vincent mansion when he was a kid. There she was in another shot, right next to hubby, who'd also been dead forever, killed in some lumbering accident they'd tried to claim was the company's fault.

As for the brat, there was an entire *gallery* of pictures documenting practically every moment of his existence, it looked like, starting with the day he'd been born.

Everywhere he looked, faces. Smiling. Smirking. Laughing at him. Laughing because *she* had pulled one over on him. She'd swiped the kid from right under his nose, and now he couldn't find either one of them.

Hatred stoked the rising flames of his anger. They were nothing but trash, all of them. He'd practically plucked his wife out of the gutter to marry her, and look what gratitude it had gotten him. Her whole worthless family, laughing at him. Thinking they were better than he was.

He would show them.

He grabbed the nearest picture of the kid off a bookcase. "I'm gonna find you," he warned in a singsong. "You can run, but you can't hide. You're going to come home soon, and then you're going to be punished for all the trouble you've caused."

Frustration gnawed his guts like a hungry wild animal. It was starting to get to him, the pressure of acting the role of panicked, hand-wringing parent in front of everyone. He slammed the photo back onto the bookcase, facedown, and that's when he spotted the one that had been hidden behind it.

Sheri and Hollister, cozied up together on a picnic blanket, arms around each other. America's sweethearts. Must have been taken nearly ten years ago, but that didn't diminish the fury that boiled through his blood. Sheri had belonged to *him,* to Derek Vincent. Bought and paid for, the most luscious babe in town, and she'd been all his.

But she'd tricked him. She was supposed to present him with a son, an heir, and instead she'd passed off another man's brat as his.

He thought he'd beaten Luke Hollister eight years ago. That had been half the fun of wooing sweet Sheri. But in the end, Hollister had had the last laugh, hadn't he?

"No," he snarled.

Now Hollister and Kristen had conspired to steal the kid that by rights should belong to *him.* He was dead certain Hollister was involved. Who else would she go running to for help? How else could she have eluded capture for so long?

They were probably laughing at him right now, thinking they had the upper hand, gloating that they'd won. Knowing he would never tell the cops Hollister was in on the kidnapping, because then the cops would ask why.

The thought of people laughing at him was intolerable.

He snatched the picture of the two lovebirds off the bookcase. His hands shook so the hated images blurred in front of him.

Whatever it took, whatever he had to do, he would not let them win.

"No," he snarled again. "No. No. NO!"

He dashed the picture to the floor as a raging cauldron of fury and hatred and frustration boiled over inside him. Glass shards flew everywhere.

Then he was grabbing pictures as fast as he could, hurling and smashing in an orgy of destruction, an endless series of shattering explosions that sounded like artillery fire.

He would wipe those superior smiles off their faces. Every last one of them.

If Luke didn't watch out, he could get used to this.

When he'd returned to the cabin late that afternoon, he'd felt like one of those TV dads from the fifties. Cody had burst through the screen door to greet him, eager to tell Luke about the family of rabbits he'd seen hopping into the woods earlier. Kristen had a smile waiting for him just inside the door, while the mouthwatering aroma of a home-cooked meal drifted from the kitchen.

The only thing missing from this touching family scene was the husbandly kiss. Maybe that was why Luke had felt such a strong impulse to take Kristen in his arms and give her one. He restrained himself, however, along with the urge to call out, "Hi, honey, I'm home."

The pleasant illusion of family life continued through dinner. Afterward, Kristen insisted on doing the dishes by herself so Luke could play checkers with Cody. He saw what she was up to—maneuvering him into playing dad, hoping to strengthen the bond between him and Cody. Luke didn't object, though. Truth was, he kind of enjoyed playing dad. Even though it was only temporary.

For cryin' out loud, he wasn't cut out for fatherhood! Yet even as he cautioned himself how unlikely he was to wind up with Cody once all the legal dust had settled, Luke couldn't help imagining a future far different from the footloose bachelor life-style he'd led so far.

Lots of men raised kids by themselves. It wasn't easy, but Luke had never lacked self-confidence when it came to getting the job done. Might be kind of fun to raise a kid, teach him stuff, take him to ball games, that kind of thing. They would sort of be a team. Maybe someday the kid would even want to follow in his old man's footsteps.

Of course, there would be one time-honored member missing from this family portrait....

No matter how hard he tried to focus on the checkers game, Luke's glance kept sneaking toward the kitchen. From where he sat on the couch he had an unobstructed view of Kristen's sexy backside while she stood at the sink. Thick auburn hair cascading down her back...narrow waist tapering into the snug-fitting slacks Luke had chosen for her in such a frenzy of indecision...

The gentle swell of her hips certainly filled them out nicely. Now that Luke had a chance to study Kristen at his leisure, he noted how differently she was built from her sister. Kristen was shorter, for one thing, with lush curves in all the right places. She had square shoulders and strong limbs, so she didn't look as if a good gust of wind could blow her right over. She radiated health and wholesomeness.

Now that Luke thought about it, Sheri had been too darn skinny. She'd had an ethereal, vulnerable, damsel-in-distress quality that had made men want to take care of her. Kristen gave the impression she would haul off and punch any man in the nose who dared suggest she needed his protection.

For the first time, it dawned on Luke how difficult it must have been for her to turn to him for help.

He wouldn't let her down. No matter what drastic action he had to take, no matter whose powerful toes he had to step on, he was going to make damn sure that she and Cody were safe from now on.

Clack. Clack. Clack. "I won!" Cody cried, leapfrogging a red checker over the last of Luke's black ones. He bounced up and down in his chair, hugging himself with glee. Luke had more or less tried to let him win, but he hadn't had to try very hard. The kid was a natural.

With his two new adult-size front teeth, Cody resembled a beaming chipmunk. Luke would have gladly emptied his pockets and shelled out his last dime to buy a smile like that. "You sure did, Slugger!" He reached over the coffee table and gave Cody a high-five slap, then held up his hand for the little guy to reciprocate.

Cody smacked Luke's palm with enthusiasm, if not perfect aim. "I captured all your pieces!" he crowed.

Luke lowered his brows in mock suspicion. "You sure you never played this game before?"

"Nope." Cody whipped his head from side to side. "I never did."

"Never did what?" Kristen emerged from the kitchen. Her cheeks held a rosy glow from the hot dishwater. Luke hadn't gotten around yet to demonstrating how the dishwasher worked.

"Play checkers," he explained.

Damp tendrils framed Kristen's face like wisps of copper. When she got closer, Luke could smell the soap fragrance rising from her skin like warm perfume. She looked all flushed and steamy, as if she'd just stepped out of the shower.

Or risen from his bed.

Whoa, get a grip! Luke warned himself. This is supposed to be family hour, remember?

"Bedtime, sweetie." Kristen good-naturedly rumpled Cody's hair.

Luke couldn't help speculating what his own response would be if Kristen ever said that to *him.* Certainly a lot more eager than Cody's.

"Aw, Aunt Kristen. We were gonna play best two out of three." He cast a sideways glance at Luke as if beseeching him for support.

"We'll finish the tournament tomorrow," Luke said, climbing to his feet. "Let's see, right now the score is one to nothing in my favor, right?"

"In *my* favor," Cody corrected indignantly, poking himself in the chest.

"Oh, yeah, that's right." Luke snapped his fingers. "I never was very good at math."

"Do I hafta go to bed right *now?*" Cody scuffed his new sneaker on the Berber rug.

"'Fraid so, kiddo. Soon as we put away the checkers."

"But I'm almost better," Cody protested. "Aunt Kristen even took my bandage off today." He pointed to his forehead, where a nasty abrasion appeared to be healing nicely. "My head hardly hurts at all anymore."

Luke made an enormous effort to conceal the anger frothing inside him. Not at Cody's stalling tactics, but at the evil bastard who'd hurt him, who didn't deserve such a great kid for his son.

He tapped his wristwatch. "Your aunt Kristen said it's bedtime. Go brush your teeth, and then we'll come in to say good night."

"Oh, *okay.*" Cody hung his head and dragged his feet as if Luke had just sent him to his room for a week.

He felt awful. Man, this parenting stuff was tough! He wanted to call Cody back and tell him he could stay up as late as he wanted, that Luke would play checkers with him all night long if that would make him happy.

The mournful click of the bathroom door struck his ears like a rebuke of betrayal.

"You're really getting the hang of this," Kristen said solemnly. But the twinkle in her eye gave her away. "Your only mistake was, you forgot to make him put the checkers away *before* you sent him to bed."

Luke groaned. "Is this supposed to get easier?"

"Yes. No." She shrugged. "Gosh, how do I know? I'm feeling my way, too. Just like you are."

"You seem to have a natural knack for mothering," Luke commented while they picked up the checkers. "How come you never married and had kids yourself?"

Yikes, he hoped that didn't sound like a come-on! He didn't want to give Kristen the wrong idea, make her think he cared one way or the other about her love life. Idle curiosity, that's all it was.

Kristen dropped a couple of checkers on the floor. When she ducked to retrieve them, Luke glimpsed the dismay that tightened her features. Obviously she didn't appreciate his prying.

"Uhh..." She let his question hang awkwardly in the air while she wriggled under the couch to reach a black checker that had rolled away.

Luke tried not to stare at her seductively swaying bottom. He wasn't successful. Darn it, he had to stop lusting after her! Worse, he had to stop mentally casting her as his co-star in some corny TV series. Kristen might have been born to play the role of wife and mother, but not on the Luke Hollister Show, thank you. His was strictly a solo act.

Her face was red with either effort or embarrassment when she crawled out from under the couch. "I guess I just never met Mr. Right," she said with a false-sounding laugh. "Isn't that the standard answer?"

"Yep." Luke put the cover back on the game box, kicking himself for asking in the first place. But he had to admit, he still wanted to know. It wasn't as if Kristen lived like a princess locked up in an isolated tower. Luke didn't have much patience for gossip, but over the last eight years he hadn't been able to help overhearing about various boyfriends she'd dated.

None of the relationships had seemed to last very long. Strange. Although Luke had once had reason not to trust her, Kristen had never struck him as the flighty type—not like Sheri. She was caring, generous and loyal to a fault, as Luke had painfully discovered. She had plenty to offer any man. A small town like Whisper Ridge didn't exactly supply an unlimited smorgasbord of bachelors, but Luke was still mystified that no one had snapped her up yet.

Even if Kristen *were* waiting for Mr. Right to come along, family and commitment were clearly important to her. Luke found it surprising she hadn't settled down with anyone yet. He would be a lucky man, whoever he turned out to be.

An unpleasant weight settled in Luke's chest. It took him a few seconds to identify it as jealousy.

Jealous? *Him?* No way. Sheri's two-timing had cured Luke of the green-eyed monster for good. You had to make a certain emotional investment in a woman before jealousy could enter the picture, and he was never going to risk such a foolish investment again. Luke Hollister might make mistakes, but he didn't make the same one twice.

That weight in his chest didn't go away, though.

"Guess it must be time to check on Cody, isn't it?" He stored the checkers box back in the cabinet where he'd found it.

Kristen appeared relieved that he'd changed the subject. "Know any good bedtime stories?" she asked.

"Uh, you mean like 'Goldilocks and the Three Bears'?"

Amusement tipped up her mouth. Luke couldn't believe how much he wanted to kiss her right now. The idea of her kissing anyone else drove him crazy. He kneaded his forehead with his knuckles, as if that could blot out such dangerous thoughts. Where had this sudden unreasonable possessiveness come from, anyway?

"I think Cody's a little old for the Three Bears," Kristen said tactfully as they walked toward his room.

"Well..." Luke scanned his memory banks for any tales he might have heard around the campfire as a kid. "How about a ghost story?'' He rubbed his hands briskly together. ''I remember one that used to scare the pants off me no matter how many times I heard—''

''Um, maybe that's not such a good idea,'' Kristen said. ''Under the present circumstances.'' Meaning Cody already had too many real-life fears to deal with.

''You're right.'' Luke cocked his thumb and sighted down his index finger at her. ''Maybe storytelling ought to be *your* department.''

Kristen arched her brows suggestively. ''I thought maybe you'd like the practice, is all.'' She sashayed into Cody's bedroom, a mysterious smile clinging to her lips.

Now, what the heck had she meant by *that?*

''You did great,'' Kristen assured Luke. ''Cody loved your story.''

They sat at the dining room table, drinking coffee. Luke had his chair tipped on its back legs like one of those rebellious kids in school who ignores the teacher's warnings until he finally topples backward.

He blew a scornful gust across the top of his coffee. ''All I could come up with was a rehash of some dumb detective show I watched on TV last week. Not exactly the Hardy Boys.''

''You made the effort, that's what counts.'' Kristen smiled. ''Kids don't care if the stories you tell them aren't great works of literature. You don't need to entertain them, you just need to show you care.''

She wondered if Luke even realized how much he cared for Cody. It gladdened her heart to observe the gentle look on his face while he interacted with his son. Tenderness wasn't exactly a trait she'd ever associated with Luke before. This new side of him was strangely attractive.

''You seem to be quite an expert on kids, considering you don't have any of your own.'' Immediately Luke backtracked. ''I didn't mean that the way it sounded.''

''That's me, the old-maid aunt,'' she said lightly.

"Kristen, come on. I meant it as a compliment." He let his chair fall forward with a bang. "For God's sake, even if you *were* an old maid, you're the sexiest one I've ever seen. All I meant was that you're so great with Cody...."

Sexy? *Her?* No, Kristen thought. Her sister had been the glamorous one, the sexy one. Still, Luke's words warmed her insides even more than the coffee she was sipping. "Thank you," she murmured. "For saying that about Cody. He means everything to me. I want so much to give him back some of the love he was robbed of when Sheri died." Because it's my fault he doesn't have a parent who loves him.

Except maybe, just maybe, Kristen could give Cody a father who did.

"He's lucky to have you for an aunt." Luke covered her hand with his.

Kristen dropped her gaze to that big, steady, competent hand. It felt so good on top of hers, both soothing and tingling at the same time. She loved how his palm felt, roughened with calluses. She loved the look of his strong, square fingers, their clean, blunt nails chipped from hard work. She loved the solid, warm weight of his flesh resting on hers. She loved—

Kristen tensed, spilling some coffee on the table. "Oops! Clumsy. Better get something to wipe that up before it stains the wood." She hastily withdrew her hand from Luke's and scraped back her chair. All at once his touch unsettled her, as if his hand was slyly beckoning her down a path fraught with peril.

Don't go there, an urgent voice warned. Once you start down that road, there'll be no turning back.

She brought a paper towel from the kitchen to mop up the small puddle of coffee. "Did you find out anything new about Sheri's death this afternoon?" Better to focus on something practical, rather than dwelling on the impossible. She and Luke hadn't been able to discuss his investigation while Cody was present.

"No." Luke tracked Kristen's movements with his eyes.

Why had she turned jumpy as a cat all of a sudden? "I thought of something that might be worth following up, though."

"What's that?"

"Here, sit down. You're going to wear a hole in the table with that paper towel." He nudged her cup in her direction.

She slid cautiously into her chair, as if she expected him to shove it out from under her at the last second. What had made her so nervous? She picked up the cup without scooting her chair back to the table.

"All right. See what you think about this." Luke got down to business. "If Derek drove Sheri to Lookout Road and sent her car over the cliff, he must have left his own car at the Vincent mansion, right?"

"Right."

"Then how did he get home to retrieve it?"

Kristen traced her thumb along the curve of her cup handle. "Walked, I suppose. He could hardly have risked hitchhiking or calling someone for a ride, because anyone who picked him up could have placed him near the scene of Sheri's accident."

Luke nodded. "That's what I figured. So this afternoon I drove from Lookout Road back to the mansion." Cruising past the massive iron gateway in front of the Vincent ancestral home, he'd half expected to be trapped by a blockade of police cars, hauled out of his truck at gunpoint and arrested. In reality, though, the cops had no reason to suspect him of any role in Cody's disappearance. Not yet, anyway.

"The distance Derek would have had to walk is about three miles, according to my odometer," Luke said. "If he cut through people's backyards, a little less."

"So he could easily have made it home in less than an hour."

"Yes. But what occurred to me was—"

"Someone might have seen him." An eager spark lit up Kristen's face with hope.

"Exactly. Now, if we can figure out a rough approximation of the route he took, maybe we can find a witness who spotted him that day." Luke emitted a curt laugh. "I imagine the sight of Derek Vincent hotfooting it past your house is something that would stick in most people's minds, even after a year."

Kristen jumped up. "I'll get a pencil and paper, so we can draw a map."

Heads bent together, they went to work sketching one. Though with the smell of Kristen's hair teasing his nostrils, it was hard for Luke to keep his mind on the task at hand. She tucked a silky ribbon of it behind her ear to keep it from dangling in the way, revealing a dainty earlobe that stirred a number of intriguing scenarios in his imagination.

She was awful cute when she concentrated, her pert nose all scrunched up, that adorable pleat between her eyebrows, the tip of her tongue peeking out from between lush, ripe lips. Luke shifted discreetly in his chair. A growing pressure in his loins was starting to make him uncomfortable.

Well, what else could he expect? It had been ages since he'd been in such close contact with a woman, let alone one with enchanting eyes and a gleaming sweep of coppery hair. His libido had gotten quite a workout these past few days, being near Kristen. But his body's reaction was simple biology, that was all. A fact of nature. The birds and the bees, et cetera.

Luke refused to consider the possibility it might be something more.

"Okay," Kristen said, indicating with her pencil. "It looks like these are the houses you should check, along this street, down this block, then along here."

Luke steered his concentration back to their plan of action. "Yeah, that makes sense to me. I'll start going door to door tomorrow, looking for anyone who might have seen Derek pass by on foot that day."

Kristen tapped the pencil eraser on the map and gave him a worried frown. "This is really a long shot."

Luke grimaced in acknowledgment. "That's the only kind we've got, unfortunately. The odds have been against us from the beginning."

"You...don't want to give up yet, do you?"

"You mean let Derek get away with murder? With beating up a poor, defenseless kid? Hell, no." Anger propelled Luke from his chair.

Kristen rose slowly. "You believe me now, don't you?" She folded her arms and peered at him closely. "That Derek killed Sheri?"

Her question stopped Luke in his tracks. In the beginning he'd mainly meant to humor Kristen for a while, to keep her from absconding with Cody before he could sort out what was really going on. As developments had unfolded, however, he'd had to admit there could be substance to her suspicions. And now…

"Yes," he answered slowly, aware of the big commitment he was making. "I do believe you."

He rasped a hand across his face. "I didn't *want* to believe you," he admitted. "You were right about that." His fingers curled into fists. "In spite of what Sheri did to me, I never wanted her to get hurt, to suffer." A harsh laugh erupted from his throat. "I won't pretend I was noble enough to wish her all the happiness in the world, but I certainly didn't wish her harm. So I didn't want what you told me to be true. I couldn't stand the idea that the guy she'd dumped me for had beaten her."

The senseless cruelty of it swept over Luke. He slammed his fist to the table, nearly knocking over his half-full cup of cold coffee. "Why did she have to go and marry that son of a bitch, anyway?" He wheeled toward Kristen, grasping her shoulders as if he could shake the answer out of her. She didn't flinch, although her eyes opened very wide and her cheeks turned pale.

"Why?" Luke demanded. "I've never understood all these years, and now I have to know. *Why,* Kristen? Tell me why Sheri married him."

Chapter 10

Kristen had asked herself the same question countless times over the years. How could her sister have picked Derek over a wonderful guy like Luke? Luke, who'd been crazy about Sheri since high school. Luke, who'd wanted to marry Sheri after he got his construction business established so he could support a wife and family.

Luke, who still hadn't gotten Sheri out of his system, judging by the haunted shadow in his eyes, the lines of pain that chiseled his handsome features with turmoil.

Kristen brought her hand to his face in a gesture meant to comfort. The faint stubble of his whiskers created a delicious friction beneath her fingertips. No matter how innocent her motives started out, it seemed every time she touched him set off an undercurrent of hopeless yearning inside her.

Hopeless because guilt would always stand in the way of her happiness. Hopeless because she could never compete with her sister's ghost.

"Sheri never truly explained to me why she married Derek,'' Kristen said quietly. ''I think...in the beginning...she was simply flattered by his attention.''

Luke's grip locked on Kristen's shoulders. ''When did she first start seeing him behind my back?''

Oh, Luke, I don't want to hurt you.... ''He came into the diner during Sheri's shift one day. Yes, I know, it wasn't his usual hangout,'' she agreed in response to the skeptical slant of Luke's dark brows. ''His car got a flat tire while he was on an errand for his father down the street. This was when his father was still alive and running the company, of course.''

''Yeah.''

''Derek came into the diner to kill time while he waited for the automobile club to come fix his flat.''

Luke's expression registered disbelief. ''What, he couldn't change a tire by himself?''

''Well...maybe he didn't want to get his suit dirty.''

Luke snorted. ''Probably didn't know where to find the tire jack.''

''Whatever the reason, he came into the diner and ordered coffee. Sheri waited on him.''

Beneath Kristen's palm, a muscle quivered along Luke's jaw. ''And it was love at first sight.'' Sarcasm roughened his voice.

''No.'' Kristen framed his face with her other hand. ''Sheri never loved Derek. That much I *do* know for sure.''

His eyes were hard and cold as chips of blue ice. ''Then why the hell did she marry him?''

''That's what I'm trying to explain.'' Kristen sighed. She wasn't sure she would ever understand the workings of her sister's mind. As far as she was concerned, what Sheri had done was incomprehensible.

''The reason Derek was attracted to *her* is obvious,'' Kristen continued. ''Sheri was beautiful. Vivacious. She bubbled over with personality. She just...sparkled.''

Luke didn't deny it. No surprise there. Clearly he was still under her sister's spell.

Kristen dropped her hands from his face. It was too tempting, knowing she had only to exert the slightest pressure to tilt his head down to hers, to bring their mouths together. It was insane, this consuming desire for a man who would never be free of another woman's memory.

Yet Kristen couldn't bring herself to tarnish her sister's image. Even though there was no excuse for Sheri's behavior, at least she could paint her actions in the most favorable light possible. "Derek started dropping by the diner on a regular basis," she told Luke. "Flirting with Sheri, leaving huge tips to impress her. Later on, he gave her expensive gifts."

"This all went on while I was out of town working?" Luke put a gap between them. "Back when I was taking any job I could get, no matter how far away, just to gain experience?"

Kristen nodded unhappily. "You were only coming home to visit on weekends. Sheri...well, Sheri liked lots of attention."

Luke hissed through his teeth. "Tell me about it. We used to spend the whole weekend arguing about how I was neglecting her. She never understood that I was doing it for *us,* to give us a solid financial future." His lip curled. "I guess Sheri figured out a way to ensure her *own* financial future, huh?"

"You make her sound so calculating," Kristen protested. "Sheri wasn't like that."

"No?" Luke walked over to the picture window and studied the darkness outside. "She forced you to lie about her whereabouts whenever I called the apartment you shared, right?"

"Well, not exactly *forced*—"

"She deliberately hid any sign our relationship was in trouble, so that I couldn't go and wreck things between her and Derek, didn't she?"

Kristen hesitated. "I suppose."

"And for her grand finale, didn't she sneak off and elope without a word of warning, so that I had no chance to stop her?" Luke raised his shoulders. "What would you call her, then, besides calculating?"

Kristen wedged her nails into her palms. "Luke, she was scared!"

He frowned. "Scared? Of what?"

"Scared of living the same kind of life our mother did! Struggling to make ends meet. Working herself to the bone and still coming up short when the bills were due every month. Agonizing constantly that she wouldn't have enough money to feed her children!"

Luke glowered at her. "*I* would have provided for us," he said indignantly. "My wife wouldn't have had to work like a slave. My children would never have gone hungry."

"Of course not." Kristen spread her hands in a pleading gesture. "But look what happened to our mother. Our father was a good provider, too, until he died in that accident. Deep down inside, I think Sheri was terrified something like that might happen to *you.*"

Luke jammed his fingers through his hair. "Let me get this straight. You're telling me she married Derek because she was afraid I might die and leave her penniless?"

"I'm saying Sheri was afraid of being poor. Even though our mother tried to shield us from her financial troubles, we still grew up with a vague threat of disaster always hanging over our heads."

"So do lots of kids in this town." Luke jabbed his thumb toward his chest. "Including me."

"I know." The Vincent Lumber Company had historically held down wages so that it was difficult for employees, like Luke's father, to get ahead. "But Sheri was still convinced that people looked down on us because we never had nice new clothes or the latest hit record album. She *hated* being poor, and she—she was impatient, too."

Luke made a disdainful noise. "Too impatient to wait for *me* to become a success, obviously, once a better prospect came along to offer her instant wealth."

Kristen leveled her gaze at him. "You were always a success, Luke," she said softly. "Success isn't about money."

Surprise briefly rearranged his features. ''Yeah, well, you should have told that to your sister,'' he mumbled.

''I did.''

Now he looked even more taken aback. ''What do you mean?''

''I told Sheri she was making a huge mistake, marrying Derek. That she ought to wait and marry you, that she would never be happy with him.''

Luke's jaw fell open. ''You did?''

''Of course.'' It had been difficult, urging her sister to marry the man she herself had had such a crush on. But above all else, Kristen had wanted what was best for Sheri. And Luke had been the best. He still was.

She gave a helpless shrug. ''You know what Sheri was like, though. Once she got an idea into her head—''

''You couldn't blast it out with dynamite.'' Luke nodded in rueful understanding. ''But at least you tried.'' He studied Kristen with a kind of dazed wonder, as if he'd never truly seen her before. ''I guess I should thank you. I never knew you'd tried to talk Sheri out of it. In fact, I'd always assumed...aw, never mind.''

''You assumed that I encouraged Sheri to go after Derek?'' Kristen edged closer. ''That the two of us were in it together, conspiring and giggling behind your back so Sheri could snag the richest bachelor in town?''

''Uh...'' Luke ran a finger under his collar. ''Something like that.''

His discomfort was so apparent, Kristen had to smother a smile. ''Well, I guess in all fairness, I can't blame you for thinking the worst of me. I did cover up for Sheri, after all.''

Luke shook his head. ''Only because you were trying to be loyal to your sister.''

''True, but I still shouldn't have done it.'' Kristen laughed in bewilderment. ''We seem to have switched sides on this issue.''

A grin played across his mouth. ''Maybe we're just bothering to see each other's viewpoint for the first time.''

"Maybe."

Luke kept contemplating her as if seeing her in a new light. His look held a mysterious intensity, a penetrating gleam of speculation that made Kristen shiver.

"Cold?" he asked.

Cold? With Luke standing so close, looking as if he wanted to kiss her, making her blood simmer and her heart beat faster? If they stood here like this much longer…

"A little," she said.

"I'll build us a fire."

There were a few logs left in a brass holder beside the huge stone fireplace, but most of the wood was stacked under a shelter behind the cabin. Luke immediately set to work ferrying logs in from outside. Kristen stood by the door so she could open it each time he came back with his arms full.

This was another one of the qualities she lov—er, admired about Luke, the way he plunged right into the task at hand, with his no-nonsense, get-the-job-done attitude. His every move was efficient, purposeful, economical. No wasted effort. He moved with the smooth, muscular grace of a tiger, sinews flexing as he hunkered down to add each load of wood to the growing pile on the slate hearth. He barely broke a sweat.

There was something so essentially physical about Luke's basic nature. He had an ease with his own body, a bold self-confidence that had attracted Kristen from the first moment her sister had brought him home. He'd been a few years ahead of Kristen in school, enough older so that she'd barely noticed his existence before. But the minute he'd stepped across the threshold of the small rented Monroe house, he'd dazzled Kristen like a dashing storybook hero—Rhett Butler and Lancelot and Indiana Jones, all rolled into one.

He'd utterly charmed Mama with his polite conversation, while Sheri rolled her eyes at Kristen behind their mother's back. He'd brought Mama a present, a bouquet of tulips and daffodils he'd probably swiped from a neighbor's garden on his way over.

When Luke had been formally introduced to his new girlfriend's kid sister, he'd actually spoken to Kristen like a human being, instead of barely glancing at her and then ignoring her, the way the other boys Sheri had brought home usually did.

His hair had been cut short for the track team, but one rakish lock had straggled across his forehead, above those dreamy blue eyes that had focused straight on Kristen as he'd said those first magic words to her: "Hey, you hang out with Tricia Hansen, don't you? Her brother's a pal of mine."

Kristen's heart had thumped wildly. He'd noticed her! Palms sweaty, cheeks hot, brain in a fog, she hadn't been able to find her voice to reply until Sheri had elbowed her in the ribs, dislodging a totally feeble "Yuh."

Luke had nodded knowingly. "I thought you looked familiar." Then he'd smiled at her, a quick flash of white teeth that had melted the few scattered remnants of Kristen's swooning senses. And from that moment on, she'd been lost.

Not that she hadn't dated other boys, and later, other men. Earlier this evening, Luke had asked why she'd never gotten married. The truth was, Kristen had received several proposals over the years. But somehow she could never picture spending the rest of her life with the guy who'd proposed. Sitting across the dinner table from him every night, waking up next to him every morning...the idea always made her shudder.

Kristen's relationships had all run pretty much the same course, with or without a proposal. In the end, she'd always discovered some lack, some fault, some fatal flaw in her current beau that made her realize this wasn't the man for her. Mr. Right still hadn't appeared.

Kristen had assured herself that she was just being selective, that it was good to have high standards when it came to choosing your life's partner. But now, analyzing her unimpressive romantic track record, she began to suspect that all along she'd been subconsciously comparing every man in her life to Luke.

She'd tried to fall in love, she really had! But not one of her suitors had ever measured up to Luke. She'd never found anyone else who made her palms sweaty and set her heart fluttering like a lovesick butterfly, who sent a thrill racing through her just by entering the same room, who turned her tongue so thick with desire that she stammered whenever he was near.

Kristen had never found love. And years ago she'd vowed never to marry for any other reason. Her sister had made that disastrous mistake, and paid for it with her life.

After Sheri's death, Kristen had given up looking for love forever. Her conscience demanded it. *She* was the one who'd pushed Sheri into making her fatal decision to leave Derek. How could she keep seeking the happiness her poor sister had never found?

Especially when the only man who could make her happy was the same man Sheri should have married.

Standing by the fireplace, Luke located some matches in a decorative canister on the mantel. He knelt to ignite the pile of kindling and crumpled paper he'd assembled. In seconds the fire blazed into life.

"Mission accomplished," he announced, dusting off his hands as he pushed himself to his feet. "I'll have you warmed up in no time."

That's what Kristen was afraid of. Luke had the ability to send instant heat rushing to every cell in her body. And it didn't have anything to do with the fire.

She had to douse her feelings for him, quick. Before they grew any stronger.

Security at Vincent Lumber was a lot tighter than it had been in the old days. As far as Luke knew, nary one antilogging protester had ever set foot in Whisper Ridge, but Derek apparently wasn't taking any chances.

The entire complex of buildings had been surrounded by chain-link fence, topped by an eyesore of barbed wire. A guard was stationed at the front gate twenty-four hours a day. Employees had to flash their official, high-tech company ID cards to get through. Everyone else had to wait while the guard checked the list of approved visitors on his clipboard. If your name wasn't on it, you didn't get past him.

Unless, of course, you called in a couple of favors and persuaded the cousin of a friend to sneak you through the guard gate hidden in the back of his catering truck. Which was how Luke entered the company premises that night.

He crouched in a small space next to the refrigerator compartment, inhaling the faint whiff of old hamburgers from the nearby griddle. Every night—technically morning, he supposed—at 1:45 a.m., Danny Navarro drove his takeout-stand-on-wheels into the Vincent Lumber compound to sell semihot food to the night-shift workers during their 2:00 a.m. dinner break. That allowed Danny fifteen minutes to warm up the griddle, organize the hamburger patties and microwave burritos, and fold out the metal panels that formed the sides of his truck, turning them into counters.

No worker who wanted to keep his job would dream of leaving his post to slip outside even one minute early, so the parking lot was deserted when Luke hopped out of the back of Danny's truck at 1:48.

''Thanks,'' he whispered.

''Shh!'' Danny whipped his head around to peer over his shoulder, as if he expected a jackbooted security patrol to descend on them any second. ''Just get out of here.'' He waved his hand in a frantic shooing gesture.

''I owe you one,'' Luke promised in a low voice. He ducked his head and scuttled between the rows of parked vehicles, keeping a low profile as he headed for the concealing shadow of the nearest building.

Behind him he could hear the unceasing racket of the mill, the shrieking whine of metal cutting through lumber, the rumble of the big machinery that carried the logs along conveyor belts, through a procession of saw blades and planers and sorting areas until what had once been a majestic tree was transformed into stacks of varying-sized boards.

People were at work in some of the other buildings, too, like the one where trimmed trees were blasted with jets of water to remove their bark, and the kilns where the boards were dried. No one worked night shift in the main office, though. That building was dark inside.

The outside, unfortunately, was lit by a perimeter of bright security lights, which made Luke's job trickier. Luckily, he'd installed a number of alarm systems during his career in construction, so it shouldn't take him long to figure out how to disable this one.

He worked quickly, ears half-cocked for approaching footsteps. Derek's paranoia hadn't yet reached the point of round-the-clock security patrols, but Luke could still be noticed by a loyal employee who would alert the guard that someone was breaking into company headquarters.

Finally! He got the alarm disconnected. At least, he hoped so. He would find out soon enough.

He skirted the building until he found a side door partially concealed in an alcove. At least a casual passerby wouldn't spot him at work there. He'd brought an assortment of tools, figuring if he couldn't manage to pick the lock, he would just remove the blasted thing.

Just for the heck of it, he decided first to give the old credit-card trick a shot. He extracted a slim plastic rectangle from his wallet, slid it between the door and its frame, wiggled it around and…

Presto! The credit card nudged the latch aside so Luke could open the door. Derek needed to hire some new security consultants.

Luke took a step inside the building and tensed, straining his ears for the sound of an alarm. Nothing. He released the air from his lungs in a whoosh and closed the door behind him.

After a couple of wrong turns, a few dead-end corridors, he finally located Derek's office. Geez, there was enough mahogany paneling in here to restock an entire rain forest! Apparently the local Douglas fir wasn't fancy enough for the presidential suite.

Now, would Derek's appointment book be out here in his

secretary's desk? Probably. If not, Luke could check Derek's, though somehow he couldn't imagine the great man himself deigning to write down his own daily schedule.

He rounded Vanessa Taylor's desk. All at once the significance of what sat on top of it sank in.

A computer. Luke froze in the act of yanking a drawer open. A horrifying possibility had hit him. What if Derek's appointments weren't recorded in a nice old-fashioned book? What if Vanessa kept them stored on that scary-looking computer?

Luke gulped. He didn't know the first thing about computers and had made it a stubborn point not to learn. He hated the foul contraptions! All those electronic blips and bytes—give him a good solid pencil and a real piece of paper he could hold in his hand any day.

Now, maybe, his blissful ignorance was going to cost him.

"Rats," he muttered under his breath. "I should have brought a twelve-year-old kid with me."

Kristen's eyes were as wide and green as the pine-covered slopes outside the cabin. "But how did you get out the gate afterward?"

Luke had to admit, he rather enjoyed having her gape at him as if he were James Bond or something. "I just strolled right past the guard and waved. He could hardly stop me from *leaving* the premises."

"But he must have reported you to Derek! Now he'll know you sneaked into Vincent Lumber last night."

"Who cares?" Luke flipped his hand in dismissal. "Derek's hardly going to report me to the police, is he? I mean, the guy may be a vicious slimeball, but he's not stupid. He must have figured out right away that I was there to dig up some dirt on him. The last thing he wants is for the cops to question me about what I was looking for."

"I guess you're right." Kristen perched at the opposite end of the couch, one knee drawn up on the cushions so she was half facing Luke.

He'd returned to the cabin at the crack of dawn to report

the results of his nighttime foray. Kristen had met him at the door in her nightgown. Obviously she'd been asleep, but so lightly that the sound of his truck had awakened her. Luke had no doubt that if it had been someone besides him coming up the driveway, Kristen would have grabbed Cody out of bed, fled through a back window, and been racing away through the woods before the driver even turned off the engine.

She was still wearing her nightgown now, although with a sweater over it to ward off the morning chill. Her long, luxurious hair was strewn across her shoulders in attractive disarray. Whenever she moved her head, coppery shimmers reflected the morning sun streaming through the window.

Luke was trying not to ogle her bare legs. But he couldn't help imagining how exciting it would be to skim his hand along the sleek curve of her calf, to slip beneath the hem of her nightgown, to stroke his fingers along her slender thigh....

Whoa, boy. Turned out he didn't actually have to carry out his fantasy to become excited.

He shifted position, discreetly edging a throw pillow over his lap. What he really wanted was to slide over there and nuzzle Kristen's neck, gradually ease her beneath him, and then make love to her until the couch springs broke.

Aside from the fact Kristen would probably slap his face, however, there was also the practical matter of Cody wandering into the living room, rubbing sleep from his eyes.

Man, but he needed a cold shower, and fast! Luke couldn't remember the last time he'd been this turned on by a woman. He felt the way he had as a teenager, except back then he'd had the excuse of rampant hormones to justify his single-minded lust.

It was that darn nightgown Kristen was wearing. He should have bought her a nice, floor-length flannel one with long sleeves and a high neck. Actually, this nightgown was fairly demure. The problem was, Kristen could make a flour sack look sexy. No wonder he had to keep fighting the urge to take her in his arms and ravish her.

She was a beautiful, vibrant woman and he was a red-blooded adult male. It was only natural for him to feel powerfully attracted to her. Simple biology, that's all it was. Chemistry. One of those physical sciences. Nothing at all to do with emotional involvement.

That's what Luke told himself, anyway. Because any other explanation was too disturbing to contemplate.

"I may have found what we were looking for," he told Kristen, corralling his thoughts back to a safer topic. "The computer had me worried for a minute, but it turned out Derek's secretary keeps his appointment book right there in her desk."

Luke felt a little guilty, the way he'd played up last night's suspense solely for Kristen's benefit. The awestruck admiration in her eyes had tempted him to spice up the details a bit, to make his performance sound like an amazing feat of derring-do. In fact, the whole adventure had gone ridiculously smoothly.

He drew a scrap of paper from his jeans pocket. "Derek only had one appointment the morning Sheri was killed. Here's the guy's name."

Kristen took the paper, examined it, crinkled her nose. "Ed Rayford." She handed the paper back to Luke. "I don't recognize the name."

"I did a little more snooping through Vanessa's files while I was there last night," Luke admitted modestly. "Rayford represents a company in Sacramento that sells do-it-yourself redwood deck kits."

"I noticed there was a phone number written below his name."

"Found it in the files." Luke glanced at the paper again before stuffing it back into his pocket. "I'm going to call the guy this morning, see if he can tell us anything about Derek's actions the morning Sheri died."

Kristen twirled a coil of hair around her finger and nibbled on an anxious frown. "What if he backs up Derek's alibi? What if he says, 'Yeah, I was in a meeting with Mr. Vincent all morning and he never left'?"

Then our chances of proving anything against Derek are that much slimmer, Luke thought. But he didn't want to add to Kristen's worries. "Then we'll find some other way to nail the bastard," he said cheerfully. "Don't forget, we still might find someone who saw him on foot near the accident that day."

Kristen tugged her hair. "That's still not enough evidence to make the police arrest him."

"No, we've got a ways to go. But it's a start."

"I just wonder..." She sighed, peering at the lock of hair as if checking for split ends. "Never mind."

Uneasy concern nudged Luke between the shoulder blades. "You're not getting discouraged, are you? After all, this whole plan was your idea."

"I know." All at once her brow cleared as if her troublesome thoughts had fled.

Which only made Luke *more* uneasy.

She closed her sweater over the front of her nightgown as she stood. "How about some breakfast?" she offered with a smile that struck him as just a shade too bright. "Cody will be up soon. I promised him pancakes this morning."

"Sounds good." Luke watched her pad barefoot across the rug. Breakfast was the last subject on his mind at the moment. Kristen's abrupt change of demeanor had stirred a disturbing suspicion.

What if she was having second thoughts about trying to prove Derek had killed Sheri? So far they hadn't uncovered one solid piece of evidence to take to the cops. The search for Cody was expanding. He and Kristen couldn't hide here in the cabin forever. Each passing day increased the odds of discovery.

What if Kristen had decided it was too risky to stay here any longer? Luke was well aware her highest priority was protecting her nephew, even if it meant giving up her quest to win legal custody by proving Derek a killer.

Legal or illegal custody—all that mattered to Kristen was

that Cody was safe. Which meant she wouldn't hesitate to flee with him if she sensed danger closing in.

Luke wanted Cody safe, too. But the alarm he felt right now forced him to admit that was no longer enough.

For the first time, he realized he didn't want to lose either one of them. And that deep personal insight scared Luke half to death.

Chapter 11

Cody stood by the window, watching Luke drive away after breakfast. He'd been so excited to see Luke when he woke up this morning. His reaction had torn Kristen up inside.

On one hand, she was overjoyed to see the warm bond of affection growing between father and son. On the other hand, it killed her to think that soon she might have to rip that precious relationship up by its roots.

She didn't know how much time they had left, but she knew it was running out. Sooner or later, searchers would get around to checking this cabin. And by the time that happened, Kristen planned to be someplace safe. Someplace far, far away.

Even if it meant separating father and son forever. Even if it meant never seeing Luke again.

"Cody?" Kristen sat on the couch and patted the cushion beside her. "Come sit with me for a little while." She'd cleaned up the breakfast dishes, got Cody dressed, changed out of her nightgown. She could no longer delay the unpleasant conversation that lay ahead.

Cody came over from the window. "Luke said he's gonna

bring a baseball and a mitt for me next time he comes, so we can play catch."

"Did he?" Cody's eager announcement surprised her. Making promises about the future wasn't exactly Luke's style. And how long did he think they were going to stay here, anyway? This wasn't a summer vacation.

Once again, the growing closeness between Luke and Cody caused her mixed feelings.

Cody bounced down beside her. "How long till Luke comes back, Aunt Kristen?"

"I don't know, sweetie." She took his hand in hers and surreptitiously scanned his arms for bruises. Most of them had faded. A playful tousle of his blond hair allowed her to check his forehead. That abrasion appeared to be healing nicely. But Kristen knew that her nephew's most serious, lasting injuries were ones she couldn't see.

"There are some things you and I need to talk about, Cody." She tried to reassure him with a smile, but dread immediately clouded his sunny expression, as if he'd just been sent to the principal's office. Though she hated what she had to do, the questions needed to be asked. "Can you tell me how you got hurt the other day? When you had to go to the hospital?"

His hand jerked as if she'd scalded him. Kristen tightened her grasp. "It's okay to tell me the truth, Cody. To tell me what really happened."

Apprehension gave his features a pinched, haunted look. "I fell out of a tree," he said in a voice so soft she had to strain to hear.

"I know that's what you're *supposed* to say." Leading the witness, Counselor. "But I need to know how you *really* got hurt."

His eyes darted rapidly back and forth. "I fell out of a tree. That's really what happened." His claim was so insistent, Kristen might have been tempted to believe him, if it weren't for his obvious distress.

She could have grilled him for more specific details, tried

to tear holes in his story, but she just didn't have the heart for it. Besides, Cody's reaction confirmed what she'd already known.

"Okay. Let's talk about something else, shall we?"

Relief made his shoulders sag, but it was short-lived.

"On the day your mommy died," Kristen asked gently, "were you and she going to go someplace in the car?"

Cody stiffened. "I...don't remember." He started drumming his heels against the sofa.

"Are you sure? Try to remember, sweetie. It's important. Did Mommy tell you that you and she were going to drive someplace together?"

"I—" Cody was breathing rapidly now, big gulps of air "—I can't remember. I don't know."

He might be telling the truth. The trauma of his mother's death could easily have wiped out the memory of the events preceding it.

Kristen hated to push him, but so much was at stake. "Your mommy didn't pack any clothes for you?"

"No."

"Maybe tell you to bring your favorite teddy bear?"

"No."

Kristen shifted gears. "Did your daddy come home from work that morning?"

"No, no!" Cody whipped his head from side to side.

"You didn't see him at your house, before your mommy died?"

"No!" Cody wailed. His eyes were wild with fear, his feet kicking a drumroll of agitation. "I didn't see anything! Honest! I didn't see anything!" He struggled free of Kristen's grasp.

"Cody, honey, come back!"

Panic put wings on his feet. He sped across the living room before Kristen could catch him, flew into his bedroom and slammed the door.

She found him huddled on the floor of the closet, sobbing. Guilt weighted her shoulders as she slid down the wall to sit next to him. She felt like a monster. "Cody," she crooned, wrapping her arms around him. "I'm so sorry, baby. I won't ask you any more questions."

His tears soaked the front of her blouse. Kristen hugged him closer, rocking him back and forth. "Shh," she whispered into his hair. "Everything's going to be okay...."

But deep in the pain-filled labyrinth of her aching heart, Kristen knew things were far from okay.

Coming back to the cabin was starting to feel like...coming home. Luke didn't much appreciate that feeling, but he didn't know what to do about it, either. He was in too deep to back out now, even if his uncompromising sense of justice would have allowed him to turn his back on the ugly violence Derek had gotten away with so far.

Committed. There was that bear trap of a word that never failed to set Luke quaking in his boots. Yet somewhere along the way, without deliberately intending to, he'd committed himself to seeing this mess through, to doing his best to ensure justice was served.

Besides, Kristen and Cody were counting on him. How could he let them down?

Luke pulled up the driveway and switched off the engine. He couldn't deny a little twinge of disappointment when Cody didn't burst out the front door right away. Luke had dug up a softball and a couple of mitts as promised, and he had to admit, he'd kind of been looking forward to a quick game of catch before supper.

Supper. For Pete's sake, what was he turning into here—Mr. Homebody? Next thing he knew, he'd be signing up for the PTA.

Oddly enough, the idea didn't repel him nearly as much as it would have once.

He found Kristen in the kitchen, assembling a salad. She hadn't run out to greet him, either, even to make sure he wasn't some unwelcome visitor. He guessed by now she must recognize the sound of his truck.

"Something smells good," he said, sniffing the air appreciatively. "Did you by any chance make enough for me?"

"Of course." The smile she gave him was distant, though, as if she had her mind on other things.

Good grief, wasn't anybody around here glad to see him?

Luke had good news he figured would make her smile for real. "I finally tracked down Ed Rayford this afternoon." He set the softball and mitts on the counter dividing kitchen from dining room.

"Who?"

"The guy Derek had a meeting with the morning Sheri died."

"Oh, right." She tore a lettuce leaf into pieces. "What did he say?" From all the excitement Kristen displayed, they might as well have been discussing the weather.

Well, just wait till she heard. "When Rayford arrived at Vincent Lumber that morning, Derek wasn't in his office," Luke said. "Vanessa, the secretary, told Rayford that Derek had forgotten a file he needed for their meeting." Luke could barely contain the triumph in his voice. "She assured Rayford that Derek would be back soon, that he'd just *run home* to get the file."

"Home?" Kristen perked up a little. Hardly the gleeful victory dance Luke had expected.

"Yep. And get this." He leaned over the counter. "Rayford told me he had to wait nearly an *hour* before Derek finally showed up. He was just about to leave when Derek rushed in, looking 'red-faced and out of breath,' according to Rayford."

Kristen had stopped tearing up lettuce now.

"Not only that, but what really ticked off Rayford was that Derek hadn't even brought the file back with him. He just looked blank when Rayford mentioned it, then got hold of himself and mumbled something about not being able to find it."

Kristen pursed her lips. "So Vanessa did lie. Derek *was* out of his office that morning."

"And the time frame fits," Luke pointed out. "The cops

estimated Sheri's accident occurred between ten and ten-fifteen in the morning, which falls during the period Derek was away from his office. Rayford remembers impatiently checking his watch every minute or two. He's positive it was five minutes to eleven when Derek finally showed up.''

''Which would have given him time to jog back to the house after sending Sheri's car off the road, pick up his own car and drive back to the office just before Rayford was about to give up and leave.'' Kristen nodded thoughtfully. Then she picked up a paring knife.

Luke had figured that right about now he would be whirling her through the air in celebration. Instead, he was watching her slice a cucumber.

''Uh, I don't get it,'' he said. ''This is our first big break. I thought you'd be more excited about it.'' Then a dismaying thought jolted him. What if Kristen didn't care any more about proving Derek guilty of murder, because she'd already decided to take Cody and run?

Luke came around the counter as if to physically restrain her on the spot. ''Look, I know finding this witness doesn't solve all our problems—''

''No, but it's important evidence that the police might actually listen to.'' Kristen set down the knife and turned to him. ''It's very good news. I'm sorry I wasn't more enthusiastic about it. It's just...'' Her glance slipped sideways past Luke, as if she were seeing something far off in the distance.

Alarm ricocheted through him. He had to convince her to stay, to give him more time. He didn't want to lose—

''It's Cody,'' she said.

Luke felt the bottom drop out of his stomach. ''Is he okay? Where is he? What's happened?'' As his arms shot out to grab Kristen, he knocked the softball off the counter. It bounced a couple of times on the dining room floor and rolled to a stop beneath the table.

''He's fine,'' Kristen said quickly, reaching up to touch Luke's wrist. ''Nothing's happened. I mean, something did happen to upset him, but it was my fault.''

"I'm sure you didn't mean to." Luke squeezed her shoulders. She looked so forlorn he wanted to go ahead and take her in his arms. But he knew where that might lead, and it was a route neither of them wanted to follow. "Tell me what happened."

Her fingers clamped around his wrist. "I confronted Cody and asked him to tell me the real reason he ended up in the hospital."

"Oh, boy." Luke sighed. "What did he say?"

"The same thing he's said from the beginning. That he fell out of a tree."

"But you still don't believe him."

"Luke, you should have seen his face." Kristen broke away and scooped up the salad bowl as if carrying it to the table had suddenly become her greatest priority. "He was scared to death. Now, why would he have been so terrified if he really *did* fall out of a tree?"

"You're right, of course." Luke followed her into the dining room.

"Derek must have threatened him, and threatened him good, to make him stick to that story." Her features hardened with anger. "I was hoping that after Cody had been safe from Derek for a few days, he would feel secure enough to tell me the truth." Her eyes flashed emerald sparks. "Obviously, he's learned from past experience that Derek carries out his threats."

Something hot and dangerous stirred in Luke's belly. Like a hibernating grizzly starting to wake up.

Kristen stalked back to the kitchen, the flat heels of her loafers pounding out a furious tattoo. "I also asked Cody what he remembered about the day his mother died. I originally tried to talk to him about it right after the accident, but he got nearly hysterical, so I dropped it."

She yanked open the oven door. "Then, of course, Derek stopped me from seeing Cody, so that I never got a chance to bring the subject up again." She removed a covered casserole dish and dropped it with a bang on top of the stove. "Cody could know something important about that day. He might have seen Derek come home, or overheard their final...argument.'' Kristen slammed the oven door shut. ''At the very least, he could have confirmed that Sheri was planning to take him somewhere in the car that day.''

Luke edged back into the kitchen. ''What did Cody say today, when you asked him?''

''He claims he can't remember anything.'' Kristen flung down the pair of potholders with disgust.

''Maybe he can't.'' Luke knew it wasn't Cody she was frustrated with.

''Maybe.'' Kristen shook her head. ''But something about that day throws him into an absolute panic.''

''Kristen, his mother died. Is it any wonder he gets worked up, thinking about it?''

''No.'' She pressed quivering fingertips to her temples. ''But his reaction...it was exactly the same as when I asked how he got hurt the other day. As if what actually terrified him wasn't the memory, but fear that he might somehow let the truth slip out.''

Kristen's shoulders slumped as if all the anger had drained out of her at once. ''I was so hoping I'd be able to coax some meaningful information out of Cody, something that would help us put that bastard behind bars.'' She covered her face with her hands. ''But I just can't bear to put him through the third degree again.''

This time Luke didn't hesitate to put his arms around her. ''We'll find some other way,'' he promised. He tipped up her chin. ''Hey, we're starting to make progress, aren't we?''

Her eyes glittered with uncertainty, with tired hope. ''But not enough.'' She slipped her arms around his waist.

''Look, tomorrow I'm going to find a witness who saw Derek running home from the scene of the accident.'' Luke settled her more snugly against him.

A reluctant smile plucked at her mouth. ''You sound pretty sure of yourself.''

''Actually, I'm considering giving up the construction business to become a private eye." He tilted his head so their foreheads bumped gently together. "Wanna be my assistant?"

"Thanks, but I couldn't settle for less than a full partnership." Her lips twitched mischievously.

Luke grinned. "That's what I was afraid of." He kissed the tip of her nose, just to tease her. Then, when he saw her eyes light up, he kissed her cheek for good measure. And from her cheek, it was such a short distance to her lips, how could he pass it up?

He couldn't.

Kristen tensed briefly, as if in surprise, even as she parted her lips to welcome him. Luke adjusted the angle of his head to kiss her more thoroughly. Somewhere in the back of his mind he knew this was a bad idea, but it was easy to ignore that warning voice when Kristen's soft breasts nestled against his ribs, when her tongue twined around his with velvet sweetness, when the eager hunger in his loins urged him to give his hands free rein.

Heat poured through him. She tasted like honey and smelled like wildflowers. Desire buzzed in his ears like a swarm of bees irresistibly drawn to her delicious nectar. He felt dizzy, reckless, drunk with the intoxicating feel of her body beneath his hands. No matter how long he kissed her, Luke suspected it would never be long enough to satisfy the soul-deep craving she aroused inside him.

"You feel so good," he breathed into the delicate hollow below her ear. Kristen shivered, arching her back with pleasure. She teetered slightly, and Luke realized she was standing on tiptoe to kiss him.

So tiny, so beautiful, so filled with passion. He circled her waist and lifted her onto the counter in one smooth motion. She gasped softly, eyes flaring wide at her abrupt change in position.

Now they were almost eye to eye. Luke wedged himself between her thighs, cupping his hands around her bottom to mold her closely against him. He brought his lips lightly to hers once...twice...three times, boldly rubbing his abdomen against her so she could feel how much he wanted her.

She let out a faint moan. Her eyes were half-closed, heavy-lidded and sultry as if she were drugged with the same erotic potion that held Luke in its spell. He wove his hands through her hair, the silken strands rippling over his fingers like water.

Man, but he wanted to take her! Right here on the kitchen counter, or on top of the dishwasher, or on the floor in front of the sink—Luke didn't care. His desire for her was blazing out of control, setting him on fire, burning away the boundaries of his self-restraint.

Crazy? Potential disaster? He didn't care. Something this big, this powerful had a will of its own, and Luke was tired of fighting it. He wanted Kristen and—make no mistake about it—she wanted him. The way she was kissing and caressing him back proved it. Why shouldn't they find pleasure with each other?

Luke combed forward wavy streamers of her long auburn hair, luxuriating in its thick texture while he let it sift over her shoulders. Kristen nuzzled her nose against his and purred. He licked his tongue lightly, seductively over her kiss-swollen lips, savoring their exquisite flavor. He brought his hand to her breast.

A fresh surge of desire rocketed through him as he began to knead her pliant flesh. The nipple was pebble-hard already. Even through two layers of blouse and brassiere, he had no trouble locating it with his thumb. Gently he stroked the hardened tip.

Kristen drew in a harsh, jittery breath. Luke peered steadily into her eyes, alert for the slightest flicker of resistance. All he saw was a mirror image of his own turbulent need.

The image blurred and filled his vision as he brought his mouth to hers and kissed her again. He felt a new eagerness in her response, almost an impatience. He lifted his other hand so both breasts nestled in his palms like warm, ripe peaches. Luke's mouth watered when he thought of tasting them.

Once that delightful possibility occurred to him, he wasted

no time turning temptation into action. He located her nearest blouse button immediately, then ran into problems. His uncooperative fingers were shaking so much he had trouble unbuttoning it. Old Cool Hand Luke was definitely out of practice.

Dimly his ears registered a distraction somewhere, but the pressure straining his jeans spoke louder. Then out of the blue someone shoved him hard in the chest so that all at once he wasn't kissing Kristen anymore.

It was Kristen, of course, who'd shoved him. She was staring at Luke with a kind of dazed, horrified embarrassment, cheeks stained crimson, breasts heaving with each ragged breath. Instinctively he angled his sights downward. He'd managed to get one button halfway out of its hole.

Kristen's face turned an even brighter red, if that were possible. She braced her hands on the counter and launched herself to the floor, stumbling so that she crashed into Luke.

"Whoa, easy there." He steadied her elbow.

She wrenched away as if he'd zapped her with several thousand volts. Hastily she started smoothing her blouse, her hair and her dignity back into place.

Then Luke himself heard what had dashed such a sudden, icy bucket of water on their sizzling embrace. A puzzled exclamation drifted from the direction of the dining room. "Hey, a softball! Where'd this come from?"

Kristen's ears must be sharper than Luke's. He hadn't heard Cody's approaching footsteps.

"Aunt Kristen? Is Luke here?"

They had about two seconds to wipe the guilty expressions off their faces before Cody came into the kitchen. "Hi, Luke!" A big smile broke across his face as he held up the softball. "You remembered!"

"Sure did, Slugger. Look, I brought mitts, too."

"Cool! Can we go outside and play ball?"

"Uh..." Luke sidled a glance at Kristen. Her cheeks were still pink, her blouse slightly crooked. Nothing a seven-year-old would notice. "I think dinner's about ready, isn't it?"

Kristen turned to fuss over the casserole dish she'd removed from the oven right before things had *really* heated up. "There's still a little time. Go ahead. I'll call you when it's ready."

Luke suspected it was *Kristen* who wasn't ready. Not ready to sit down at the dinner table next to a man she'd been locked in a hotblooded embrace with only moments ago. He didn't blame her. In his current worked-up state, even an innocent request like "please pass the salad dressing" would sound charged with sexual connotation.

"We'll be outside." He touched Kristen's arm, trying to convey all the things he couldn't say in front of Cody.

She didn't turn around. "Have fun," she said over her shoulder.

"Let's go." Luke offered Cody one of the softball gloves. He wasn't too sure he was capable of throwing a ball with much accuracy at the moment. He was still shell-shocked from the stunning force of his desire for Kristen. Why, he'd been ready to make love to her right there on the kitchen counter, never mind the consequences!

It wasn't like him to toss aside his self-control like that, to let passion get the best of him. He'd definitely been without a woman for too long. This past year he'd been so wrapped up in trying to save his business, he hadn't had any time for female companionship.

His long abstinence must be the reason Kristen affected him so powerfully. It must explain how she'd slipped into his blood like an addictive drug Luke couldn't get enough of. How she'd gotten under his skin so that he tossed and turned between the sheets at night, tormented by aching, unsatisfied need, wishing she was there next to him.

No, not need. Luke Hollister didn't *need* anyone. He didn't *want* to need anyone.

Ever.

"Why, yes," the old woman said, shifting her dentures so they clacked softly. "Matter of fact, I did see him come by here once."

Eureka! Luke had just struck paydirt.

Her name was Mildred Peeples, and she was the eighth person Luke had spoken to that morning. Lace doilies covered every square inch of furniture in her small one-bedroom house, which sat in a quiet lane located between the Vincent mansion and the scene of Sheri's accident.

Luke had begun their interview the same way as he had the previous seven. Would she mind thinking back about a year ago? Had she ever seen Derek Vincent passing by her house on foot, maybe even through her backyard?

Before now, all the answers had been the same, and Luke had been getting discouraged. Then he'd noticed the rocking chair drawn up to Mildred Peeples's front window, and spied the pair of binoculars sitting right next to her cup of tea and her crocheting.

They were both seated on her couch now, a faded antique monstrosity whose ancient springs kept jabbing Luke's hindquarters no matter which way he shifted, like the bones of an emaciated horse.

The moment Mildred Peeples recollected that yes, she had seen Derek Vincent, Luke completely forgot his discomfort.

"You're sure it was him? Derek, I mean."

Miz Peeples glared over her spectacles like the stern schoolteacher she'd once been. "Yes, young man, I'm sure. I may be ninety-one years old, but I'm not senile."

"No, ma'am. I just meant—"

"Lived in this town nearly my entire life, haven't I? I've seen four generations of Vincents running that mill, and believe you me, I know one when I see one." She bobbed her gray head with a curt *hmph.* "Besides, he was wearing a business suit. Who else in this town dresses up so fancy?"

"Then you...didn't see his face?" Luke wondered how reliable those ninety-one-year-old eyes were.

"I didn't say that, did I?" She poked one shaky, arthritic finger in the direction of the front window. "I wondered what a man in a suit was doing, scurrying down my street like an escaped criminal, so I picked up my binoculars and took a closer look.'' She cleared her throat delicately. ''I use them for bird-watching.''

More like neighbor-watching, Luke thought. Bless her nosy heart. ''And through the binoculars you recognized Derek Vincent?''

''Well, of course! Isn't he practically as famous around here as the president of the United States? I may not get out much anymore, but I could certainly recognize Mr. Derek Vincent, yes, indeed.''

''You said he seemed to be in a hurry?''

''Like a pack of hounds was chasing him, right along the sidewalk out there. He was walking just as fast as he could, though I could tell he was itching to break into a run. 'Why, whatever's put those ants in his pants?' I wondered.''

Luke bit his lip to keep it from twitching. ''And this was about a year ago when you saw him?''

She made an impatient swipe through the air. ''One year, two years, I can't remember. Might've been just a month ago.'' She jostled her teeth again. ''When you get to be my age, young man, you start to lose track. Why, I read just the other day it's thirty years since man first landed on the moon. Thirty years! Land sakes, you could have knocked me over with a feather. Time goes by so fast. My goodness, it doesn't seem like it could have been more than...''

Luke was only half listening by now. It was a shame she couldn't pinpoint any closer the day she'd seen Derek. She seemed pretty definite it had been him, though. Would she be willing to testify, or at least talk to the police? She probably had dozens of relatives in town who would be vulnerable to Derek's revenge.

On the other hand, she seemed pretty lonely, judging by the eager way she was bending Luke's ear. Could be she didn't have any relatives. But he didn't want to place *her* in danger, either. He wouldn't put it past Derek to arrange an accident to silence her permanently, and who would look too closely into the death of a ninety-one-year-old woman without any relatives?

He heard her say the word *accident,* and the verbal echo of his own thoughts snagged his attention.

"That's how I remember, because afterward I thought, 'that poor man, here I saw him on the very same day his wife was killed,' and I wondered later whether he'd already heard the terrible news by then, but I don't think so, because he didn't seem upset, exactly, just in an awful hurry."

Pins and needles of excitement prickled the back of Luke's neck. "Let me get this straight," he said, forcing a calm he didn't feel into his words. "Are you telling me that the day you saw Derek Vincent walking by your house was the same day his wife died?"

"Isn't that just what I've been saying?" She clicked her tongue in disapproval. "Have you been woolgathering, young man?"

Luke was feeling pretty pleased with himself as he drove back from Pineville that afternoon. Kristen had asked last night if he could do some more shopping, which he took as a hopeful sign she wasn't planning to skip town right away.

As long as he was in Pineville, he'd stopped by the construction site, where Andy Driscoll had assured him things were running smoothly. Maybe Derek was too busy looking for Cody to bedevil Luke's business with any more disasters for a while.

Luke could hardly wait to get back to the cabin. He planned to stop in town and pick up a pizza, then play a quick game of catch with Cody while dinner reheated in the oven. Later, while Cody was washing up, Luke would surprise Kristen with the great news that he'd found a witness who could place Derek on foot near the scene of Sheri's accident.

Luke could hardly wait to see the look on her face.

He could hardly wait to see *her,* period.

"Enough of that," he warned himself. There weren't going to be any more frenzied encounters in the kitchen, or anyplace else for that matter. Pure, straightforward sex was one thing. No promises, no recriminations afterward. No sticky emotional entanglements to snare him like a spider's web.

Unfortunately, what Luke felt for Kristen had gone way beyond that. Which was why he didn't dare make love with her.

He didn't want to get trapped.

"Okay, stop thinking about her. Focus on something else." He reached for the dashboard and cranked up the radio volume. Over the next rise the Whisper Ridge city-limits sign came into view. The local station was playing some corny country-western tune about unrequited love.

Luke switched off the radio. "Any other bright ideas, Hollister?"

Cody. He would think about him for a while. Nice kid. Cute. Smart. And he had a pretty good arm, too. He was about the right age to start Little League, wasn't he? What a kick it would be to sit up in the bleachers with a bunch of other parents, watching Cody come up to bat, hollering insults at the umpire when he called "Strike!" on a pitch that any blind knucklehead could see was low and inside.

Other parents? Whoa! Luke got so rattled he nearly swerved into the ditch. For a second there, he'd veered dangerously close to thinking of Cody as his.

No. He didn't want that to be true. Because that would mean—

All at once a car came out of nowhere, cutting across the truck's path like a deer bolting from the brush alongside the road. Luke slammed on his brakes, slued sideways, and once again nearly wound up in the ditch.

The pickup skidded to a stop on the gravel shoulder. Luke's heart was thudding like a jackhammer. Adrenaline beat out anger, but not by much. Where had that maniac come from, anyway? It was almost as if he'd been lying in wait—

With a harsh screech of rubber, the car angled to a halt in front of Luke's truck, blocking access to the road. His initial glimpse of the vehicle had been blurred by speed and surprise, but now he recognized it immediately.

The hair stood up on the back of his neck. Like an animal spoiling for a fight.

Luke flung off his seat belt, every muscle in his body tensed to leap from his truck. As he grabbed for the door, it flew open.

"Where is he, Hollister?" Derek Vincent snarled in his face. "What the hell have you done with my kid?"

Chapter 12

Derek must really be losing it. Luke couldn't believe the guy would have the audacity to ambush him out in the open like this, on a well-traveled highway just outside town.

But if he wanted a fight, Luke would be more than happy to give him one. "I don't know what you're talking about," he said calmly. Though calm hardly described what he was feeling. Inside he was furious, still shaken up by the near-collision Derek had caused.

"Don't play dumb with me," Derek said, glaring down his aristocratic nose. "Cody. You know where he is, and you're going to tell me, or by God, I'll—"

"You'll what?" Ignoring the fact Derek was blocking his exit, Luke went ahead and climbed out of his truck. Derek backed up, but maintained an aggressively short distance between them. "You'll turn me in to the cops, is that what you were about to say?"

Contempt oozed through Derek's muddy brown eyes. "All I have to do is give the word, and they'll drag you off to jail so fast your heels will be smoking." A whoosh of exhaust from a passing car lifted a few platinum strands of his expensive haircut.

"But you don't dare give the word, do you?" Luke planted his feet at a belligerent stance. "Because then the cops might ask me why someone would take Cody in the first place."

A fleck of spittle appeared at the corner of Derek's mouth. "That bitch took him so she could get her hands on my money."

"That the story you're telling the cops?" Luke wanted to laugh. "Funny, but the news reports haven't mentioned any ransom note, have they?"

A vein throbbed at Derek's temple. "She's trying to frame me, spreading lies about me, hoping I'll be forced to set up a trust fund for the kid that *she* can control."

"Interesting theory." Luke tucked his hands under his armpits and nodded thoughtfully. "Sorry I can't help you, though." He turned to get back in his truck.

"Not so fast." Derek's hand clamped down on his forearm.

Luke gave him a stare that could have melted granite. "Let go of me."

"Tell me where they are."

"I said, let go of me." The cold fury in Luke's tone must have revealed his intentions more vividly than any threat.

Derek released him, puckering his mouth as if he'd just sampled a bad batch of caviar. His tie was askew and his hand-tailored shirt was coming untucked from his trousers. The guy was losing it, all right.

"Then I'll just follow you," he said with the frustrated bravado of the schoolyard bully he'd once been. "Sooner or later you'll lead me right to them."

"It's a free country," Luke said, feigning a so-what shrug. He'd already been extremely careful whenever he drove out to the cabin. Now he would have to double his efforts.

Derek wiped his mouth with the back of one starched white cuff. "You're making a big mistake messing with me, Hollister."

"Yeah? What are you going to do, burn down my *house* this time?"

It was an impulsive shot in the dark, but it found its mark. As soon as Luke saw guilt slither across Derek's face, he knew Kristen's guess had been correct. Derek *had* been pulling the strings behind all of Luke's business problems.

Luke bunched his fists, instinctively gearing up for the thrashing Derek deserved. He was so mad he could hardly see straight. The son of a snake had nearly ruined him! Not to mention what he'd done to Sheri and Cody.

But if Luke meted out punishment right now, he might very well wind up in jail. And if he was stuck in a cell, Kristen and Cody would have to fend for themselves. He couldn't risk it. Derek's eyes ricocheted back and forth like pinballs. Clearly he was preparing either to duck or run. But then he spotted something in the back of Luke's pickup that sidelined his fear.

"What have you got here?" He grabbed one of the sacks Luke had stowed next to his toolbox, a sack bearing the name of a Pineville department store. Before Luke could stop him, he ripped it open and waved a woman's blouse through the air like a matador brandishing his cape in front of a bull. "Well, look at this, huh?"

Luke advanced on him. "Give me that."

"Revamping your wardrobe, Hollister?" Derek flung the blouse at him.

Luke had to dive for it, giving Derek a chance to paw through the sack some more. Price tags fluttered as he yanked out miscellaneous articles of women's and boys' clothing. "Kristen got you buying her clothes now?" He flung the items to the ground, spilling some of them into the roadway.

Luke scrambled to retrieve them.

"Do you just get to pay for them," Derek taunted, "or does she let you take 'em off her, too?"

Luke stuffed the clothes inside his truck.

"Come on, 'fess up, Hollister." Derek tried to dodge him, bobbing and weaving like a drunken boxer. "You screwing Kristen, too, just like you screwed her sister?" His sneering face was purple. "Is she as good in bed as our sweet Sheri was, huh?"

Luke seized the front of Derek's shirt and nearly hoisted the creep off his feet. He'd never wanted to kill a man before, but by God, it would sure feel good right now.

"Shut up," he said softly, feeling like his lungs were about to explode from the rage he was holding inside his chest.

"Get your hands off me, or I'll report you to the cops," Derek ordered in his usual haughty tone. But Luke could see the fear swimming through his eyes.

"Go right ahead," Luke said through his teeth. "I'm sure they'll be fascinated by some of the things I can tell them. Like how Sheri really died. Like the way you've abused Cody." He jerked Derek closer so they were nose-to-nose. "Like whose son he really is."

Derek turned pasty white. He goggled at Luke, his mouth opening and closing soundlessly like a stunned fish's. His knees sagged, so that Luke had to work harder to keep him upright. "You—you—you—"

Luke shoved him backward in disgust. He was pleased to see his dirty handprints on Derek's formerly spotless shirt-front. "You sorry bastard. You don't deserve a great kid like that." He jabbed a warning finger at Derek's car. "That thing's going to need a lot of expensive bodywork if you don't move it out of my way. Fast."

He climbed back into his truck and slammed the door. Derek must have recovered quickly, because by the time Luke keyed on the ignition and shoved the pickup into gear, Derek's car was scuttling backward, making room for Luke to drive over onto the road.

Barely pausing to check for oncoming traffic, Luke peeled out of there in a hurry, tires spitting up gravel behind him. He had to grip the steering wheel in a choke hold to keep his hands from shaking.

It hadn't been Derek's threats or sneering insinuations that had rattled him so badly. Or even the fact that Derek knew for certain now he was hiding Kristen and Cody.

No, what had Luke all shook up was what Derek *hadn't* said.

He hadn't denied that Cody was someone else's son.

"Oh, boy! Pizza!"

Standing on the front porch, Kristen watched Cody jump up and down with excitement as Luke lifted a flat cardboard box out of his truck.

"Hey, Slugger! Want to carry this into the house for me?"

"Yeah!"

"It's sausage and mushroom. You like that kind?"

"Sure." Cody nodded enthusiastically.

Kristen had to giggle. Kids' tastes were fickle as the breeze, of course, and she and Cody had been apart for a year. But as far as she knew, he *hated* mushrooms.

When she passed him on her way to help unload the groceries, her nephew was carefully setting one foot in front of the other, balancing the giant pizza as if it were a tray of dynamite. Kristen smiled at his concentration. Clearly he took very seriously the responsibility Luke had handed him.

Luke was lifting grocery bags out of the back of his truck. Kristen came up behind him, trying to ignore how his muscles flexed beneath his short sleeves, how the light glinted off his black hair like sparks of obsidian. She'd never noticed before how sexy the nape of a man's neck could be, that bare, vulnerable patch of tanned skin just above his collar and below the ends of his hair.

Kristen pulled up short. Good grief, what was wrong with her? She had no business fantasizing about the nape of Luke's neck or any other part of his fabulous anatomy. But ever since last night in the kitchen, when she and Luke had had their hands and mouths all over each other, his body had practically become an obsession.

It was as if that wild, unrestrained encounter had unlocked a wellspring of sensual awareness Kristen hadn't even known existed before. All day long, colors had seemed brighter, sounds clearer, flavors more intense. She noticed the weight and texture of her clothes against her skin, found herself studying the grain in a piece of wood, marveling over nature's workmanship.

And she couldn't stop remembering the heat and feel and scent of him. Or imagining what it would be like to—

"Here, let me carry some of those," she said, abruptly derailing that tantalizing, dangerous train of thought.

When Luke turned around, the expression in his eyes quickly erased any of Kristen's lingering fantasies.

"What's wrong?" she asked.

Luke handed her two sacks of groceries. "Oh, nothing." He peered around her to make sure Cody was out of earshot. "I just had a rather unpleasant run-in with Derek, that's all."

"What?" Kristen nearly dropped the sacks in alarm.

Luke grabbed two more out of the truck. "A little man-to-man talk."

"Luke, what did he do? What did he say? Did he try to hurt you?"

He snorted. "He wasn't fool enough to take a swing at me, if that's what you mean." He gestured into the cab of the truck with his elbow. "Only damage he did was getting some of your new clothes dirty."

Kristen glanced through the window and saw a tangled pile of clothing on the seat. "What? How...?"

"He forced me off the road just outside of town. Accused me of hiding both of you." Luke set off briskly across the driveway. "Then he spotted the department-store sack in the back and ripped it open. So now he knows."

"Oh, my God." Kristen tagged close on his heels. "Luke, this is terrible! We'll have to find another hiding place, think of a new plan—"

"No, we won't." He halted so quickly at the top of the steps that Kristen bumped into him. He lowered his voice, mindful of Cody nearby. "This doesn't change anything. I don't intend to let Derek follow me here, and he's still afraid of turning me in to the cops, for fear of what I might tell them."

A haunted look crossed his face. Not fear, exactly. Kristen couldn't imagine Luke being afraid of anything. But something was definitely preying on his mind.

"Is there more you're not telling me?" she asked.

"No. Of course not." But his slight hesitation and the way his gaze angled away from hers told her he was lying.

The bags were growing heavy in her arms. But they were nothing compared to the weight of knowing that Luke was hiding something from her.

"Tell me," she insisted. "I have a right to know. Cody's life could depend on it."

She should have known it was pointless to press Luke. When he dug in his heels, there was no budging him. "It's got no bearing on Cody's welfare." He clamped his jaw as if to squelch any further discussion.

"What's bothering you, then?"

His dark brows gathered like thunderclouds. He juggled his grocery sacks, shifting from one foot to the other in irritation. Then a calculating gleam settled into his eyes and his stormy expression lifted.

"All right," he said. "I didn't want to worry you. But when I was in town just now, I noticed some new posters the cops have put up."

Really, Luke had to be the world's worst actor. The most gullible soul on earth could see right through him, and Kristen was far from gullible. This poster stuff wasn't what was bothering him at all.

It bothered Kristen plenty, though, when she heard the rest of it.

"It isn't just Cody's picture plastered all over the place anymore," Luke said. "It's yours, too."

"Mine?" she gasped.

His mouth quirked into a grim curve. "According to the posters, the cops now consider you their prime suspect in Cody's kidnapping."

Kristen sagged back against the porch railing. Dismay set her stomach churning. "Oh, no."

"Look, so what?" Luke set his sacks down to take hers before she dropped them. "The cops have suspected you all along. They searched your shop, didn't they? The only difference now is they've gone public about it."

"Then why do I feel like a hunted animal all of a sudden?" Kristen hugged her midsection, but it didn't calm the nausea. "I can't believe my picture is on a Wanted poster, like a common criminal's."

To her surprise, Luke burst out laughing.

"What's so funny?" she demanded, injecting some starch into her tone.

"You *are* a criminal," he pointed out with a grin. "At least according to the letter of the law." He clicked his tongue in admiration, giving her a head-to-toe once-over. "But there's certainly nothing common about you."

Kristen made a sour face. "Gee, thanks."

"I haven't even mentioned the reward Derek's offering for your capture."

"What? A *reward?*" The churning in her stomach returned to full boil.

"Well, not for you, exactly. For 'Information Leading to Cody Vincent's Return.'" Luke winked. "Fifty thousand dollars. Not bad, huh? Of course, that's only pocket change for a guy like Derek, but still..."

"Luke, how can you joke about this? Now everyone in town will be looking for us—"

"They already are." Luke elbowed open the door. "And they haven't found you yet, have they? Come on, let's go eat pizza. I'm starving." He jerked his head toward the cabin's interior and stood there waiting for her. "If you're a good girl and clean your plate, for dessert I'll tell you about the new witness I found today."

"*What* new witness?"

"Huh-uh-uh, pizza first."

"Lu-u-u-ke!" she groaned with exasperation.

It wasn't till later that Kristen remembered she still hadn't found out what was bothering him.

* * *

"Screwdriver." Luke held out his hand. Cody placed the tool into it.

Luke tightened the screws on the lower panel of the dishwasher. Kristen had mentioned the appliance was leaking around the bottom, so after the three of them had eaten their fill of pizza, Luke had asked Cody to help him fix it.

"Me?" Cody had scrunched up his forehead in doubt. "But I don't know how."

"I'll show you. You can be my assistant and hand me the tools."

"Okay."

Now they were about finished. Luckily the problem had turned out to be just a loose connection between the water inlet valve and the incoming water line. Luke had had to point out to Cody which tool was the pliers, but then it had only required a few twists of the wrist to tighten the connection.

Once the lower panel was back on, Luke lay on his back and stuck his head under the sink. "Wrench." He held out his hand.

Efficient as an operating nurse, Cody slapped the tool into his palm. Luke turned the water back on, then crawled out from beneath the sink. "Okay, buddy. Time to test this thing out." He dusted his hands on his jeans. The dishwasher was already loaded. Luke poured in some soap, closed the door and set the dial. "Let 'er rip!" He stood back to let Cody start the machine.

"Um..."

"Just pull out that gizmo."

"Oh." Gingerly, Cody turned on the dishwasher.

It roared into life. "Okay, now you watch and see if any water leaks out the bottom, while I pack up my tools." Luke had to grin at the way Cody stood somberly at attention, eyes riveted on the floor as if he expected a rattlesnake to crawl out from under the dishwasher. He sure was a good kid.

But is he my kid?

That question had hammered in Luke's brain for hours, ever

since his run-in with Derek. Why hadn't he reacted indignantly when Luke had implied Cody didn't have any Vincent blood running through his veins? Wouldn't a real father have hotly denied his kid was someone else's and taken an outraged swing at anyone who hinted otherwise?

Instead, Derek had turned almost gray with shock and fear. Fear that his secret would be revealed? Fear that the whole town would snicker at him when word got out his wife had borne another man's child?

And if Derek wasn't Cody's father...well, there was pretty much only one man who could be. Sheri may have had her faults, but sleeping around hadn't been one of them.

Luke's insides coiled into a knot. Jesus, what if it was true? What if Cody *was* his?

Up till now he'd dealt with the possibility by refusing to think about it. He'd had plenty of other problems to deal with first. Besides, he'd had good reason to believe that either Sheri or Kristen had been lying.

Kristen's accusation echoed through his memory. *You don't want to believe Cody's your son. Because then you'd have to face the fact that your child has been raised by a man you despise. That your old enemy has been abusing your son.*

His son. His own flesh and blood. Trapped all these years under the same roof with a monster who mistreated him. Deprived of a real father's love.

Not to mention everything Luke had missed out on. Childhood years that had slipped away, gone forever. Cody's first tooth. His first step. His first word.

A white-hot rage dug its claws into Luke, making him tremble. Kristen was right. He *didn't* want to believe. Because he was afraid of what he would do with the truth. Afraid of what the truth would do to *him.*

He glanced down and saw he was clutching his wrench as if he meant to destroy something with it. He forced his fingers to uncurl and dropped it back into his toolbox. Thankfully Cody was still fixated on the floor in front of the dishwasher.

Luke quickly rearranged his features so he wouldn't scare the pants off the kid if he suddenly turned around.

"Any sign of water yet?" He clapped a hand on Cody's shoulder, forcing himself to sound cheerful.

"Nope."

"Well, it's made it through the first cycle. I'd say we fixed it."

"We did?" Cody finally looked up, his blue eyes filled with amazement. "I never knew you could fix stuff like this. I thought you hadda call a repairman."

Luke chuckled. "Well, I guess some people do."

Cody rubbed one sneaker against the other. "One time when I was little, *our* dishwasher broke, only my dad, he didn't know how to fix it."

Luke was surprised. Not that Derek couldn't fix the dishwasher—the guy probably didn't know one end of a screwdriver from another. But this was the first time he'd ever heard Cody mention Derek.

Cody's chin started to quiver. "Mommy teased him 'cause he didn't know how to fix it. Then Daddy got real mad." Cody's breathing came in fast gulps. "He—he—he—"

Before Luke even knew what he was doing, he crouched down and put his arms around the boy. Cody trembled against his chest. After a moment, his thin little arms slid hesitantly around Luke as far as they would go.

A strange pressure expanded behind Luke's ribs, making it hard to breathe. He couldn't believe how fragile this small human life felt. How precious.

Helplessly he patted Cody's hair as the boy buried his face in Luke's shirt. "It's gonna be all right," he muttered over and over. "Shh..."

By God, no one was going to hurt this kid again. No one.

After a minute or two, Cody sniffled and drew back to rub his eyes. Luke loosened his hold, but kept him in the circle of his arms. "You okay?" he asked gruffly.

Cody nodded. He sniffed again. "Yeah."

Luke wasn't sure what he should do now. So he let the boy

go and pushed himself to his feet. "Hey, what say we go find your aunt Kristen? Maybe we can rope her into a checkers tournament."

"Luke?" Cody's cheeks were tearstained when he looked up.

"Yep?"

"Know what I wish?"

"What's that, pal?"

Cody glanced down again, nudging his toe against Luke's toolbox. He mumbled shyly into the neck of his shirt, so softly Luke could barely hear him. "I wish *you* were my dad."

Luke didn't know what to say. Not that it mattered. Because right now his throat was closed up so tight, he couldn't have spoken a word if his life depended on it.

Kristen closed Cody's door behind them and smiled at Luke. "You're getting better at those bedtime stories," she whispered. "I could hardly wait to hear how that one ended myself."

His mouth formed the semblance of a smile, but Kristen could tell his heart wasn't in it. All evening long he'd drifted in and out of these preoccupied moods. She wished he would open up and tell her what had happened today that weighed so heavily on his mind.

Might as well wish for the moon. Luke was hardly the opening-up type. He wasn't the kind of man to bare his soul, to unburden himself by sharing his troubles. No, he preferred to handle them all by himself.

It was one more way he asserted his solitary self-reliance, made sure he was dependent on no one. Another way he kept his freedom.

Obviously, after what Sheri had done to him, it was also Luke's way to avoid getting hurt again. That was one of many things Kristen had learned about him during the last week.

Maybe *that's* what was bothering him. Concern about putting his heart at risk again. Because Kristen could see that, much as he might resist it, Luke was getting awfully attached to Cody.

"How about a beer?" he asked, crossing the dining room. He'd brought some to go along with their pizza.

"No, thanks." She walked over to the picture window in the living room, even though it was too dark to see anything outside. How many more nights would they spend here?

How much longer before they found proof that would put Derek in jail? Or before someone discovered them? Or before Kristen had no choice but to take Cody and run? The more time passed, the more likely one of the last two outcomes seemed.

Kristen knotted her fists and pressed them into her thighs. She would never, ever let Derek have Cody back. She would *not* let anyone find them.

Which made fleeing from Whisper Ridge seem more and more like her only option. Every day the noose was tightening. Derek's reward, the posters with her picture on them—what next? The FBI's Most Wanted list?

She and Cody would have to escape soon, before it was too late. And she would have to hide her intentions from Luke, so he couldn't try to stop her.

He would never let Cody go now. Whether he'd admitted that to himself or not.

"Think I'll build a fire," Luke said from across the room. "It's getting kind of chilly in here."

Kristen drifted over to watch him. "You're a regular Boy Scout," she said after a minute, when the flames leaped into life.

"Ha! Not me." Luke stood up from the slate hearth and brushed off his hands. "Not that I mind helping little old ladies across the street."

That reminded Kristen of the new witness Luke had told her about after dinner. "Do you think Mrs. Peeples will agree to testify against Derek?"

"Hard to say." Luke sat cross-legged on the rug in front of the fire. "You said you knew her, right?"

"Slightly. I mean, she was retired from teaching before I even started school, and now she's pretty much a shut-in. But I've delivered flowers to her a couple of times. Once when she was in the hospital last year." Kristen lowered herself beside Luke. The cozy crackle of the flames warmed her skin. It was nice, sitting in front of the fire with him.

"She have family in town?"

"I don't think so," Kristen replied. "I believe her children moved away after they grew up, and her husband died years ago." She searched her memory. "As best I recall, the flowers were ordered by people from out of town."

"Well, that's something in our favor, at least." Luke reached for his beer bottle.

"You mean, because Derek won't be able to threaten her family to stop her from testifying against him?"

"Exactly."

Kristen sighed. "Do you really think we're ever going to find enough evidence to convince the police to arrest Derek?"

Instead of swallowing, Luke abruptly set his bottle down. "Doubts? Coming from *you?* This was your idea in the first place."

"I know, but—"

Luke took hold of her shoulders. "Kristen, don't give up on me now. We're making progress." His blue eyes blazed like reflected flames. "We're going to nail that bastard. We're going to make sure he never hurts anyone again."

"But we still don't have any real proof that he killed Sheri! All we have are a jumble of facts and witnesses that coincide with our theory of what happened." Kristen didn't believe it was a theory. She *knew* how Sheri had died. But the law wouldn't give any weight to her own personal conviction. "Even if we persuade the police to arrest Derek, his defense attorney would make mincemeat of our case. Or even more likely, get it dismissed before it came to trial."

Luke scooted closer, so their knees were touching. His square jaw slanted at a stubborn angle. "We're going to find more evidence. We're not going to let Derek get away with murder. We're going to make him pay for what he did to my—to Cody.''

Kristen blinked at him. That slip of the tongue had revealed more than he'd intended, of that she was sure. Had Luke finally accepted the fact that Cody was his?

She raised her hand to his face. ''Oh, Luke.'' How ironic. Now that he'd finally found powerful, personal reasons of his own to fight Derek, Kristen's own determination was suffering a crisis of confidence. ''We're running out of time,'' she said, unable to keep the despair from her voice.

Luke's fingers tightened on her arms. The fire cast flickering shadows that threw his stern, unyielding expression into even sharper relief. But, amazingly, the flames also revealed a trace of fear. ''I won't let you take Cody and disappear from my life,'' he said, barely moving his lips.

What was he saying? Was this a threat? A plea? A commitment? Beneath her fingertips Kristen felt the taut bowstring of muscle along his jaw. His gaze held her mesmerized while she tried to make sense of what she read in his eyes.

Slowly, inexorably, he drew her toward him. Kristen's heart beat faster. Whatever unreadable message his dark features conveyed, it was one she'd never seen before.

Heat enveloped her. Not from the fire, but from the closeness of Luke's body and the furnace of her own quickening desire. The gap between them narrowed, even as warning sirens erupted in the sensible part of Kristen's brain. Pull back! Pull back before it's too late!

She could taste his breath on her lips now, feel his own accelerating pulse beat where her fingers touched his neck.

Tomorrow she might have to leave him forever. This might be the last time she saw him, her last chance to find out whether Luke really was the one man on earth who could show her the true meaning of passion.

Pull back! Pull back!

Kristen brought up her other hand and wove her fingers through his hair. He let his eyes drift shut, angled his head to press a kiss into her palm. She felt his tongue flick across her flesh, and a shudder of tingling pleasure rippled through her entire body.

When Luke opened his eyes again, what Kristen saw there made her catch her breath.

Then everything dissolved into a blur and the room began to spin, as he crushed his lips to hers and stole the rest of her breath away.

Chapter 13

Luke couldn't stop himself. He didn't *want* to stop himself. He was tired of fighting the powerful chemistry that had been brewing between him and Kristen all week, gaining strength, becoming more impossible to resist.

Ever since she'd sought refuge on his doorstep, his life had been turned upside down. His whole belief system had been rocked to the core, filled with doubt and uncertainty by answers to questions he'd never even thought to ask before. Sheri's death turned out to be murder, not an accident. The troubles plaguing his business were rooted in sabotage, not bad luck. Would they ever be able to prove Derek guilty of either?

And the one question that tormented Luke above all others…did he have a son?

All Luke was sure of right now was that he wanted Kristen. More than he'd ever wanted another woman. And he wasn't going to fight it anymore.

He angled his head to deepen their kiss, seeking her tongue with his. She kissed him back with the same hot, hard, questing urgency that was driving him toward the edge. Her fingers curled through his hair as if to pull him even closer.

Luke obliged. He dragged her against him so she was half sitting on his lap, their arms and legs tangled together. ''Mmm, Kristen...'' he muttered between her lips. He slid his mouth from hers to explore the soft, delicious curve of her neck, tickling her earlobe with his tongue, kissing her hair, then working his way backward.

With a sound that was half moan, half sigh, she let her head fall back, exposing the slender, creamy column of her throat. Luke could feel purring vibrations as he traced a path with his lips, down to the opening of her blouse collar. He nuzzled her there for a moment, inhaling the warm, feminine scent of her.

Then he brought his face to hers again, seducing her with his mouth, running his tongue across her teeth while his fingers teased open the first blouse button.

He wasn't as clumsy as he'd been the last time he'd tried this. One by one, the buttons popped open as if by magic. Kristen held herself motionless, as if trying to make his task easier. But once Luke slipped his hand inside to knead one lace-covered breast, she strained against him, arching her back and releasing a pent-up sound of pleasure.

A shock wave of heat rushed through his loins. Whoa, easy now, he cautioned himself. He intended to make this as good for Kristen as he knew it would be for him.

Gently he eased her back to lie on the rug. He settled beside her, propping himself on one elbow while he continued to kiss her. That left one hand free to continue his sensual explorations.

Kristen gasped softly when he caressed her breast again. Darn it, he wanted to touch *her,* not some frilly piece of underwear! He skimmed his fingers along her bra until he found the clasp. She wriggled slightly to give him easier access. Luke felt a surge of satisfaction at this sign that she wanted this as much as he did.

The clasp slowed him down for a few moments while he fiddled with it. Meanwhile Kristen was driving him wild with her kisses and increasingly bold caresses. He had to restrain himself from simply tearing the bra off her. It might get him what he wanted, but would certainly cost him any points for subtlety.

"Want some help?" she whispered. He felt her smile against his mouth.

"What, and miss half the fun?" He grinned back. "I mean to undress you, my sweet. No matter how long it takes."

Her eyes flared wide, turning a deeper shade of green. "Take your time," she murmured.

Long, slow seductions had always been Luke's specialty. He understood the value of anticipation...how holding himself back, dragging the tempo, made the grand finale so much better for both of them.

What he didn't understand was why he was so impatient this time. Why he could hardly wait to feel the friction of bare skin against bare skin, to join their bodies, to become one with her.

He was the same person he'd always been. The difference must be Kristen.

At last! The clasp of her bra came free. With unsteady fingers Luke pushed the filmy material aside and closed his hand over her warm, quivering flesh. A shudder ran through Kristen. She sucked in a little hiss of air.

Her nipple was a taut, tender peak. Luke stroked it lazily with his thumb, loving the almost panicky look of pleasure that slid over Kristen's face. Her thick auburn hair spilled across the rug like a luxurious curtain, woven with copper threads that shimmered in the firelight.

He glanced down to watch himself in action. His hand, dark against her pale flesh. Callused where she was smooth. Hard where she was soft.

All at once he wasn't content to touch her. He wanted to taste her, too. He pushed himself into a position where he could lower his head to her breast. Kristen groaned. Luke swirled his tongue around the rosy tip, teasing, flicking, drawing her into his mouth.

Kristen fisted her hands in his hair. Her ragged breaths tickled the side of his face, interspersed with delicious little whimpers he took for encouragement.

Now touching and tasting weren't enough. He wanted to see her, too. All of her. Every lovely square inch of her. He eased one sleeve off her shoulder.

"Luke, wait," she said breathlessly. "We can't—"

For one agonizing second he was afraid she was calling a halt to their lovemaking.

"Not out here." Her gaze darted in the direction of Cody's room.

Luke understood at once. He rearranged her blouse, letting his hand linger a moment on her breast. Then he levered himself to his feet—not an easy task, considering the stiffened condition of his lower anatomy.

He extended his hand to help Kristen. As she rose, he swept her up into his arms in one continuous motion. She let out a soft whoop as her arms came around his neck.

Sweeping her off her feet. So this was what it felt like, Kristen thought. All her life she'd wanted to know. Now, the reality was turning out to be even more heart-stopping than her wildest fantasy.

She buried her face in Luke's shirt, savoring the heat and smell of him. Against her cheek she could feel the rapid-fire thudding of his heart, the rise and fall of his chest. Whatever reservations she might have still harbored about making love with Luke had gone up the chimney in a whirlwind of smoke and fire.

Right or wrong, this was their one night together. And Kristen wasn't going to spoil it by letting guilt or regret intrude. Tonight there was only Luke.

He elbowed his way into her bedroom, kicking the door shut with his foot. Amazing how effortlessly he carried her, how light and graceful she felt in his arms! Almost as if she were floating.

He laid her gently on the bed, treating her like a precious

object of spun glass. He switched on the bedside lamp. ‘‘Be right back.’’

‘‘Where—?’’

But he’d only crossed the room to lock the door. In seconds he was back, towering above her, studying her with a look of such intensity that she blushed. She had to flatten her hands against the bedspread to keep them from yanking her blouse closed.

A comma of black hair fell across his forehead. ‘‘I could stand here and look at you all night,’’ he said soberly. A twinkle gleamed in his eye. ‘‘But I’ve got a better idea.’’

‘‘Luke…’’ She reached for him.

He dove onto the bed, seized her, rolled her over on top of him. ‘‘You’re so beautiful,’’ he said, pushing her hair back from her face. He kissed the tip of her nose. ‘‘Corny, I know. But it’s true.’’

Kristen had never considered her looks all that special. Certainly not compared to her glamorous sister’s. But Luke made her *feel* beautiful. Sexy. Wanton.

She took hold of his wrists and pinned them back against the pillows. Then slowly, deliberately, she lowered her head as if to kiss him. Desire leaped into his eyes.

She flicked her tongue lightly across his upper lip, pulling back quickly when he tried to capture her mouth with his. A smile spread across her face, a kind of smile she’d never felt there before. ‘‘Patience,’’ she whispered. Then she began to rotate her hips against him, reveling in his hard arousal and the excitement that exploded through his eyes.

‘‘Kristen,’’ he said in a warning tone.

She leaned forward to nibble his lower lip, to drop tiny seductive kisses along his jaw, his neck, his ear. Her breasts brushed against him, her taut nipples fairly aching for his touch.

He let her torture him until *she* was the one who couldn’t stand it anymore. As soon as she released his wrists, Luke used his newfound freedom to whisk off her blouse and bra.

He urged her to sit up, to straddle him so he could get a better look at her.

Kristen forgot all about her self-consciousness the moment Luke lifted his hands to cradle her breasts. Sheer, excruciating bliss radiated through her as he kneaded her, brushing his fingers across her nipples, undulating his hips beneath her so that she swayed gently up and down as if riding the crest of a wave.

With shaky hands, she found his belt buckle. Opened it. Tugged out his shirt. Once she'd made it that far, Luke grabbed the fabric and peeled the shirt off over his head.

Kristen gulped. This wasn't the first time she'd seen his naked chest, but it was the first time she'd had the right to touch it. To skim her fingers across it. To lower her mouth and use her tongue to explore the muscular contours, the bristly dark hair, the flat male nipples—

Luke clamped his hands to the sides of her head. ''Better stop now, my sweet,'' he said in a raspy voice, ''or this party's gonna be over mighty quick.''

Kristen pushed herself up on her arms and batted her eyelashes at him. ''What's the matter?'' she asked innocently. ''Can't take it anymore?''

''I'll show you what I can take,'' he growled.

In one swift movement he was on top of her, fumbling with the zipper of her slacks. Well, turnabout was fair play, wasn't it? Kristen reached for the fly of his jeans.

Luke won the race, but only with Kristen's help. She raised her hips off the bed so he could drag off her slacks and panties in one fell swoop. Before Kristen could start to feel self-conscious again, Luke swung to his feet and shucked off his jeans and briefs. He stood revealed in the lamplight, skin burnished with a golden glow, proud and erect in all his glorious masculinity.

Oh, sweet heaven...

Kristen swallowed. He was even more magnificent than she'd imagined.

"I want you," he said. "But I need to make sure that you want this, too."

More than anything she'd ever wanted in her life. "Yes," she whispered. No looking back. No looking ahead. Only the here and now...

He climbed onto the bed with her and took her in his arms. His nude body felt so strange yet so familiar at the same time. Hairy skin and hard muscle, heat and bone and sinew, the warm, alive vibrancy of blood pumping through his veins.

"We're a perfect fit," he told her, coaxing her arms around his broad shoulders, nuzzling her neck, molding her against him.

"Perfect," she echoed dreamily.

Then he resumed where he'd left off, tangling his hands through her hair, using his mouth to arouse her, twining his legs around hers. Kristen drew in a sharp breath that filled her lungs with the sweaty, wonderful, musky scent of him. His whiskers rasped against the sensitive skin of her breasts while his tongue played across their tips.

Kristen dug her fingers into his shoulders. "Oh, Luke..."

Desire unfurled inside her so that every nerve in her body tingled, every cell craved his touch. She inched her fingers down his backbone, acquainting herself with every sexy knob and hard angle. Though her limbs felt heavy and molten, they were constantly in motion, as if instinct had taken control of her actions.

To her delight, she discovered ways to touch him that made him groan, that made him stiffen with pleasure, that made his breath come hotter, faster against her skin.

"Better cut that out," he said through his teeth when she curled her fingers around his rigid, pulsing flesh. "Or else I—"

"Now," she whispered in his ear. "Luke, please, I'm on fire for you....."

"Ah, Kristen..."

Though she could see by the strain in his features how much

it cost him to hold back, he brought his hand below her belly and gently opened her with his fingers.

Kristen arched her back with a gasp. "Luke, I mean it. I—I..." Then she couldn't speak anymore as he continued his intimate caresses, sending incredible ripples of sensation radiating outward from the secret core of her being.

Pressure built inside her. She groped for him, clinging to the edge by her fingernails. Through the dizzying mists of rapture she felt him watching her, studying her every reaction, responding instantly.

"Luke..." She mouthed his name but no sound came out. Something hot and urgent ignited inside her, an oncoming explosion she was powerless to resist.

He must have seen the change in her face. Quickly he raised himself above her and found her mouth with his. He nudged against her, adjusted his position, then eased forward in a slow-motion thrust.

When he entered her, Kristen shattered into a million pieces. Dazzling, white-hot ecstasy seared through her, obliterating all thought, all control, leaving only emotion and pure physical sensation in its wake.

Luke continued to move above her, creating spasm after spasm of intense pleasure with each stroke. Kristen had never felt like this before. Yet with an instinct as natural as breathing, she matched her rhythm to his so they moved together as one.

When Luke's face came back into focus, she saw mounting excitement straining his rugged features. His eyes bored into hers as if he could see straight through to her soul. "So good," he gasped. "Can't...much longer..."

He thrust faster, deeper. Kristen traced the rigid curves of muscle flexing along his arms as he held himself above her. A bead of sweat dripped off his forehead onto hers. All at once his eyes filled with wonder, as if he'd just glimpsed the most awesome, incredible sight in the world.

"Kristen..." Her name emerged in a groan. Then the long,

lean length of his body went taut as he surged into her again and again, his handsome face contorted with passion.

"Yes," she hissed in his ear. "Oh, Luke, yes..." He filled her with joy, with triumph, with a primitive female satisfaction that was older than time.

He belonged completely to her. For these few moments, anyway.

Gradually his rocking motions subsided. Heat continued to roll off his body in waves. The tendons in his neck convulsed as he swallowed big gulps of air, trying to catch his breath. Then he toppled over to one side and crashed onto the mattress next to her.

"Wow," he said.

He squinted blearily at the ceiling and shook his head as if to clear it. When he turned to look at Kristen, his eyes were still glazed with wonder. "That was..." He slid his arm beneath her shoulders and tilted her against him. He blew a stream of air through his teeth. "Words fail me. Incredible doesn't begin to describe it."

Kristen draped her arm across his ribs. She felt as content and satiated as a cat who'd just lapped up an entire bowl of cream. "Mmm, that goes for me, too."

Luke kissed her temple as if the effort exhausted him. "I mean, that was utterly fantastic." He blinked in disbelief, then craned his neck to peer at her suspiciously. "You've been holding out on me."

Kristen fluttered her lashes and offered him an angelic smile. "We haven't even been on speaking terms for eight years, much less..."

"Oh, yeah. That's right, I forgot." He scratched his head. "*Why* was I mad at you, again?"

She pinched a clump of his chest hairs and pulled.

"Ouch!" Re-energized, he levered himself on top of her again. "You're a feisty one, aren't you?"

"When the situation calls for it." A warm thrill zigzagged all the way through her, making her toes curl with pleasure. She couldn't believe she was in bed with Luke, exchanging cozy postcoital banter, as comfortable with each other as long-time lovers.

Something they could never be in reality.

Kristen pushed that depressing thought aside. She wasn't going to spoil this lovely, glowing aftermath by thinking about the future. Or their lack of one.

She linked her hands behind his neck and brought his head down for a kiss. She knew Luke wasn't in love with her, that mere physical attraction had been the driving force behind his lovemaking. But he'd acted so tender, so considerate, so...so *connected* to her in ways that had seemed to go beyond the physical. Didn't that mean he must feel *something* special for her?

He kissed her back with gusto. "Mmm." He bumped his nose against hers. "You're amazing, do you know that?"

Luke certainly made her *feel* special. Beautiful. Sexy. As if he didn't just view her as Sheri's kid sister anymore, but as a desirable woman in her own right.

"In fact, you'd have completely knocked my socks off," he said with a grin, "if I'd been wearing any at the time." He hooked their ankles together and wiggled his bare feet next to hers.

Kristen would have felt silly telling Luke how wonderful he'd been. He'd no doubt been complimented on his sexual prowess by women far more experienced than she was, whose praise meant a lot more.

So she told him the truth. "No one's ever made me feel the way you do," she said softly. "Never." *Never again,* cried a tiny, faraway voice.

All trace of amusement fled from his eyes. "Kristen." He tightened his arms around her. A mixture of helplessness, of regret, of some yearning quality Kristen couldn't identify shimmered across the rugged landscape of his face.

He brought his mouth to hers. But his kiss was different this time. Gone was the urgency, the need, the deliberate, seductive dueling. Instead his kiss had a tender, poignant sweetness to it. A wistfulness. A sense of...finality.

Almost like a goodbye.

Kristen forced herself not to clutch Luke's neck and cling to him. Neither of them had made any promises. Neither of them could.

So maybe that's what this was.

Goodbye.

Luke had rolled over so many times during the night, his sheet was twisted around him like the knot of a hangman's noose. As the first gray light of dawn seeped through his bedroom window, he punched his pillow as if his lousy night's sleep had been all *its* fault.

I have to leave.

He'd never minded saying those words to a woman before. In fact, he'd rather prided himself that that was his motto. Making love to a woman was one thing. Spending the night in the same bed with her, though—that involved a certain whiff of domesticity and a level of commitment Luke wanted no part of.

He'd always figured the best way to make this clear was to pull on his pants and make his departure as soon as it was polite. Hey, he was just being honest, right? Even though it would have been a lot easier sometimes just to roll over and start snoring, he didn't want to risk giving the lady any wrong ideas.

So Luke's normal policy was to get dressed, thank her for a good time—although not in those words, of course—and head out the door before night turned into morning. Then he could spend the yawning drive home congratulating himself for being so upfront about his intentions. Or *lack* of intentions, to be accurate.

Why, then, had he felt like such a heel when he'd finally gotten around to telling *Kristen* he had to leave?

After all, last night had been one time Luke had genuinely had a compelling reason not to stay. Both he and Kristen had agreed it was important for him to keep up the pretense that he knew nothing about Cody's disappearance, by sticking to his usual routine as much as possible. In other words, sleeping in his own bed every night.

The truth was, however, that last night was the first time in years Luke had *wanted* to spend the night in a woman's bed. He'd actually *wanted* to wake up in the morning to find Kristen asleep next to him, her gorgeous hair spread out on his pillow, her beautiful green eyes all heavy-lidded and sexy when they finally fluttered open.

Most of all, he'd wanted to be able to make love to her again while the sun came up, to seduce her awake with sleepy kisses and lazy caresses until they were both wide-awake and panting for each other.

He'd even wanted to share those lingering, meaningful glances with her across the breakfast table.

Luke rolled over onto his stomach with a groan and dragged the pillow over his head. Man, he had it bad this time. And he didn't see how any good could possibly come of it.

He was *not* going to let Kristen become that important to him. No way. Huh-uh. He'd learned his lesson. Mrs. Hollister's son didn't need to get burned twice by the stove to figure out not to touch it again.

But whether Luke liked it or not, Kristen was going to stay part of his life in the future, because of Cody. Cody was the link that had brought them together, and he was the bond that would forever connect them. Luke was determined to play a role in the boy's life from now on. He hadn't figured out what kind exactly, but any role at all would inevitably mean ongoing contact with Cody's devoted aunt. With Cody's smart, sexy, irresistible—

"Aargh!" With a roar of frustration, Luke hurled his pillow across the room. He shouldn't have made love to Kristen. What if she assumed it meant more than it had?

Okay, maybe it *had* been about more than just sex. But that was all the more reason for Luke not to let it happen again. He couldn't risk getting any more emotionally involved.

Look at how far she'd already gotten under his skin! Whenever he wasn't with her, he was *thinking* about her, for Pete's sake! This was exactly the type of entanglement he'd sworn to avoid.

Even now he was obsessing about her, wondering if it had really been good for her last night, worrying whether or not she was going to read too much into their passionate encounter. No wonder he hadn't been able to get any sleep.

He would just have to find some excuse to avoid making love to her again. No matter how many cold showers he had to take.

He would never be able to live with himself if he kept leading Kristen on like this, letting her think there might be a house with a white picket fence in their future.

Bad example. *His* house had a white picket fence. Okay, letting Kristen think they were going to set up housekeeping someday. That the unexpectedly enjoyable simulation of family life they'd fallen into at the cabin might eventually become permanent.

He'd accidentally let down his guard, that was all. Yesterday, for the first time, Luke had let himself fully consider that Cody might be his. And then the kid had to go and say that stuff about wishing Luke was his dad. No wonder Kristen had been able to slip past his emotional defenses!

All right, that wasn't fair. Kristen wasn't trying to trap him, to trick him into making promises. She was too worried about Cody, too wrapped up in her own guilt about Sheri's death to dream about happily-ever-after.

Last night had been a big mistake for both of them. There wasn't going to be a repeat performance. And the sooner Luke spelled that out for Kristen, the better.

Chapter 14

Kristen sat on the front steps, watching afternoon shadows creep across the driveway. Cody was in his bedroom, playing with the video game Luke had bought him, but the close confines of the cabin had finally driven Kristen outside.

Ever since she'd awakened this morning and realized what she'd done, she'd been edgy and anxious. Jittery from lack of sleep. Tormented by regrets, by doubts and questions about what to do now. The cabin walls had felt like they were closing in on her.

She propped her elbows on her knees, dropping her chin onto her hands with a sigh. She couldn't be in love with Luke. She just couldn't.

Bad enough that she'd made love with him last night. That had been a one-time occurrence, something that would never happen again. In the glaring unforgiving light of day, though, Kristen had to face the unfortunate fact that what she felt for Luke would go on forever.

Somehow, despite her best efforts to resist it, she'd fallen in love with him. But she would never find happiness with him. Her conscience wouldn't allow it.

Sheri's life had been cut brutally, tragically short, thanks to her. Kristen's life would continue, but why should she be allowed to find the joy and fulfillment her sister never had? Cody had been the one shining star in Sheri's unhappy universe. He was the one person Kristen could let herself care about now, the one person she intended to devote her life to completely.

She couldn't let anyone else into her heart. But somehow, Luke had found his way in.

Why did the one man she would ever care for have to be the same man her sister had loved? The same man who'd loved Sheri? Somehow, that made it even worse. Not because Kristen was jealous. But because Luke was a constant reminder of how Kristen's actions had cost Sheri her life.

A blue jay scolded her from the branch of a nearby sugar pine. Kristen peered up at him, shading her eyes against the westering sun. ''Why can't I just take Cody and fly away like you?'' she asked. ''That would solve all my problems at once.''

Cody would be safe. Derek would never find them. And Kristen would never have to face Luke again, or see the reflection of her own guilt whenever she looked at him, or fight the overwhelming temptation to give in to her desire for him.

She braced her arms behind her, drumming her fingers on the step while she went over her options again. Stay. Go. Not a very long list.

How were she and Cody going to escape from this cabin without Luke's help? Help he would never give them now. Well, Pineville was only twelve miles away. If worse came to worst, they could always walk, hiding in the ditch alongside the road whenever a car came into view. Cody seemed much stronger now. If they waited till dark, they could probably make it to the battered-women's shelter by morning.

But what if the people there didn't believe her story? They would have heard about Cody's disappearance. What if they became convinced Kristen was actually a kidnapper, and called the police? Not likely, but possible. Kristen drummed her fingers faster. They needed to get someplace far away, quick, where no one would recognize them.

There were other vacation homes near Blackberry Lake, even some places where people lived year-round. This was the kind of area where people didn't bother much with locking their cars. Sometimes they even left their keys in the ignition. Kristen might be able to steal a car, drive it out of this part of the state, then abandon it once they got to a big-city airport or train or bus station.

She figured auto theft would be a pretty minor charge to add to her criminal portfolio, compared to kidnapping.

Hitchhiking was out of the question, unless she could come up with foolproof disguises for herself and Cody. Even a long-distance truck driver who stopped to pick them up on the highway would probably have heard about them.

Luke *had* left her his cellular phone. She could order a pizza, hijack the delivery truck—

''All right, let's not get ridiculous now,'' she said, clicking her tongue. But the truth was, Kristen would do whatever it took to protect her nephew. So the fact that she was stranded here with no transportation, no money and no place to go didn't really enter into her deliberations of whether or not she should make a run for it with Cody.

But the idea of separating father and son nearly broke Kristen's heart, not to mention her own anguish at the thought of never seeing Luke again. She couldn't let Cody and Luke's growing attachment or her own feelings delay her too long, though, blinding her to the need to leave until it was too late.

She ought to leave *now,* tonight, after Luke had gone home, so they would have a head start before he discovered they were missing. Once she fled with Cody, it wouldn't be just Derek and the police who were after them.

Kristen chewed her fingernails. Once she took that drastic step, there would be no going back, no way to change her mind. It would be too risky to return.

Dear God. She couldn't bear to picture the look on Luke's face when he realized they were gone. He would never forgive her, never stop hating...

Then she detected the sound of his pickup turning off the road. The familiar rumble was unmistakable to her now, after all the times she'd listened for his return. She clung to her perch on the step. How would Luke behave toward her now, after last night's reckless, uninhibited lovemaking?

Hot crimson blossomed in Kristen's cheeks. Would this be the last time she waited for him, the last time she heard his truck come up the driveway? Would she and Cody be hundreds of miles away from him by this time tomorrow?

Butterflies circled wildly through her stomach in a blizzard of agitation. Luke coasted to a stop. When he climbed out of the truck, Kristen's heart clenched like a fist at the welcome sight of his face. Jet-black brows above eyes as blue as the sky, the handsome sculpture of his chiseled features, the confident, almost cocky way he held his head...

If Kristen had still had any doubts she loved him, they were vaporized by the force of emotion that slammed into her while she watched Luke stride toward her. Shakily she rose to her feet. He was hardly beaming her an eager lover's smile, but he wasn't frowning at her, either. She started down the steps. Of course, that was because Luke didn't realize what she was planning to—

"Oh!" Kristen let out a yelp of surprise. Her foot had somehow missed the next step so that all at once she was tumbling forward. She grabbed the railing at the base of the steps and at least saved herself from pitching facedown onto the driveway.

"Ouch!" Now the pain came, shooting up from her ankle. Her foot had landed funny.

"Are you all right?" Luke was there in two seconds, sliding his shoulder under her arm to support her.

"I..." She tested her ankle and winced. "No, I guess."

Darn it, if only she hadn't been so jumpy and anxious, so

distracted about Luke and her decision to leave that she hadn't paid attention to where she was stepping…

"We'd better get you inside." Just like last night, he swept her into his arms to carry her.

The vivid reminder unsettled Kristen even further. "I can walk," she insisted.

"Not very well, from what I saw." He shifted her so she had no choice but to put her arms around his neck. Either that, or let them dangle like a rag doll's.

She was acutely aware of the rise and fall of his chest, his pulse beating in his throat, his eyes fixed on hers with a concerned intensity that made her feel even more awkward. "This isn't necessary," she repeated.

"I don't mind." He winked. "It's not like I've never done this before, remember?"

She remembered. Whoo, boy, how she remembered.

"I'll take a look at it once we're inside. Probably just a sprain." He started up the steps.

A sprained ankle. Wouldn't that be peachy keen? Just when she might need to hike twelve miles through the night with—

The screen door banged open like a rifle shot.

Luke hesitated, then kept climbing. "Hey, Slugger." His smile was puzzled. "Where're you going so fa—"

"Put her down!" Cody shouted.

Astonished, Kristen whipped her head around to stare at him. Luke froze at the top of the steps. Cody's face was bleached white except for two scarlet spots that blazed on his cheeks. His blue eyes were enormous. Angry. Full of fear.

"I said, put her down!" he yelled again.

Then he rushed forward and kicked Luke in the shin.

It must have hurt like the dickens, but if Luke were as shocked numb as Kristen was, he'd probably barely felt it.

"Cody!" she cried. "What on earth—"

"Now! Put her down right *now!*" Cody began to pummel Luke with his fists.

Kristen could feel each blow reverberating through Luke's

body. She tried to wriggle out of his arms, but he kept her securely against his chest, holding her out of the way as if he feared Cody might attack her, too.

"Let go of her!" Cody shrieked.

"Luke, do as he says," Kristen exclaimed. "I can stand."

Tears streamed down Cody's cheeks. His face was beet red now, his eyes crazed with near hysteria. "Let her go! Put her down!" He kept hitting and kicking Luke. "Don't take her away!"

"Okay, buddy, I'm putting her down." Luke lowered Kristen near the porch railing as gently as he could with Cody raining blows on him. "You sure you can stand?" he asked her.

"I'm sure." She clamped her teeth against the sudden knife blade of pain and gripped the railing for support.

"Easy now, kiddo. Easy." Luke dropped to his haunches and managed to capture Cody's flailing fists. "That's enough of that now." He made an effort to speak calmly, but Kristen could tell he was as shaken up as she was. "You want to tell us what this is all about?" he asked.

Cody was crying so hard he could barely speak. "Don't...take..."

"Shh, it's okay." He moved to put his arm around the boy, but Cody ducked away.

"Honey, listen to me. Whatever it is, it's going to be all right." Kristen let go of the railing and hobbled toward them, ignoring the scream of protest from her ankle. She eased herself down into a sitting position and stroked Cody's hair.

His sobs subsided a little. Since he didn't reject her touch, Kristen patted his back, squeezed his shoulder. His limbs vibrated as if high-tension wires ran through them. What in heaven's name could have upset him so?

"Shh," she repeated over and over until she felt some of the panic ebb from his body. When it became clear he wasn't going to take a swing at Luke again, she opened her arms and said, "Come here."

Luke released her nephew's wrists and Cody spun into her

arms, seizing her around the neck as if he would never let go. He whimpered something into her collarbone. "What was that, sweetie?"

It took some more cajoling until she could finally pry his arms from around her neck and get him to look at her. His eyes were swollen, though calmer now. His face was smeared with tears. Kristen smoothed back his hair. "What were you trying to say just now, Cody?"

He sniffed, rubbed his nose with his wrist. He sidled a furtive glance in Luke's direction. Still in a crouch, Luke spread his hands and gave Kristen a mystified look.

"I didn't want him to take you away," Cody said in a tiny voice. His head was bowed so that he appeared to be addressing the floorboards.

"Take me away? You mean Luke?" Kristen tipped up his chin so she could hear him.

"Uh-huh." Cody bobbed his head once and gulped.

Kristen struggled to understand. "Honey, Luke wasn't going to take me anywhere. He was just trying to help me into the cabin, because I hurt my ankle."

Distress jumped back into his eyes. "But he carried my mommy away like that!"

"Who did—Luke?" Kristen's brow puckered in bewilderment. She checked Luke for confirmation and saw he was just as confused as she was.

"No." Cody shook his head and looked down at the ground again. "My daddy."

Something ice-cold congealed inside Kristen's chest. The first stirring of suspicion. "When, Cody?" She grazed his cheek with the back of one finger. "When did you see your daddy carrying your mommy like that?"

He pinched his lips together and refused to look up. The same suspicion must have dawned on Luke, judging by the ominous set of his jaw. But he obviously realized Kristen would have to be the one to coax answers from Cody.

"Sweetheart, this is very important." She braced her hands

on his shoulders. "I need you to tell me when it was you saw your daddy carrying your mommy."

She could feel a terrible conflict tearing at him. His body was rigid with resistance, trembling with indecision. "Cody..."

"When she died," he blurted out. "It was that day."

Luke made a faint sound in his throat.

Kristen forced herself not to react. "You saw your daddy carrying your mommy on the day she died?"

He nodded, still averting his eyes.

"He was carrying her the same way Luke was carrying me just now?"

Another nod. His mouth was compressed into a tight hyphen as if to prevent any more words from spilling out.

"Why was he carrying her, Cody? Do you know?"

An uneasy shrug.

"Did he—was your mommy hurt?"

Silence.

"Cody..."

"I heard him hitting her." He spoke so softly Kristen could barely hear him. But the impact of his words registered loud and clear.

Her stomach dropped with a sickening lurch. "Your daddy was hitting your mommy that day?" Dear God, what a horrible nightmare that a child should have to give such testimony! But he was the only one who could.

He nodded.

"What happened? Why was he hitting her?" There was no sane answer to that question. Certainly nothing an innocent child could make sense of. But anything Cody could tell them might be important.

He scuffed one sneaker against the weathered wood of the porch. "He came home while we were getting in the car."

Kristen moved her head closer to hear him. "Were you and Mommy going someplace?"

He nodded. "On a trip. Just me and her, she said. She

packed our suitcases and was putting them in the trunk, and then Daddy came home.''

Kristen swallowed the bile that rose in her throat. ''And where were *you?*''

''Sitting in the car.''

''What did your daddy do?''

''He grabbed Mommy's keys and opened the trunk again. Then he started yelling at her.''

''Did he hit her?''

''No.'' A sniffle. ''Not right then.''

''What did he do?''

Cody lifted his head and met her eyes. ''He grabbed open my door and told me to get in the house. So I did.'' The ghost of terror haunted his face. ''Then he made Mommy come in the house, too. I ran into my room and shut the door. I—I was scared.''

The vise around Kristen's heart tightened another notch. ''What happened next?'' she asked softly.

''I heard Daddy yelling. Mommy was crying. Then I—'' A sob hitched in his chest. ''—I heard him hitting her.''

Kristen unfortunately didn't need to ask how Cody had recognized that ugly sound. ''Then what happened?''

''It got quiet. An' then I heard a noise outside in the driveway, so I looked out my window. My daddy was getting the suitcases out of Mommy's car.''

Pack a suitcase for each one of you, but don't do it ahead of time, Sheri. Derek might find them. Just figure out what you're going to take, and throw everything in at the last minute, right before you leave to meet me.

Oh, Sheri, Kristen mourned silently. I should have told you not to pack anything! We could have bought new stuff later. All that mattered was escaping with your lives....

''You all right?'' Luke asked sharply. They were the first words he'd uttered since this heartrending interrogation had begun.

Cody flinched. Kristen somehow kept her voice level after

giving Luke a reassuring nod. "Did your daddy take the suitcases into the house?"

"Yeah." The anguish in his eyes was almost unbearable to witness. "I kept looking out the window so I could see when he went back to work. But then he came out of the house and he was—he was carrying Mommy." He shot a frightened glance at Luke.

"Was..." Kristen swallowed. "Could you tell if your mommy was hurt? Was that why he was carrying her?"

One lone tear slid down Cody's cheek. "I think she was asleep," he said. "Her eyes were closed and she wasn't moving. I guess that's why he was carrying her. 'Cause she was asleep."

It took every ounce of Kristen's self-control to hold back the sob that welled up inside her.

When Luke saw she couldn't go on, he asked quietly, "Where did your...dad put your mom?"

Luke's question agitated Cody. He starting breathing faster. "In the car," he said, edging away from Luke. "He put her in the back seat, lying down so she could sleep."

"Then what?"

"He drove away. I watched out the window a long, long time. My daddy came back, but he didn't have Mommy's car anymore." All the color had leached from Cody's complexion.

"He was walking?" Luke asked.

"Yes." Cody's chest heaved rapidly. "I never saw Mommy again! He carried her away and she died and I never saw her again!" His face crumpled into a mask of tears.

Kristen bundled him into her arms and held him close, stroking his small, quaking back. Miraculously, she found her voice. "Is that why you were so scared when you saw Luke carrying me? Because you were afraid he would take me away and I'd never come back?"

Cody nodded against her shoulder.

"Honey." She let him cry for another minute, then gently peeled his arms from around her so he could see into her eyes. "You never have to worry about me going away forever. I'm never going to leave you. I'll always be around to take care of you, and Luke—''

Even now, she was hardly entitled to make promises on his behalf, was she? ''Luke is our friend,'' she told Cody. ''He would never do anything to hurt either one of us. Do you believe me?''

Cody nodded reluctantly, his tearful gaze darting back and forth between the two adults.

''Good.'' Kristen gave him another hug. But when she tried to stand, her ankle nearly gave way. She gratefully accepted the quick offer of Luke's hand. ''Cody, maybe you could give me a little boost, too.''

''You can't tell him!'' Cody burst out.

Kristen sank back onto the porch, jarred by the note of panic in his voice. Luke kept her hand firmly in his. ''Can't tell who what, honey?''

''I wasn't s'posed to tell! Please, please don't tell him I did!'' Cody's teeth were chattering with fear.

''Sweetheart, calm down. Who are you talking about?''

''My d-daddy. H-he saw me looking out the window when he was carrying Mommy to the car.'' That disturbing gleam of hysteria came back into his eyes. ''When he—when he got home, Daddy told me never never never tell anyone I saw him. He said I'd get in big trouble. He said—he said...'' Cody hiccuped with fear. ''He said if I told, he'd k-kill me!''

Luke's grip cinched so tight Kristen nearly cried out. But it wasn't the physical pain that made her gasp. It was the horror of these terrible secrets Cody had had to live with for so long.

Both adults were speechless for a moment. Then Luke clamped his hand on Cody's shoulder. ''He's not going to hurt you,'' he said in a low voice that made the hair stand up on the back of Kristen's neck. ''Never. You don't have to worry. I promise.''

Cody stared up at him as if hypnotized. Probably because he was too terrified to move. Luke's face was dark with outrage. Fury glinted in his steely eyes like crossed swords. Kristen knew he was trying to reassure Cody, but frankly, if anyone had ever aimed a look like that at her, she would have run screaming in the opposite direction.

"I won't let anyone hurt you, ever again," Luke said through lips that barely moved. He tightened his grip on Cody's shoulder. "Do you understand?"

Cody's eyes were the size of silver dollars. Something akin to awe crept over his face. He blinked twice, then nodded.

"Good." Luke rested his big hand on top of Cody's head for a moment, like a solemn benediction. Then he turned to help Kristen to her feet. "Let's get you inside, shall we?"

As she limped into the cabin, Luke and Cody on either side of her like a pair of bookends, Kristen felt as if she'd witnessed a miracle. Luke Hollister, making promises?

I won't let anyone hurt you, ever again.

It certainly sounded like a lifetime commitment to her.

Except Kristen still might decide she had no choice but to flee with Cody, bad ankle or no. Which meant Luke would never see his son…or her…

Ever again.

"Luke, it's out of the question!"

Round and round they'd gone on this, ever since putting Cody to bed. Luke's frustration was approaching the hair-pulling stage. He paced back and forth in front of the sofa, where Kristen sat with her sprained ankle propped on the coffee table.

"For cryin' out loud, what more do you want?" he demanded. "We've got an eyewitness now, someone who actually saw Derek carrying Sheri's body out to the car that morning."

"But he's only a child! What if the police don't believe him? What if they think we put him up to the story?"

"We've got other corroborating evidence." Luke ticked off witnesses on his fingers. "The guy Derek was supposed to meet with that morning, who can break his alibi for the time Sheri was killed. Mildred Peeples, who saw him running by her house on foot. And you, your testimony that Sheri planned to leave Derek that day.''

Kristen winced as she adjusted the ice-filled towel wrapped around her ankle. ''My word doesn't count for anything, or the police would have arrested Derek long ago.''

Luke fisted his hands. ''They won't be able to ignore it when they hear all our other evidence.''

''*What* evidence? An identification made by a ninety-one-year-old woman with bad eyesight?'' Kristen's face held a hopeless gleam that worried Luke. ''And maybe what's-his-name, Rayford, won't say anything incriminating against Derek because they have business dealings.''

''Obviously, Cody's testimony is the most damning evidence we're going to find.'' Luke dropped to a half-sitting position on the arm of the couch. ''What else do you suggest we do, besides go to the cops with it?''

He didn't like the guilty, secretive way Kristen's glance slid away from his. He didn't like it one bit.

The foot that *wasn't* on ice started to tap. ''We'll just have to wait some more, that's all.''

''Wait for *what?*'' Luke landed on the couch beside her. He'd felt it prudent to keep a safe distance between them, to make sure there was no repeat of last night's reckless lovemaking. But that hardly seemed a danger now, not when they were at such loggerheads. ''We've already got the evidence we need to force the cops to arrest...that creep.'' He couldn't even bring himself to say the name, not after listening to Cody this afternoon. Pronouncing it would leave a foul taste in his mouth.

Kristen shook her head. ''We can't be sure they'll arrest Derek right away.'' Her mouth twisted bitterly as she curled her fingers around Luke's wrist. ''What we do know for certain is that the first thing they'll do is arrest *me*.''

Even now, when so much was at stake, he felt a surge of electricity snap through him. His desire for Kristen hadn't dimmed one bit, even with the knowledge that he would never have her again.

"The second thing they'll do," she said with a catch in her throat, "is hand Cody straight back to Derek."

Luke covered her hand with his. "We'll hire a lawyer. Someone who can get a court order and make sure that doesn't happen."

"Court orders take time, even if we could find a judge willing to rule against the most powerful man in the county." Kristen shuddered. "How long do you think it would take Derek to take revenge on Cody, especially when he finds out what Cody told us today?" She snapped her fingers. "*That's* how quick he could hurt him."

"I promised Cody, and I'm swearing to you now. I won't let that happen." Luke had done his best to rein in his anger so they could have a rational discussion—not that Kristen was its target. But at times like now, when he let himself think about what Derek had done to Cody, how he'd hurt him, threatened him, made him live in terror, it was all Luke could do not to punch his fist through a wall.

Kristen scanned his face as if she could see the violence simmering inside him. Maybe she could. "You won't be able to protect him, no matter how much you want to," she said despairingly. "Not if Derek gets his hands on him again."

"Going to the authorities is the only way out of this mess," Luke insisted. "You can't keep hiding here forever."

"I can't risk it!" Kristen cried. "It's my fault Sheri is dead. How can I put her son back in danger, even if I *didn't* love him more than my own life? Even if it means my sister's killer goes unpunished?"

Luke grabbed her arms, feeling instant remorse when she winced at the jostling of her ankle. "You're not responsible for Sheri's death," he said sternly. "It was your idea to prove *Derek* guilty of murder, wasn't it? Isn't that why you came to me for help?"

Her eyes skittered back and forth across his face. Shifting emeralds that conveyed her fear, her guilt...and another element Luke couldn't identify. "Yes," she said slowly. "That was one of the reasons."

He didn't bother asking about the others. "Then why have you changed your mind? Why now, when we're so close to success, when we finally have the proof we need?"

Kristen hesitated, then dropped her hand helplessly to his thigh. "I didn't know Cody would turn out to be the proof," she said. Luke felt the imprint of each individual finger through his jeans. "I—I guess I always envisioned that Derek would be in jail before we came out of hiding."

He caressed her hair. So long and lush, so silky smooth, so exciting when it tickled his bare chest....

He cleared his throat. "It definitely would have been preferable if things had worked out like that," he admitted. "But that's not how it happened. Cody turned out to be the key to everything. And he's going to have to tell his story to the police before they'll arrest Derek." Luke had been right. The name did leave a foul taste on his tongue.

Kristen's resistance transmitted itself through her fingertips, into his muscles. "Then we'll have to find another way," she said. Her chin came up stubbornly. "I won't put that darling little boy in danger."

"Do you think that's what *I* want?" Luke launched himself to his feet in exasperation. Just as well. He'd been seriously considering trying to win their argument with a few well-placed kisses.

"Of course not. But if we do it *your* way—"

Just then his cell phone rang, startling them both. Their heads pivoted simultaneously toward the counter that divided kitchen from dining area.

Luke crossed the room. "Expecting any calls?" he asked with a wry smile.

Furrows pleated Kristen's forehead. "It's rung a few times since you left it here, but I've never answered it."

He picked up the phone. "Hello?" he said cautiously. Dumb. Whoever was on the other end couldn't see where Luke was.

It was Andy Driscoll, his foreman. Luke listened for about

thirty seconds without saying a word. The one he uttered when he hung up was unprintable.

Kristen was watching him, eyes wide with mounting alarm. "Luke, what is it?"

"I've gotta go," he said, heading for the door. "Someone poured sugar into the gas tanks of the dump truck and backhoe I've had parked over at the construction site in Pineville." Blistering anger crawled up his neck like a bad rash. "Andy says both engines are wrecked."

The door banged shut behind him, cutting off Kristen's exclamation of dismay.

Chapter 15

No matter how much Kristen's heart resisted the idea, reason told her it was time to run.

Luke wanted to take Cody to the police. Kristen could see his logic, but logic wouldn't protect Cody from Derek. No matter how much it cost her, no matter how much it hurt Luke, she couldn't risk letting Derek get his hands on her nephew again.

In the hour that had passed since Luke had stormed out of the cabin after Andy's phone call, Kristen had gone over her decision again and again. Postponing it wouldn't make any difference. It was time to wake up Cody and go.

An awful weight settled over her as she pushed herself off the couch, like a giant pair of invisible hands pressing down on her shoulders, urging her to stay.

Oh, Luke, I'm so sorry. But I can't. For Cody's sake.

She moved gingerly toward her bedroom, favoring her sprained ankle. She would never make it all the way to Pineville on foot now. After she packed a few things, she would have to stea—er, borrow a car from one of the neighboring cabins.

She tried not to picture Luke's face when he returned in the morning. He would be angry and upset about the vandalism to his construction vehicles—Derek's latest handiwork, no doubt. He would come charging into the cabin...

And find them gone.

Luke, Luke, forgive me! Kristen brushed tears from her eyes as she stuffed a few articles of clothing into a shopping bag. *I gave you your son, only to steal him away just as you were finally starting to believe he was yours....*

She stood stock-still and gazed at her neatly made bed, remembering. Was it only last night she and Luke had lain there together, bodies connected in a feverish tangle of desire, sharing such passion, such bliss?

Kristen pressed trembling fingertips to her mouth. Passion and bliss she would never know again. As for Luke...

A tiny shard of doubt poked its way into her mind. What if Luke hadn't truly shared her feelings? She knew he didn't love her, of course. But what if he'd only made love with her to keep her from fleeing with Cody? What if his tender words and intimate caresses had all been an act?

Luke didn't want to lose Cody now. Whether he'd admitted it to himself or not, Kristen's nephew had become very important to him. Maybe their lovemaking had just been a calculated attempt on Luke's part to seduce her into staying.

Kristen didn't want to believe he could be so cold-blooded. Certainly the Luke she'd come to know in the past week, the Luke she'd fallen in love with, would never have faked his feelings to get what he wanted. He hated deceit of any kind.

But when it came to Cody's welfare, Kristen herself had never hesitated to resort to whatever extreme measures were necessary. How could she judge Luke for using her, for employing whatever tactics he could, to keep his son from vanishing?

Kristen gathered her things and left her room for the last time—the room where she'd discovered the joyous, fulfilling ecstasy she'd never known before. The place where she'd finally found the love she'd been seeking all her life. Pain seared through her, making her injured ankle feel like a twinge in comparison. She would never see Luke again.

If only she could cling to the belief that he'd made love to her with ulterior motives, maybe that would ease the hurt a little. Maybe it would ease her conscience a tiny bit, too, over the fact that she was about to steal his son.

"Cody?" She was preparing to give her nephew a gentle shake to wake him when he rolled over with a groan.

"Aunt Kristen?" He blinked against the overhead light she'd turned on. "My tummy hurts."

"Does it?" Clumsily she dropped to her knees beside the bed and smoothed his hair off his forehead. His skin felt clammy. "You barely touched your dinner tonight. Did your tummy hurt then?"

"A little, I guess." He winced. "But it hurts worse now."

"Where does it hurt, exactly?"

He pulled up his pajama top and touched his belly button. "Right here."

Kristen tried not to become alarmed. Kids got stomachaches all the time, didn't they? He would probably be fine in a little while. Then they could leave.

"Try lying on your tummy and see if that feels better." She stroked Cody's back, moving her hand in circles, waiting for him to drift off to sleep. He would be fine when she woke him again, she assured herself.

Except Cody never really went back to sleep. One hour passed. Then two. By then Kristen had lugged in some sofa cushions to make herself more comfortable beside his bed. Cody tossed and turned restlessly, moaning whenever he rolled over.

Kristen's concern increased as the night dragged on. She curved her hand around his forehead. It felt hot to the touch. He wasn't burning up, but he definitely had a fever now.

Fever. Fever meant infection. Was it possible Cody had some internal injury from Derek's beating that hadn't healed properly? That had become infected because Kristen had taken him out of the hospital?

Dear God. He'd seemed to be recovering so well...but there was definitely more wrong with him than an upset tummy.

Maybe it was just the flu. Maybe if she could get him to take some of the children's pain medication that was still left...

When Kristen came back with it, Cody was awake, looking up at her with glazed eyes. "My tummy still hurts," he said. "I feel like I wanna throw up."

"Oh, sweetie..." She sat on the edge of the bed so she could hold the glass of water for him.

"Ow!" Cody clutched his abdomen. "It hurts when I move."

This didn't sound like the flu.

She noticed he was holding a different spot than he'd complained about before. "I thought it hurt around your belly button," she said, making sure not to jostle him while she felt his forehead again. Still hot.

"Now it hurts here." His hands were covering the lower right side of his abdomen.

Kristen didn't know what to do. Should she give him the medicine? Have him sip water? Weren't there some injuries where it made the patient worse if you let him eat or drink anything?

She couldn't stand to see Cody suffer. He looked awful. Something was terribly wrong with him.

Minutes ticked away while she tried to figure out what to do. Minutes that might be crucial if Cody were as seriously ill as he seemed. Tears leaked from beneath his eyelids. He let out another pathetic moan. His face was chalky white.

Dear God, what if he died? What if she sat here dithering all night long, until it was too late to save him?

That horrifying possibility decided her. Except she really had no decision to make, not anymore. What other choice was there?

She took great care not to jiggle Cody as she got up. Once

on her feet, she hobbled across the room as fast as she could. Heading for the kitchen, and Luke's cell phone.

Luke got to the hospital first. He paced back and forth in front of the emergency entrance, waiting for the ambulance to arrive.

Dread churned through his bloodstream. Kristen had sounded frantic when she'd phoned to tell him that something was wrong with Cody and she'd already dialed 911. He caught a glimpse of a clock through the glass doors, its hands creeping toward 2:00 a.m. All hell was going to break loose around here when people saw Cody and Kristen. No doubt the ambulance crew had already recognized them. Would they have radioed ahead to the cops? No. Probably not. But it wouldn't take long for *someone* to contact them.

Right now, though, the police were the least of Luke's worries. Kristen would never have brought Cody out of hiding unless he was in pretty bad shape. The authorities Luke could deal with—somehow. But the idea that Cody might die was too awful for him to handle.

"Hurry up, come on, where are you?" he muttered, shoving his shirttails into his jeans. He'd leaped out of bed and left home so fast he'd barely had time to get dressed.

He cocked his head and froze when he heard the distant wail of a siren. His apprehension increased along with its volume. It seemed to take forever before flashing red lights pinwheeled around the corner and the ambulance braked to a quick, smooth stop right in front of him.

Luke was around back, hauling open the doors before the driver even killed the ignition. The guy riding inside with Kristen and Cody elbowed him aside as his partner arrived to help lift out the gurney. A solid fist of fear planted itself right in the middle of Luke's chest.

Cody looked terrible. Eyes closed, face contorted with pain, skin as pale as the sheet tucked over him. He was breathing rapidly and moaning. To Luke's panicked eyes, the boy looked far more weak and wan than the night Kristen had first brought him to Luke's doorstep.

So much had happened since that night....

Luke longed to touch him, but was afraid to. Then the ambulance crew was whisking Cody toward the emergency entrance and Kristen was climbing out of the ambulance, leaning on Luke for support, digging her nails into his shoulders as she landed on the ground beside him. Her face was a taut mask of fear.

"He's so sick." She clamped her hand to her mouth as if to hold back a sob. "I sat up with him for hours, hoping he'd get better, but he only got worse, and then I couldn't think of what to do. I didn't have any choice but to..." Her eyes darted wildly around while they hurried after the gurney, as if she expected to see a ring of cops with their guns pointed right at her, ready to snatch Cody away.

"You did the right thing," Luke assured her. He gave her waist a comforting squeeze with the arm he was using to take some weight off her ankle. "He needs medical care. That's more important than anything else right now."

The glass doors opened automatically as they rushed into the hospital. Up ahead they could see Cody being wheeled into an examining room. By the time they arrived at his side, a doctor and two nurses were already working on him. They were all people Kristen recognized. People who knew Cody had been missing, who knew Kristen was suspected of kidnapping him. After all, this was the same hospital she'd taken him from.

But the emergency-room staff was too professional to react with anything more dramatic than raised eyebrows. For now, anyway.

"What were his first symptoms?" Dr. Barnett asked Kristen.

She listed them for him, forcing herself to recall them as precisely as possible. Luke kept his arm securely around her the whole time. She noticed the two nurses exchange a brief, curious glance.

"So he didn't have a fever when the pain first started?" the doctor asked.

"No. I mean, I didn't have a thermometer to take his temperature, but he didn't feel hot at first."

"Does it hurt when I press here, Cody?" The doctor palpated his bare abdomen.

"No," Cody replied in a tiny, choked voice.

"How about he—"

"Ow!" Cody howled in pain.

Luke tensed as if about to lunge forward and shove the doctor aside. His arm tightened convulsively around Kristen.

The doctor gave a curt nod. "Appendicitis." He tugged down Cody's pajama top with an apologetic smile. "Sorry I had to hurt you, buddy. Terry?" He glanced at one of the nurses. "Could you have Surgery notify whoever's on call?"

"Right away, Doctor." Her rubber soles squeaked as she spun efficiently around. On her way out of the examining room, her eyes met Kristen's for a split second. Then she hastily shifted her gaze elsewhere.

Something about that quick, speculative look suddenly reminded Kristen she had a price on her head. Never mind. Derek's reward offer was the least of her worries right now.

"Is he going to be all right?" Luke demanded. He had his arm cinched so tight around Kristen it was difficult to breathe.

The doctor raised one eyebrow, as if surprised by the life-or-death intensity of Luke's concern. "He'll be fine," he replied, directing his answer at both of them. "But he needs surgery as soon as possible, before his appendix ruptures."

Kristen didn't know whether to be relieved or frightened. Surgery? Cutting open her precious nephew with a scalpel? But plenty of people had their appendixes out, didn't they? No big deal. Except when it happened to someone you loved.

Dr. Barnett ruffled Cody's hair. "We're going to take you upstairs to the operating room and fix you right up, okay, pardner?"

Panic leaped into Cody's pain-filled eyes. "Aunt Kristen?"

"I'm right here, sweetheart." She stepped quickly forward to hold his hand.

"Don't let them take me!"

"They have to take out your appendix to make you better," she explained in as soothing a voice as she could muster.

Cody's lower lip trembled. "Can—can you come with me?"

"I'm afraid not, honey." She patted his hand. "But the doctors and nurses will take very good care of you."

"No! No!" Cody's agitation increased. "Don't leave me, Aunt Kristen! I'm scared! I don't wanna go without you."

Tears spilled down his temples into his hair, his ears. Kristen felt a quivering in the back of her throat, a sting behind her eyelids that warned her she, too, was about to start crying.

She'd done everything in her power to protect him. But in the end, it hadn't been enough. The police were probably already on their way to arrest her. Luke wouldn't be able to stop Derek from taking Cody home as soon as he recovered from surgery. Eventually, of course, blood tests would prove Luke was Cody's real father, but by that time, there was no telling what dreadful harm Derek could have inflicted on Cody.

She'd made a terrible mistake. She should never have gone to Luke for help. She should have fled far away with Cody as quickly as possible, so that at least he would have ended up in a hospital where no one recognized either of them.

Cody was clutching her fingers so hard she had to fight to keep the pain from showing in her face. "Don't leave me," he pleaded, sobbing. "I don't wanna go away from you...."

Dr. Barnett cleared his throat, raising his voice to be heard. "Tell you what, Cody." He shot a meaningful look across the examining table at Kristen. "Your aunt can stay with you while we're getting you ready. Then she can wait right outside the door during the operation, okay? You'll see her as soon as you wake up."

Cody's sobs slowed a little. He peered up at Kristen for confirmation. She, in turn, looked at Dr. Barnett, to make sure she'd understood his unspoken promise not to call the police for now. The doctor gave her a slight nod. "Gail?" He spoke to the other nurse. "I think you'll agree that plan would be best for our patient, right?"

Uncertainty stitched her lips into a tight seam. Clearly she understood exactly what she would be agreeing to. Finally she gave a shrug of assent. "Yes, Doctor."

Kristen sent her a grateful look. "All right, honey?" She leaned over and stroked Cody's flushed cheek. "I'll stay with you as long as I can, and I'll be right outside while they do the operation." She didn't want to promise to be there when he woke up. That would be hours from now, and a lot could happen during that time.

Cody hiccuped. "'Kay." Then his gaze shifted past her. "Can Luke come, too?" he asked in a small, hopeful voice.

Luke stepped next to Kristen and winked at Cody. "Just try and stop me, Slugger."

Apparently Dr. Barnett had no intention of doing so. With a tilt of his head, he motioned Kristen and Luke aside for a private talk. "Clearly it would traumatize the poor kid to be separated from you right now." He aimed a stern look at Kristen. "So I'm going to hold off notifying the police until he's out of surgery. But that's as much as I can do. Is that clear?"

"Yes. I understand."

"Maybe this is for the best," Luke told her in a low voice.

If only Kristen could believe that. "Thank you," she told the doctor.

He was twisting his stethoscope, studying them both with puzzled curiosity. "I can hardly *wait* to hear *this* whole story," he mumbled with a shake of his head.

The hospital might delay contacting the police, but Luke knew there was no way they weren't going to notify Derek. No matter how much Luke hated the idea, Cody was legally Derek's son. Under normal circumstances they would have needed him to sign a consent form, but because this was an emergency, they wound up whisking Cody into surgery before Derek had shown up yet.

Luke sat with Kristen on a couch in the waiting area. He had his arm wrapped around her, but he wasn't sure which of them this was meant to comfort. Every time Kristen heard someone approaching, she jumped about a foot in the air, as if she expected Derek to come barreling around the corner breathing fire.

Personally, Luke was kind of looking forward to another face-to-face confrontation with the jerk. He was tired of all this sneaking around, this hiding. He was sick of all the lies. Better if everything just exploded out into the open, in his opinion.

An opinion he knew Kristen didn't share. She dragged in another long, unsteady breath and released it in a sigh. ''If my darned ankle didn't hurt, I could pace back and forth,'' she said ruefully. ''Maybe that would help.''

Luke kissed her temple. ''Cody will be all right.'' He only wished he felt as confident as he sounded. Lots of things could go wrong during surgery.

Kristen squeezed his hand with a worried, absent smile. Her pale skin was drawn taut across her high cheekbones. Her hair looked as if she'd been distractedly plowing her fingers through it, which she had. Gray smudges rimmed her eyes with exhaustion.

She'd never looked more beautiful to Luke.

At the sound of footsteps she tensed like a frightened deer.

Dr. Barnett walked around the corner into the waiting area. ''Come on, let's go for a ride,'' he told Kristen, patting the wheelchair he was pushing in front of him.

Kristen shrank against Luke. ''What do you mean? Where?''

He pointed at her foot. ''I noticed earlier you were limping.''

''Oh, that.'' She tried to shrug it off. ''I sprained my ankle, that's all.''

''Long as you're here, we might as well take a look at it.'' He positioned the chair and extended his hand. ''Come on. I'll take you down to Radiology to have it x-rayed.''

"Oh, that's not necessary," she said quickly. "I need to stay here and wait for Cody—"

"Cody's going to be a while yet. I'll have you back safe and sound before he comes out of surgery, I promise." The doctor had her halfway into the wheelchair before she could protest again.

"Really, I'd much rather wait here—"

"Go on, Kristen." Luke took hold of her other arm and maneuvered her into the wheelchair, earning an indignant look of betrayal. "Might as well have the doc take a look at it."

"But Cody—"

"There's no sense both of us sitting around chewing our fingernails. I'll be right here the whole time." He braced his hands on her shoulders. "You go get that ankle taken care of." He kissed her forehead. "Then you can come back and chew your fingernails some more."

"Well..."

Before Kristen could protest further, the doctor was wheeling her away. Oh, well, she decided. Maybe he and Luke were right, and she ought to have the ankle taken care of now. No telling what kind of medical care would be available in prison.

After the X ray, the technician wheeled her back to the emergency room area. "The doctor will come talk to you as soon as he looks at the X rays." He parked her in the corridor near Dr. Barnett's office. The technician must be new in town. Kristen didn't recognize him. She just hoped he didn't recognize *her*. Judging by the quizzical looks he kept sliding her and the way he kept scratching his head, he hadn't quite figured out yet that he'd seen her face on a Wanted poster.

Hopefully his memory wouldn't improve. Not that it mattered. Unless Kristen wore a bag over her head, it was inevitable that people would recognize her. Even though there was a limited hospital staff on duty in the middle of the night, all it would take was one of them to call the police.

Kristen's eyelids drooped. She was worn-out from worry and lack of sleep. She yawned. As long as she had to sit here and wait for the doctor, she might as well...try to catch...a few...winks....

When she jerked awake, someone was pushing her down the deserted corridor. "Did you look at my X rays?" she asked, craning her neck to question Dr. Barnett. "Are you taking me back to—"

Horror froze her blood like ice. It wasn't the doctor pushing her. It was Derek.

"Stop!" she gasped when she could catch her breath. "What are you—"

He halted abruptly at the end of the corridor. Then he seized Kristen and hauled her out of the wheelchair, one hand clamped around her mouth so she couldn't scream. Pain speared up from her ankle as he wrestled her through the door of the stairwell, but she barely felt it. Terror was a very effective anesthetic.

The metal door clanked shut behind them. Kristen struggled against Derek, but he was simply too strong for her. Down, down the stairs he dragged her, half lifting her whenever she dug in her heels and tried to slow them down. His fingers were like iron bands over her mouth. He would have been half suffocating her even if her lungs hadn't already been straining with fear.

The touch and smell and heat of him sickened her. When she thought of what those hands were capable of doing...

At the bottom of the stairwell he hustled her roughly through the door. Kristen had never been in the basement of the hospital before.

The morgue was down here.

Luke checked the clock on the wall again. Good grief, was the thing broken? He couldn't believe how slowly time was moving.

He prowled restlessly back and forth across the waiting area. Cody was going to be in the operating room for a while, the doctor had said.

Luke was going crazy. Somehow having Kristen to talk to

had made him feel less like climbing the walls. Maybe he should have gone with her while the doc checked out her ankle. He certainly wasn't doing any good *here.*

He glanced at the clock again. Sheesh, hadn't the hospital paid its electric bill or something?

He was no good at waiting. Never had been.

With one last ferocious scowl at the clock, he went to find Kristen.

Kristen had a vague impression that besides the morgue, there were some clerical offices down here in the basement. The records department, maybe? The corridor had a silent, dimly lit stillness that hinted no one worked down here in the middle of the night.

No one who could hear her scream, even if Derek didn't have his hand bolted over her mouth.

He forced her down the empty hallway and into the first door they came to. An office. Desk, chairs, filing cabinets…

Derek kicked the door shut with his foot. "You bitch," he snarled in her ear. "I've got you now."

A whipcord of panic lashed through her. Her heart was pounding so hard it felt on the verge of exploding. Then she caught sight of an object on the desk across the room, and *click!* An idea took hold amid the terrified chaos inside her brain.

But first she had to figure out a way to get over there, to make Derek let go of her…

"First you tried to talk my wife into leaving me, then you thought you could steal my son." The caress of his breath on her ear made her gorge rise. He adjusted his hand over her mouth, loosening his grip slightly. "Now you're going to pay for—"

Kristen bit him as hard as she could.

"Ouch! Bitch!"

All at once she could breathe again. She sucked in a huge gulp of air. Then had it knocked out of her when Derek shoved her across the room.

She didn't have much control over her trajectory, but managed to land near the desk, grab the edge and haul herself upright. Her ankle nearly collapsed, but she stayed standing.

Derek advanced on her. "Look! I'm bleeding, damn you." He raised his other arm and backhanded her across the face.

The force of the blow stunned her, but she used the opportunity to sidle down the desk some more so she was blocking his view of the object that was now behind her.

She had to distract him so he wouldn't notice what she was doing. "You'll be making a big mistake if you kill me," she said, dismayed by the hysterical pitch of her voice. "Everyone will know you did it."

Derek smiled at her. And that smile terrified Kristen more than anything he'd done so far. "Oh, I'm not going to kill you," he said, arching his brows in feigned innocence. "You're going to kill yourself, by jumping off the hospital roof." He shook his head and made tsk-tsk sounds. "Such terrible injuries. After all, the hospital is four stories high." He shrugged one shoulder. "Who's to say how much of the damage occurred *before* you flung yourself off?"

The X-ray technician had informed Luke he'd left Kristen just outside Dr. Barnett's office. But there was no sign of her there now.

"Yes, I was planning to go over the X rays with her," the doctor confirmed. Luke was leaning in his doorway. "But I haven't seen her since I left her in Radiology. In fact, I was about to go check and see if she'd gone back to wait with you."

"Well, she didn't." Luke stepped back and turned his head to scan the hall in both directions. No sign of her. But down at the far end…

He loped down the hall and retrieved the empty wheelchair. No way of telling if this were Kristen's, of course. "I found this by the stairs," he told the doctor. One of the nurses was in his office now.

"Terry, have you seen Kristen recently?" the doctor asked.

The nurse frowned. ''Last time I saw her, she was sitting in a wheelchair right outside here. I assumed she was waiting for you.''

''How long ago was that?'' Luke asked.

''Gosh, I'm not sure. But it was before Mr. Vincent arrived, and that was about—'' she consulted her watch ''—oh, about ten minutes ago.''

Luke went rigid. ''Derek? Derek was here?''

''Yes, after hours all hospital visitors have to enter through the emergency room. He walked right past me. I remember thinking, oh dear, I hope he doesn't see Kristen—''

Luke reached past her and grabbed the doctor's phone. With shaking fingers he jabbed out 911. ''Hello?'' he said quickly. ''I want to report the location of a dangerous fugitive. A kidnapper. It's Kristen Monroe. She's hiding somewhere here inside Whisper Ridge Hospital.''

Apparently, an urgent call that his kidnapped son was in the hospital hadn't been earthshaking enough for Derek to lower his strict code of attire. He was dressed for murder as if he planned to chair a business meeting right afterward.

He said to Kristen, ''Everyone knows you kidnapped Cody because you were crazed with grief over your beloved sister's death. That's what I told the police.'' He showed his teeth. ''So after you failed in your pathetic attempt to steal him, who would question another unbalanced act like suicide?''

Kristen shifted her hands ever so slowly, moving them behind her. ''Luke would,'' she said, lifting her chin.

Those two words had a much greater impact than she'd intended. ''Hollister!'' Derek exploded. His face turned red. ''That son of a...'' Fury throttled him for a second. ''This is all his fault. He's been a thorn in my side way too long.'' A sneer curled Derek's lip. ''But don't count on *him* to avenge your death. He's next on my list.''

''Are you the one who burned down his business?'' Kristen raised her voice, hoping to cover the sound of what she was doing.

''Not me *personally,* you idiot.'' A look of malevolent satisfaction slid over his aristocratic features. ''Though I will take credit for dumping sugar into those gas tanks yesterday.''

Behind Kristen was a hospital intercom unit. She'd never operated one herself, but she'd seen people use them during her frequent trips here to deliver flowers. Without moving a muscle except for the hand behind her back, she lifted the receiver that you spoke into to page someone over the hospital-wide speaker system.

''Luke knows it was you.'' She was babbling now, trying to distract Derek from noticing what she was up to. ''He knows you killed Sheri, too. He's been investigating, and he's found evidence to prove you did it.''

Maybe no one would find her until it was too late. Until Derek had killed her. But by God, Kristen would make sure everyone knew that he'd murdered her sister. She would make sure he never got his hands on Cody again.

Working her fingers across the intercom unit, she felt for the button that would broadcast their voices throughout the hospital.

''Fat chance,'' Derek scoffed. ''Don't you think I know what he's been up to? I've heard how he's been snooping around town, asking questions. So what? There aren't any witnesses, except—''

Kristen kept her face perfectly neutral. Cody's life might depend on it. But Derek either saw something in her eyes, or figured it out for himself.

''Except for that stupid kid,'' he breathed. Sparks of anger whirled through his eyes, and for the first time Kristen saw a gleam of madness there as well. ''I told him to keep his mouth shut.'' His hands fisted like anvils. ''Now it looks like I'm going to have to punish him once I get him home.''

Kristen located what she prayed was the right button. With the door closed, hopefully Derek wouldn't hear their voices over the speaker in the hallway. Hopefully the simultaneous sound of their talking would cover up whatever sound filtered through.

Not that she had any choice. This was her only chance.

Kristen took a deep breath. ''Why did you kill Sheri? Was it because she was going to leave you?''

Derek gave her a withering look. ''You think I couldn't live without her? Is that it? What a laugh.'' Genuine amusement flickered across his face like the forked tongue of a snake. Then bitterness curdled his expression again.

Kristen pushed the button.

''I killed her because I found out the truth, that's why. Because she was trying to pass off that whiny brat as mine.''

Chapter 16

Luke ran from room to room, flinging open doors, switching on lights, calling Kristen's name. He ignored the hospital employees who scolded him to be quiet. Kristen's life was at stake. What did it matter if he woke up a few patients? Nurses did that anyway, always coming in to take your temperature in the middle of the night....

Right after calling the cops to report Kristen's presence, Luke had raced out to the parking lot to make sure Derek's car was still there. The cursed vehicle was locked, or he would have opened the hood and disabled the engine so Derek couldn't escape in it. No time to let the air out of the tires, either.

But at least he knew Derek must still be in the building with Kristen. The problem was, Luke didn't know whether Derek had taken her upstairs or down from the last place she'd been seen. No doubt he would have headed somewhere deserted to take whatever revenge he intended. What about the roof? Not only would no one be up there, but it would be easy to claim they'd gone there to talk out their differences in private, gotten into an argument, then a struggle, and that Kristen had fallen off the roof by accident.

Without waiting for the elevator, Luke had dashed up four flights of steps. When he hadn't found them on the roof, he'd started working his way down, intending to open every single door in this hospital until he found her.

He was just finishing the third floor when he heard Derek's voice.

"...Killed her because I found out the truth, that's why. Because she was trying to pass off that whiny brat as mine."

What the hell? Luke spun his head around wildly, trying to figure out where the voice had come from.

Then he heard Kristen. "You killed her before you put her in the car, didn't you?"

The speaker. At last it made sense to Luke. Kristen had somehow switched on the hospital intercom, only Derek didn't realize it. Now, if only she would give Luke a clue as to where she was.

Frantically he started yanking open doors again.

"She asked for it," Derek said in a self-righteous tone, as if *he* were the injured party.

Kristen could hardly contain her loathing contempt. Blame the victim. The classic technique of a batterer. What a cowardly, despicable way to justify the monstrous things he'd done.

But she had to keep him talking. "What do you mean, she asked for it?"

"She didn't just ask. She begged. She pleaded. 'Please, please let us go,'" he mimicked in a cruel falsetto. "'There isn't any reason for you to keep us here. Cody's not even your son.'" A crimson flush rose from Derek's immaculate white collar.

"How do you know she wasn't just saying that so you'd let them go?" Oh, Sheri, Sheri, my poor sister, you must have been so desperate....

"I could always tell when she was lying," Derek bragged.

"She wasn't." He cracked his knuckles. "Besides, I got proof later on. After I arranged for blood tests that showed the kid *couldn't* have been mine." He gave Kristen a vicious wolf's leer. "Not too hard to figure out whose brat he *was* though."

Luke, Luke, are you hearing this? Will I ever see you again? Or my sweet darling Cody?

"So you killed Sheri and then made it look like an accident." Though she badly wanted to spit in Derek's face, to claw out his eyes, Kristen did her best to make it sound as if she had to admire his cleverness. Maybe an appeal to his Godzilla-sized ego would buy her a little more time.

"She deserved what she got," Derek replied, fisting his hands. "I gave her my name, my money, a big house, a fancy car, a whole new wardrobe…and how did she repay me?" His color deepened to purple. "By sleeping around behind my back! By trying to foist off someone else's brat as mine!"

"She never cheated on you!" Kristen cried, no longer able to hold in her outrage. "Cody was conceived before you got married! Sheri didn't know she was pregnant when she married you!"

Derek hit her again. Kristen fought her own reflexes and stopped herself from yanking up her hands to shield her face. She had to hold the receiver off the hook, had to keep pressing the button on the intercom, on the slim chance that it was actually broadcasting.

What shocked her even more than the pain of the blow was how calmly Derek had dealt it to her. As if she were of no more consequence than a pesky mosquito.

"Sheri was trash," he said. "Just like you. Just like all the other losers in this town."

He seized Kristen's chin and forced her to look straight at him. Though she tried not to flinch, she could tell by his smug expression that he could see the terror in her eyes.

"You think I'd let her make a laughingstock out of me?" Derek's tone sounded perfectly reasonable, as if his logic were flawless. "How would it look to people, knowing she'd tricked me into raising another man's bastard as my own legitimate heir?''

''She never wanted to trick you,'' Kristen mumbled. Her mouth wasn't working quite right. ''She just wanted to get away from you.''

Derek arched his brows in mock astonishment. ''And how would *that* have looked? My gorgeous, pampered, incredibly fortunate wife, divorcing me? There's never been a divorce in the Vincent family. Never. Not one.'' He clicked his tongue. ''Think how people would have talked.''

The touch of his hand on her face made Kristen's skin crawl. He lifted his other hand and circled her neck experimentally with his fingers, as if sizing her for a necklace. ''But you were going to bring it all out into the open, weren't you, Kristen? People wouldn't listen when you told them I killed your sister. So you decided to tell them I was hurting the kid. But they still wouldn't listen, would they? So you stole him. So people would laugh at me.''

''No—''

He tightened his grip, choking off her protest.

''If you'd had your way, people would have laughed at me. Looked down on me.'' His mint-flavored breath warmed her face like the ominous lick of flames. ''I won't tolerate that, Kristen. I'm a Vincent. I own this town. And I won't stand for people laughing at me.''

Spots danced before her eyes.

The rational mask Derek wore started to crack. ''I'm sick of your interference,'' he said, gnashing his teeth. ''Sick of your whining. Your scheming. You've meddled in my business for the last time. Now you're going to get the punishment you so richly deserve.''

As he locked his grip tight and cut off her air, Kristen finally swung up her hands to defend herself. Either everyone in the hospital had heard Derek or not. Now it was time to fight for her life. She gouged with her nails, kicked wildly, struggled to wedge her fingers beneath the strangling hands around her neck.

The room started to spin. Darkness descended. Through the rushing that filled her ears, Kristen heard a dim, sharp sound from far, far away.

All at once the pressure was gone and she was free. She staggered backward, dragging in searing, blessed lungfuls of air. As her vision cleared, she saw Luke hammering Derek with his fists, over and over. With an ease born of fury he hoisted Derek off his feet and heaved him into a wall. Then he went at him with his fists again.

Kristen tried to call out, but couldn't make a sound with her damaged throat. Dear God, she had to stop him! This was going too far!

She channeled every ounce of strength into her vocal cords. ''Luke!'' she rasped. ''Luke, stop it! You'll kill him!''

She was stumbling toward him, determined to capture one of his swinging fists and restrain him, when the police burst into the room.

Although the cops had plenty more questions, Luke had insisted they wait. Right now he and Kristen needed to be by Cody's bedside so he would see them as soon as he woke up from surgery. They'd made him a promise, hadn't they?

Derek had been hauled off to jail. With a hospital full of witnesses able to verify his confession, the police had been more than willing to drop the minor matter of kidnapping charges against Kristen.

Now she sat in the chair next to Luke's while they waited for Cody to wake up. He stroked the back of her hand with his thumb. ''So you're not mad at me for turning you in to the cops?'' he teased.

''Not under the circumstances.'' She smiled back at him, and once again Luke's overwhelming relief that she was safe turned his insides to mush.

He couldn't believe how close he'd come to losing her. How much that prospect had terrified him.

''I figured the fastest way to find you was to call in some

assistance. Even though they didn't realize they were going to be saving you from Derek.''

''But *you* saved me.'' Kristen squeezed his hand. Her green eyes were luminous. ''By the way, in all the commotion, have I got around to thanking you yet?''

Man, she was beautiful! Those incredible eyes with their long dark lashes...that lush, irresistible mouth, still rosy from the frenzy of bruising kisses Luke had planted there as soon as they were alone...the tumble of gorgeous red hair that concealed most of the marks on her neck...

Luke stomped down his anger as if putting out a fire. He didn't want bitterness and rage to spoil this precious, peaceful interlude, didn't want Cody to wake up and sense bad vibrations in the air.

Derek would finally get what was coming to him. Luke's anger no longer served any useful purpose. He knew it would be a long, long time, though, before he could let go of it completely.

In the bed, Cody stirred. Both adults scooted their chairs closer, but then he retreated back into sleep.

Kristen tenderly fingered a lock of blond hair off his forehead. When she looked back at Luke, her expression was unreadable. Expectant, but uncertain. ''A hospital's the perfect place to take a blood test,'' she said softly.

Luke's gaze darted automatically to the boy in the bed. The boy he'd come to love like his own son. But what if it turned out Cody *wasn't—*

''I don't need any blood test,'' Luke told her, feeling something momentous happen inside him. ''I already know the answer.'' He touched his chest. ''In here.'' Amazingly, he realized he meant it. How long had he known the truth?

Kristen put her arms around him. When she drew back, her eyes were wet. ''I'm glad,'' she said. ''But you'll still need to take a blood test for legal purposes. If you intend to claim custody of Cody, that is.''

''But what about...?'' Luke swallowed. Kristen had given

him his son. How could he take Cody and then turn his back on the person who'd brought them together?

Kristen sensed his thoughts. "I hoped all along that someday you'd want to raise him." She touched Luke's cheek in reassurance. "Not that I don't love Cody with all my heart. Not that I wouldn't have been overjoyed to raise him myself if things…" A haunted, wistful expression shimmered briefly on her pretty features. "If things had worked out differently," she finished.

"Kristen—"

"A boy should be with his father," she said with a bob of her head, as if that ended the discussion.

Turned out it did. At that moment, Cody blinked open his eyes. The panicked confusion swirling through them dissolved when he caught sight of the two people bending over his bed.

"Hi, Aunt Kristen. Hi, Luke," he mumbled.

"Hi, Slugger."

"How do you feel, sweetie?"

"Okay, I guess. I'm sleepy." He gave them both a groggy smile. Then he perked up. "Hey, do you think they'll let me see my appendix?"

The next day Derek was officially charged with Sheri's murder and the assault on Kristen. A judge denied bail, agreeing with the prosecutor that Derek posed a flight risk. Word had spread rapidly around town about Derek's on-air confession, including the part where he'd referred to the citizens of Whisper Ridge as a bunch of losers. Public opinion was not sympathetic toward him. His defense attorney quickly filed a motion to hold the trial in a different, preferably distant county.

Later that day, another judge awarded temporary custody of Cody to his aunt, pending the results of DNA tests being performed to determine whether or not Luke was the boy's biological father. The test results would take several weeks.

So when Cody was discharged from the hospital three days after his operation, he went home with Kristen. Luke drove them to the apartment over her florist shop.

''Want to see the room I fixed up for you?'' Kristen led Cody into her bedroom. She would sleep on the couch while Cody stayed with her. She and Luke had decided to wait until the test results were official to tell Cody that Luke was his father, and that he would be living with him from now on.

Kristen's heart contracted with a painful throb at the thought of the two people she loved building a new life together. Without her. She would always be Cody's doting aunt, of course. But that's as far as her role would go. No matter how much she wished it could be otherwise.

She managed to coax Cody into lying down for a rest, even though he claimed he didn't feel like a nap. ''Doctor's orders, remember?'' Kristen unfolded the quilt draped over the foot of the bed and used it to cover him. ''You're supposed to take it easy.''

''Will you play cards with Luke and me after I get up?'' Cody had become quite a fiend for crazy eights during his stay in the hospital.

Kristen hesitated in the doorway. ''Honey, Luke might not be here when you get up. He—he has his own house to go to. And he's got to get back to his job.'' How was she going to explain that they weren't going to be like a family anymore? No more cozy meals, no more evenings playing checkers…not for all of them, anyway. From now on, only one person would be tucking Cody into bed.

She ended up promising Cody she would invite Luke to come back that night to eat with them.

It gave Kristen a funny feeling to find Luke waiting in her living room after she left Cody resting. She wasn't used to seeing him here. She didn't *want* to get used to it.

''You've sure made amazing progress straightening this place up,'' Luke said. When he'd brought Kristen back here for the first time, they'd discovered not only the mess the police had left after their search, but the hatred-filled destruction Derek had committed. All her photographs, smashed. Fortunately, the pictures themselves had survived intact. The glass and frames she could replace.

''I couldn't have done it without your help,'' Kristen replied with a grateful smile. She and Luke had taken turns sitting with Cody while he was in the hospital. At some point it had seemed convenient to give Luke a copy of her apartment key. Unbeknownst to Kristen at the time, he'd spent an entire afternoon here working on the cleanup.

''Cody napping?'' he asked.

''Not if he can help it.'' Kristen rolled her eyes. ''But the doctor said just lying down for a while is good for him.''

Luke was prowling around her living room like a caged cheetah. Kristen couldn't blame him for wanting to get out of here. No doubt he was anxious to get back to the construction project he'd neglected for so long.

He was definitely acting anxious, all right. He dragged a hand through his hair, leaving it standing in little black tufts. ''Kristen, there's, uh, something I've been wanting to talk to you about.'' He stuffed his hands into his jeans pockets, then pulled them back out.

She sat on the couch. ''If it's about Cody, let me assure you again that I have no intention of fighting you for custody or any kind of joint arrangement. He belongs with you, and—''

''No, no, that's not it.'' Luke marched back and forth some more, grinding his teeth together. Kristen watched, puzzled but amused. She'd never seen Luke so unsure of himself before.

''Aw, the heck with it,'' he muttered. ''I'm no good at this.'' He clenched his fists at his sides and planted his feet apart as if bracing for a blow. ''Kristen, will you marry me?''

The shock was so great she couldn't reply for a minute. She must not have heard him correctly. Or else too many lovesick fantasies had finally befuddled her brain, conjuring up this crazy, impossible dream. Either way…

''No,'' she said.

Luke's posture sagged for a second. He recovered quickly and crossed his arms over his chest. ''Geez, don't beat around the bush,'' he grumbled. ''Just give me a straight answer, why don't you?''

Beneath his sarcasm Kristen detected something she didn't understand. It sounded like hurt. But why should Luke feel hurt? Frustrated, maybe, because she wouldn't cooperate with whatever plan had prompted this unlikely proposal.

No doubt Luke was simply feeling overwhelmed by the prospect of instant fatherhood. He'd lived a footloose bachelor's life-style for a long time, but that was all going to change once he was awarded custody of Cody. Luke was taking on a huge responsibility, not to mention a time-consuming one. Being a parent was a lot of work. It meant he would have to fix meals for Cody, take him shopping, see him off to school...and whenever Cody got sick Luke would have to stay home from work to take care of him.

Let alone what a big dent raising a child was going to put in Luke's free time for dating.

No wonder he'd proposed. How much easier it would make his life to have a helper, a mother for Cody, a woman to take care of the domestic chores and satisfy his own sexual needs. Besides, he and Kristen got along...well, most of the time. Marrying her must have seemed like the perfect solution.

Now that she'd figured out Luke's motives, it should have been easier to refuse him. But it wasn't.

"I can't marry you, Luke." She said it as much to convince herself as him. "I can't marry anyone."

His dark brows slashed together. "That's a pretty drastic statement."

Kristen lifted her chin. "I won't allow myself to accept what Sheri will never be able to have now."

Luke frowned. "Are you still harping on that guilt stuff?"

His dismissive attitude irritated her. "Look, I know you don't understand, but—"

"You're damn right I don't understand!"

"Shh!" She whipped a finger to her lips, throwing a cautionary glance toward the bedroom.

Luke's face was the picture of aggravation. But he did lower his voice when he dropped onto the couch next to her. "Kristen, when are you going to get it through your head that you did the right thing by persuading Sheri to leave that creep she was married to?''

Kristen's mouth quivered. ''How can you call it the right thing, when she wound up dead because of me?''

''Grrr.'' Luke poked a finger in the air. ''Number one, *Derek* killed Sheri. Not you, not anybody else. That was one hundred percent his doing. Got that? Number two...'' he held up a second finger ''...just because Sheri's decision to leave ended in tragedy doesn't mean it wasn't the right decision to make.''

Kristen blinked back tears. ''I shouldn't have talked her into it.''

''Are you going to blame yourself for the rest of your life because you didn't have magical powers to see the future?''

''No.'' She sniffed. ''Of course not.''

''That's what it sounds like to me.'' Luke gripped her arms and gave her an exasperated shake. ''Kristen, no one can see the future. All we poor, dumb human beings can do is blunder through life the best we can, making decisions based on what we *do* know. On common sense. On what our conscience tells us is right.''

She *wanted* to believe Luke. Desperately. But one indisputable fact stood in the way. ''If I hadn't persuaded Sheri to leave Derek,'' Kristen said in a choked voice, ''she would still be alive.''

Luke's grip tightened. His eyes blazed with blue sparks. ''So that's your advice now to other battered women? 'Don't dare try to leave him. It's too risky. Just stay and let him keep hitting you.'''

Kristen flushed. ''No. Don't be ridiculous.''

''Sheri deserved better than that.'' Anger flashed across Luke's face. ''So does anyone who suffers violence at the hands of someone who's supposed to love them.'' His bold features were chiseled with conviction. ''Sheri made the right choice, deciding to leave. It was just a terrible coincidence that Derek came home at the wrong moment. She couldn't have foreseen that happening.'' He gave Kristen another brief shake. ''And neither could you.''

Anguish clawed at her heart. If only there were some way to go back in time, to rewind the tape and replay that awful day, knowing what she did now.

Luke framed her face between his hands. ''Sweetheart, the only reason for you to feel guilty would be if you had closed your eyes to Sheri's suffering. If you had ignored what Derek was doing to her, or advised her to make the best of it.'' He pressed a kiss to her forehead. ''But you did what was right, instead.''

Kristen's eyes brimmed with tears. A chaotic storm of confusion and grief and regret swirled through her. She clamped her fingertips to her mouth to hold back the tide of misery. ''Please, Luke,'' she said in a muffled voice. ''Just—just go.'' More than anything, she wanted to be alone now. Too much had happened too fast. She needed time to make sense of it all.

The wounded look on Luke's face made her feel even worse. ''Whatever you say.'' He sifted his fingers briefly through her hair before he stood up. The gesture expressed some kind of powerful longing that Kristen didn't understand.

On his way out the door, he paused to look back. The outline of his wide shoulders and well-muscled frame were dark against the sunshine. He arrowed his arm to point toward the bedroom. ''You saved that kid in there, Kristen.'' His voice was rough with emotion. ''If that doesn't count for something, then I don't know what does.''

Her throat closed up tight.

''Give yourself a break in the guilt department,'' Luke told her. ''Lord knows, you've more than redeemed yourself.'' With that, he closed the door behind him.

Kristen buried her face in the couch and burst into tears.

Only later did she remember that she'd broken her promise to Cody, by forgetting to invite Luke for dinner.

Luke had to admit, Kristen had been awfully generous during the past several weeks regarding the time she'd let him spend with Cody. Luke wouldn't have blamed her for hogging her nephew all to herself while she could, knowing Cody wouldn't be living with her much longer.

What Luke *didn't* want to admit was what torture it was to see Kristen every time he came to pick up Cody for an outing. It was pretty ironic, all that time he'd spent denying to himself how much he cared for her. He shuddered every time he recalled that horrible vision of Derek's hands wrapped around her neck. Nearly losing Kristen had finally rammed some sense through Luke's thick skull, made him realize that she and Cody were the most important people in the world to him.

The irony was that, once he'd finally woken up to the fact that he wanted to spend the rest of his life with her, Kristen had turned him down flat.

Luke tried to tell himself it was just his bruised ego hurting whenever he saw her now. After swearing years ago never to put his heart on the line again, he'd gone ahead and done it, only to have Kristen dance the flamenco on it.

All right, that wasn't fair. In all honesty, turning down his proposal had seemed to distress Kristen as much as it had Luke. Maybe she'd felt sorry for him. His track record with Monroe women was certainly pitiful enough to merit sympathy.

In recent days, however, Luke's disdain for self-deceit had forced him to admit that the constant ache in his gut ever since Kristen had rejected him wasn't just injured pride.

He hadn't raised the subject of marriage again. In fact, he'd barely spoken to Kristen at all, other than the polite chitchat required in front of Cody. Once in a while Luke suggested she join Cody and him for whatever activity he'd planned. Kristen inevitably declined, which should have relieved Luke. At least he wouldn't have to bother hiding his feelings for her, or keep reminding himself that the three of them weren't a family and never would be.

Still, the way Kristen avoided him kept jabbing Luke with disappointment. He missed her. Even though every moment he spent in her presence was like another twist of the knife lodged in his wounded heart.

This particular morning, however, he was going to need a lengthier conversation with her than ''hello'' and ''goodbye.'' Luke's stomach was swooping like a roller coaster when he stopped by the flower shop after dropping Cody at school. Kristen had agreed that occasional overnight visits were a good idea, to let Cody get used to sleeping at his place.

She was behind the counter, fiddling with an elaborate arrangement of...well, Luke didn't have a clue. Several varieties of orange and yellow flowers, that was the extent of his botanical knowledge.

She did a double take when she spotted him, evidently detecting something unusual in his face. Without a word she came around the counter, shut the shop door and flipped the Closed sign around.

''What is it?'' she asked, folding her arms in a wary pose.

Luke took a deep breath. The rich, sweet perfume of flowers didn't exactly settle his stomach. ''My, uh, lawyer called this morning.''

''And?'' Kristen latched onto his elbow. It was the first time she'd touched him in weeks. It felt wonderful, even though she was digging her nails into him hard enough to leave dents.

Luke backhanded a film of sweat from his brow. ''The DNA results came back.'' Unannounced, a huge grin stretched across his face. ''Cody's my son.''

As Luke said the words out loud for the first time, a surge of joy welled up inside him, so vast and powerful it nearly cracked his ribs.

''Luke, that's wonderful.'' Kristen smiled, too, but there was sadness mixed in it. ''I'm so happy for you. For Cody.'' She tilted her head. ''Did you tell him yet?''

''No.'' Luke covered her hand with his. ''I thought we could tell him together.''

''I'd like that.'' Her eyes shone with gratitude, with gladness, with...anxiety? Hmm. What was that all about? ''How do you feel?'' she asked. ''Now that you're officially a father.''

Luke tried to sort it all out. ''Happy. Relieved.'' He exhaled a balloon of air from his chest. ''Terrified.''

Kristen raised up on tiptoe and launched a swift kiss at his cheek. ''You're going to make a wonderful father,'' she assured him quietly. ''You already do.''

''Thanks to you.'' Luke knew that as long as he lived, he would never be able to repay Kristen for the miraculous gift she'd given him.

''I only did what was right,'' she said, gazing steadily into his eyes.

Luke arched his eyebrows. Had Kristen been thinking about what he'd told her? Had he finally convinced her she'd done the right thing by stepping in to stop Derek's abuse?

''This...might not be the right time to discuss this.'' She wove her fingers together and studied her hands. Her lowered lashes screened her expression. ''Or maybe it is, I don't know.''

''Discuss what?''

When she lifted her head, that nervous look was back. ''Well, um, I've been thinking about your...suggestion.''

Luke searched his memory. ''My suggestion?''

Kristen licked her lips. ''I mean, after all, it *would* make your life a lot easier to have someone help you take care of Cody. And I wouldn't mind doing most of the cooking and the housework. Well...'' She puckered her mouth. ''*Half* the housework, anyway.''

Luke blinked. Surely she couldn't mean—

''Besides, having two parents would certainly be better for Cody. That's definitely something to consider.''

''Definitely,'' Luke echoed in a daze.

Kristen lifted her chin. ''I won't pretend *I* wouldn't be getting something out of the arrangement, too. After all, you know how much I love him, how much it would mean to me to play such an important role in his life from now on—''

"Kristen..." Luke scratched his head. "Are you talking about *marrying* me?"

Blushing, she shrugged. "I know you don't love me, that Sheri will always be the love of your life, but—"

"Whoa, hang on a second!" Luke held up his hands as if she'd stuck him up at gunpoint. "Let me get this straight. You think I'm still in love with your *sister?*"

"Well...with her memory." Kristen faltered beneath Luke's narrow-eyed glare. "Maybe part of you still is, anyway." She swallowed. "Sort of."

What a dumb idea this had been, bringing up the subject of marriage at this particular moment. Obviously Luke figured she'd only changed her mind because she was about to lose Cody.

But during the last several weeks, Luke's words had echoed in Kristen's mind over and over. None of us can see the future. All we can do is make decisions based on what we do know. On common sense. On what our conscience tells us is right.

When Kristen had peered deep into her soul, she'd finally seen the truth. The truth was, if she had it to do all over again, she still would have urged Sheri to leave Derek. Because it had been the right thing to do.

Just like marrying Luke would have been the right thing to do. For all three of them.

Only now Luke was staring at her as if she'd lost her mind. "Kristen, just for the record, I haven't loved Sheri for a long, long time." He grimaced. "She did a pretty good hatchet job on my feelings when she dumped me for Derek. And the fact is, lately, well, lately I've started to wonder whether what I felt for her was ever really love at all."

"But—but the two of you were meant for each other!"

"No." Luke enfolded Kristen's hands in his. "Sheri was beautiful and sexy and a lot of fun. Unfortunately, I was so dazzled by her that I failed to notice some of her negative qualities. She was shallow sometimes, and she could be deceitful and scheming...no, don't look at me like that!" He strengthened his grip when Kristen tried to pull away. "I admire your loyalty, but you have to admit it's true.'' Luke shook his head regretfully. ''The way I feel toward Sheri now isn't hate, but it sure isn't love, either. I guess I feel…sorry for her. And grateful, too.''

Kristen frowned. ''Grateful?''

''For dumping me.'' Luke tugged her toward him and branded a tender kiss on her forehead. ''Because if Sheri hadn't dumped me, I never would have found the real love of my life.''

''The real…?'' Kristen's jaw dropped. Surely Luke couldn't mean what it sounded like he—

''See, I told you I'm no good at this stuff.'' Luke's mouth twisted with disgust. ''It just hit me that I still haven't got around to telling you how much I love you.''

Kristen caught her breath. ''You—you love—*me?*''

Luke gently stroked a knuckle along the underside of her jaw. ''Did you think I only asked you to marry me to give Cody a mother?''

''Well, actually…yes.''

He rearranged his features as if to disguise disappointment. ''Fair enough, then. You've been honest and spelled out all the reasons why *you* would be marrying *me*. I can't expect you to—''

''I left one out,'' Kristen said abruptly.

''Left out—?''

''One of my reasons for marrying you.''

A gleam ignited in his eyes. ''And that would be…?''

Kristen grabbed two fistfuls of his shirt and hauled him close enough to kiss. ''Because I love you, Luke Hollister.'' Then she flung her arms around his neck and spent the next several minutes proving it to him.

''Good thing you put out that Closed sign,'' Luke muttered eventually, nuzzling her neck some more.

Kristen released a sigh of pure rapture. ''Keep that up, and I just might close the shop for the rest of the day.''

''Mmm, I've got some suggestions about how to spend your free time.''

"Really? Let's hear them."

He whispered in her ear for a while.

Afterward, trying not to blush, Kristen drew back and said with an innocent twinkle in her eye, "So, does this mean that marriage proposal you offered me a few weeks ago is still good?"

Luke gave her a grin that sent her heart soaring. "As good as it gets, my sweet." And he sealed his promise with a kiss.

* * * * *

COMING NEXT MONTH

#925 CATTLEMAN'S PROMISE—Marilyn Pappano
Heartbreak Canyon
Guthrie Harris was shocked when Olivia Miles and her twin daughters showed up on his Oklahoma ranch—with a deed!—and claimed it was *their* home. But since they had nowhere else to go, the longtime loner let them stay. And the longer Olivia stuck around, the less Guthrie wanted her to leave—his home *or* his heart.

#926 CLAY YEAGER'S REDEMPTION—Justine Davis
Trinity Street West
Clay Yeager hadn't meant to trespass on Casey Scott's property—but he was glad he had. The emotions this ex-cop had kept buried for so long were back in full force. Then Casey became a stranger's target, and Clay knew the time had come to protect his woman. He was done with moving on—he was ready to move in!

#927 A FOREVER KIND OF COWBOY—Doreen Roberts
Rodeo Men
Runaway heiress Lori Ashford had little experience when it came to men. So when she fell for rugged rodeo rider Cord McVane, what she felt was something she'd never known existed. But would the brooding cowboy ever see that the night she'd discovered passion in his arms was just the beginning—of forever?

#928 THE TOUGH GUY AND THE TODDLER—Diane Pershing
Men in Blue
Detective Dominic D'Annunzio thought nothing could penetrate his hardened heart—until beautiful but haunted Jordan Carlisle needed his assistance. But Jordan wasn't just looking for help, she was looking for miracles. And the closer they came to the truth, the more Dom began wondering what was in charge of this case—his head or his heart?

#929 HER SECOND CHANCE FAMILY—Christine Scott
Families Are Forever
Maggie Conrad and her son were finally on their own—*and* on the run. But the small town of Wyndchester offered the perfect hideaway. Then the new sheriff, Jason Gallagher, moved in next door, and Maggie feared her secret wouldn't stay that way for long. Could Maggie keep her past hidden while learning that love *was* better the second time around?

#930 KNIGHT IN A WHITE STETSON—Claire King
Way Out West
Calla Bishop was desperate to save her family's ranch. And as the soon-to-be-wife of a wealthy businessman, she was about to secure her birthright. Then she hired Henry Beckett, and it wasn't long before this wrangler had roped himself one feisty cowgirl. But would Henry's well-kept secret cause Calla to hand over her beloved ranch—and her guarded heart?